FALLEN ANGEL

LONDON RUTHLESS: BOOK 2

SADIE KINCAID

PRAISE FOR SADIE KINCAID

'Gabriel Sullivan rocked my world'

'Omg this book is hot!!!'

'OMG, I've never read a book in a day I couldn't put it down what a fantastic love story.'

'The intense sexual chemistry is amazing between this couple that I read into the early hours'

'A perfect mix of action-filled, suspenseful storyline, with red hot scenes as well as lots of unexpected turns.'

'Dark Angel is a dark romance and has everything, hot steamy sex & passion, brilliant storyline & gritty.'

'Gabe and Sam are everything. So so hot'

'Devoured this Dark and steamy read in one sitting.'

'I LOVE Sam and Gabe! This story has it all, suspense, angst and most of all plenty of heat!!'

LONDON RUTHLESS

Have you read Book 1 in the London Ruthless Series?
Dark Angel is available here

For my boys

Chapter 1

SAMANTHA

I walked down the hallway towards the kitchen, with Gabriel's ex-wife, Jennifer following close behind me. The smell of the lasagne he was cooking for dinner filled the house, making my stomach growl. However, at that moment, I didn't feel like I could have eaten a bite. Jennifer's unexpected visit had me on edge. What on earth could she want?

I turned to her as we reached the doorway. 'He's in here,' I said, glancing down at Jennifer's stomach. She was clearly very pregnant. Her bump was considerably bigger than mine, but I knew that didn't mean much in terms of how far along she was, and it was hard to tell just how pregnant she was. I smiled at her but all that was going through my mind was why the hell was she here?

We walked into the kitchen and Gabriel turned when he heard us. He smiled at me, but then his gaze drifted to the woman standing behind me and his smile turned to a frown.

'Jennifer? What the hell are you doing here?' he asked.

I stepped aside and his eyes locked on her pregnant stomach. The look of horror on his face made my heart lurch into my throat. But, I knew that what I was thinking was impossible. He would never do that to me.

'I need to talk to you,' Jennifer said as she wiped the tears from her cheeks. Then she shot a look at me. 'Alone?'

Gabriel walked towards me and put an arm around my waist. 'Whatever you have to say to me, you can say in front of Sam,' he snapped.

She shrugged her shoulders. 'If that's what you want?'

'It is,' he replied.

'My sister kicked me out. I have nowhere to go,' she sniffed.

'And why is that my problem?' Gabriel growled.

She rubbed a hand over her swollen belly. 'Because I'm having your baby,' she said as she blinked at him.

I felt like my knees had been hit from behind with a sledge-hammer as they buckled beneath me. It was as though all of the air had been sucked from the room. Gabriel pulled me tighter and I looked up at him, waiting for him to tell his lying ex-wife that she was crazy and that she needed to get out of our house.

'That's not possible,' he scowled at her and I felt the relief wash over me.

So, it wasn't true?

But then he carried on speaking. 'I wore a condom.'

I wondered if I had misheard him. Suddenly the room started to spin as my heart started to pound in my ears. I turned to him, my legs and my voice shaking. 'What?' I asked.

He looked at me, his brows knitted in a frown. 'Sam, let me explain.'

I stepped away from him. 'Explain what?' I snapped at him. 'How you knocked us both up within a few weeks of each other?'

He shook his head. 'It's not mine. It can't be.'

'It is yours,' Jennifer interjected. 'There's been no-one else.'

Gabriel glared at her. 'Can you give us a minute?' he snapped.

She started to turn to walk out of the kitchen.

'There's really no need to leave, Jennifer. I will,' I said as I brushed past her and marched up the stairs. I heard Gabriel bark something to her but I couldn't hear what he said, and then he was running up the stairs behind me. I was in our bedroom by the time he reached me. I opened the wardrobe and pulled a large empty holdall from the bottom.

'Sam!' he shouted. 'Will you please let me explain?'

I turned and glared at him. 'Explain what? How you screwed your ex-wife?'

He reached for my arm but I shrugged him off. 'It was after we broke up,' he started. 'I thought you and me were over. I was drunk. I wasn't thinking straight. It meant nothing to me.'

'Tell that to her and your baby,' I shouted.

'There's no way it's mine. I wore a condom.'

'Oh, well then. Because accidents never happen, do they?' I looked down at my own bump.

'That was completely different. We never used protection for a start.'

I shook my head. I couldn't deal with this right now. I had to get out of there before I said something to him that I could never take back. My heart felt like it was breaking and I didn't know what the hell to do about it. I started pulling some clothes from the wardrobe and stuffing them into the bag.

'Sam. Don't do this. Don't run away from me,' he pleaded.

'I'm not running, Gabe. I'm walking. I'm walking out on you because I don't trust you any more. You lied to me –'

'I didn't lie,' he interrupted me.

'But you never told me the truth.'

'And how would that have gone, Sam? Tell me how or when would have been a good time to tell you that? We'd split up. Even after your dad's engagement party when you let me bring you home and fuck you senseless, you walked out on me again the next day. You tore my fucking heart out. And then you only came back to me because you were having my baby.'

I glared at him. 'Is that what you think? That I'm only with you because of the baby?'

He shook his head. 'I didn't mean it like that. But the baby is the reason you came back. Before you found out you were pregnant, you told me you didn't love me and you didn't want to be with me. I was fucking lost, Sam. I didn't know what to do with myself. Then I got drunk one night, and she was there. I would never ...' he trailed off.

'Well, I hope it was worth it,' I sniffed.

If what he said was true, why had he jeopardised everything we had for a meaningless encounter?

'Just stay tonight. Let's talk about this when you've calmed down,' he insisted.

'I don't need to calm down, Gabe. I need to get away from you and from her.'

'Where will you go?'

'To my dad's. I'll ask him to come and pick me up.'

He glared at me, as though he was considering whether to let me leave. 'Okay. But tomorrow, we'll talk?'

I glared back at him. 'I don't know.'

'Sam. You can't just shut me out.'

'Watch me,' I said as I brushed past him to the en-suite and started throwing my toiletries into the bag too. 'Hadn't you better go downstairs and see to your wife and child?' I snapped at him.

I saw the impact of my words on his face – full of guilt and pain. But I didn't care. He had broken my heart.

He didn't answer me. He just nodded before turning and walking out of the room.

As soon as he was gone, I pulled my phone from my pocket

and texted my dad, asking him to come and pick me up as soon as possible. Then I sank to the bathroom floor and started to cry.

Just twenty minutes earlier, I had been the happiest woman in the world. I'd believed my relationship with Gabriel was perfect. But, right now, I could see no way back from this for us.

How could I ever sit back and watch him running off to play happy families with his ex-wife?

CHAPTER 2

GABRIEL

I stared at my ex-wife as she sat at my kitchen table sipping a cup of peppermint tea, and wondered if I was dreaming.

Surely, I must be?

But, if I was, it was a fucking nightmare. Samantha had left twenty minutes ago. Her father had picked her up but he hadn't come into the house. Sebastian Donovan was my best mate and my business partner, and now he was stuck in the middle of this thing with me and his daughter. I'd promised him I'd never do that to him. I'd promised him I'd never hurt her.

As soon as his car had pulled up outside, Samantha had practically ran out of the house without a backwards glance. I'd thought about stopping her going and forcing her to talk to me, but I realised that I couldn't.

I felt fucking helpless. Samantha had every right to be pissed off with me. She had every right to hate me – I hated myself. And now, instead of eating dinner with the woman I loved more than anything else in the world, I was waiting for my ex-wife to explain how the hell she could be pregnant with my child.

'I'm sorry Samantha left. I didn't mean to come between

you,' Jennifer said as she stared up at me with her huge blue eyes.

She wasn't sorry. Not even a little bit. But I didn't tell her I knew that. 'I don't understand how this baby could be mine. We used a condom?'

'Well, they're not infallible. And you were pretty wasted. Maybe you didn't put it on right?' she offered.

'I've been using condoms for twenty-five years. I think I know how to put one on,' I barked at her.

'Well, maybe it had a tear in and you didn't notice?' she shrugged. 'All I know is this baby is due in twenty-four weeks, and that means it was conceived when we had sex. I haven't been with anyone else except you.'

I shook my head. I still couldn't believe it. This woman was a manipulative liar. She had proven that while we were married.

'Gabriel. I'm sorry to drop this on you like this, but this baby is yours.'

'So, why are you only just telling me now? Why didn't you tell me when you found out?'

'I didn't want to land this on you. I knew you were with someone else. I thought I could do it on my own. And maybe with Emily's help, I could have. But now I realise that I can't. It's too hard,' she sniffed.

I frowned at her. That didn't fit with the woman I knew. Doing this on her own? Jennifer Sloane didn't do anything the hard way. She had spent her life as a pampered princess. Sixteen years younger than her sister, Emily, she had been a surprise to their parents and had been spoiled by them and her older sister from the moment she was born.

But perhaps she had changed? Was my anger clouding my judgement?

'Why did your sister throw you out?' I asked. Emily had

always doted on her and after their parents had died, she'd been like a second mother to her.

'We had a huge fight. She doesn't approve of me keeping the baby. Or the fact that it's yours.'

'But why is it any business of hers? You're forty years old for Christ's sake. Why is she even bothered what you do?'

'Well, it was more that it's your baby. And you and I ... well, you know. She feels like you took advantage of me.'

I laughed out loud. 'Are you fucking kidding me?'

'Of course, I told her it wasn't like that. But you know what she's like?'

'What exactly do you want from me?' I asked with a sigh.

'I need somewhere to stay. I had to leave my temping job because I'm constantly tired,' she groaned as she rubbed her bump. 'I have no-one else to turn to, Gabriel. And this baby is half your responsibility.'

I clenched my fists at my sides. She had a fucking nerve preaching to me about responsibility. 'I'll provide for the baby if it's mine.'

'I know you will, and it is,' she said with a smile.

'But you can't stay here. What happened to the house?' I asked her, referring to the half a million pound house she got in our divorce.

'I had to sell it. I couldn't afford to run it on my own.'

'So, why didn't you buy somewhere smaller?'

She shook her head. 'I tried, but I had bills to pay. I couldn't find a decent job. It's not like I had an endless supply of money. I had expenses to cover.'

I gritted my teeth. I remembered all too well how quickly she used to burn through money. I'd known she wouldn't have been able to afford to keep our huge house herself, but she had demanded it in the divorce, and in the end, I'd handed it over just to be rid of her. She hated to work and she refused to do any jobs which she considered beneath her. So, it wasn't surprising that she'd blown the lot and had nothing left.

'Well, you can't stay here. This is mine and Samantha's house,' I told her. Samantha may have left, but if I had my way, it would be a very temporary arrangement and she'd be back in my arms and my bed before the end of the week.

'But I have nowhere else to go, Gabriel,' she said as her bottom lip started to tremble.

'A friend of mine has some properties,' I lied. The properties were mine, but I didn't want her knowing that. 'There's one without a tenant for the time being. You can stay there until you find somewhere more permanent. But you're going to have to find another job eventually. I'm happy to cover what I can, but you'll need to start providing for yourself too.'

'No-one will employ a pregnant woman,' she sniffed. 'And then once the baby comes, I won't be able to work. I'll have my hands full as it is.'

I frowned at her. She was as unlike Samantha as anyone could possibly be. I wondered how I had ever fallen for her. It seemed that all of the things that I'd once found attractive in her – those huge blue eyes, her neediness, her dependence on me, were now complete turn-offs. Samantha Donovan had ruined me for any other woman.

I checked my watch. It was almost eight o'clock. 'You can stay here tonight. I'll have someone move you into the flat tomorrow.'

She nodded. 'Thank you, Gabriel. I knew you would come through for me. You're a good man.'

I leaned back against the counter. I don't think a good man was how most people who knew me would describe me. And I certainly didn't feel like one right now. Not when I had broken Samantha's heart. Maybe what I actually was, was a mug!

'Let me show you the spare room,' I said.

Jennifer followed me up the stairs and I opened the door to the guest bedroom. 'You should find everything you need in here,' I said before stepping back and out of her way.

She placed a hand on my arm and squeezed lightly. 'Thank you, Gabriel. I really appreciate this,' she said with a flutter of her eyelashes. I rolled my eyes and took a deep breath.

What the fuck was I letting myself in for?

I lay in bed with my hands behind my head and wondered how my life had turned to shit in a matter of hours. I wondered what Samantha was doing right now. Was she sitting at her father's kitchen table, telling him what a complete bastard I'd turned out to be? Or was she lying in bed, thinking about me too, and wishing she was here instead?

I was relieved I hadn't had to face her father earlier. He'd been my best mate and my business partner for the past eighteen years. I had promised him I would never hurt his daughter, and I'd fucked that up royally.

Jennifer was asleep in my spare room. I'd get some of my employees to set her up in one of my empty properties tomorrow, and get her out of my house. Whether she was carrying my baby, or not, I couldn't have her here. I couldn't bear to look at her and be reminded of what I'd done.

I glanced at the empty space in the bed beside me where Samantha should be and felt a jolt of pain through my heart.

I had fucked everything up. The hurt on her face when Jennifer had dropped her little bombshell was etched into my brain. I kept replaying it over and over in my head and each time I did, it made me feel sick. I wondered if she would ever forgive me. And if she did, how would we ever learn to navigate this new dynamic in our relationship. I was going to be the father of another child before ours would even be born. How the hell would that even work?

It was clear from my conversation with Jennifer that she wanted me to be involved. It was even clearer that she expected me to pay for everything for her and the baby from here on in. Not that the money bothered me. If the kid was mine, I'd be happy to pay.

But what would I do about Samantha?

I was desperate to talk to her. I contemplated driving over there and forcibly removing her from Sebastian's house. I imagined walking into her bedroom, throwing her over my shoulder, carrying her down the stairs and putting her into my car.

If only I could.

I'd have to grit my teeth and wait until she was ready to talk to me, as much as that killed me and went against every instinct I had.

I was used to taking what I wanted when I wanted it. But I couldn't do that with her. She belonged to me and I would never let her go, but she was too stubborn and strong-willed to allow me to bully her into a decision. Besides, I loved her too much to force her to do that.

CHAPTER 3

SAMANTHA

I looked up at my dad as he handed me a mug of hot chocolate. I counted eight tiny marshmallows floating on top of the brown, frothy liquid and I couldn't help but smile.

'That always used to make you feel better when you were a kid,' he said before planting a kiss on my head and sitting on the sofa next to me. 'So, tell me what the hell is going on? You said Jennifer is pregnant and it's Gabriel's baby?'

I nodded as I tried to stop the tears from overwhelming me again. All I seemed to do lately was cry and it was bloody annoying. 'She says it's his, and I suppose she'd know?' I replied with a shrug.

'But he would never ... Not with her,' my dad shook his head.

'Well, he did. He admitted it.'

'So, he cheated on you?' he frowned.

'Well, it was when we'd broken up, so, technically no,' I sniffed. 'But it feels like he cheated on me, Dad. And with her, of all people.'

'I know, love,' he said as he wrapped an arm around my shoulder and pulled me towards him. 'He's a fucking idiot.'

'Well, I won't argue with that,' I said, forcing a half-hearted laugh as I wiped a tear from my cheek.

'What are you going to do, love?'

'I honestly don't know. I don't even have the flat any more ...'

'Well, you can stay here for as long as you like. This is your home, Sam. And my grandchild's home too – for as long as you both need it.'

'Thanks, Dad.'

We sat in silence for a few moments and I took a sip of my hot chocolate.

'You know I'd be happy to kick his fucking arse if you want me to?' my dad said suddenly. He looked at me and flashed his eyebrows, no doubt trying to diffuse the tension.

'Thanks, Dad,' I smiled. 'But, I don't think that will be necessary. And I don't expect you to choose between us either. You don't have to give him a hard time because of me. I know he's your family too.'

'A hard time? He'll be lucky if he gets off with just a kick in the nuts, love.'

I leaned against him, and nestled my face against his chest. He always smelled of his favourite Chanel cologne. He'd worn it for as long as I could remember, and I still found the smell comforting.

I knew he was joking about kicking Gabriel in the nuts. Humour was his way of trying to handle the intensity of the moment.

The whole situation was going to be almost as painful for him as it was for me and I had no idea how any of us were going to get through the next few days.

Every time I thought about Gabriel, and Jennifer, I felt like the air was being squeezed from my lungs. I kept hoping that he was going to call me and tell me it had all been a huge mistake.

How could my world have completely fallen apart in the space of a few short hours?

CHAPTER 4
SAMANTHA

I closed my laptop and leaned back in my chair with a sigh. I'd managed to distract myself all morning by burying my head in my work, but now I was feeling hungry and if I didn't eat regularly these days, I started to feel incredibly nauseous.

I wished that Nick was here. Nick Cook was my best friend of fourteen years, and my business partner. He was also the one person I felt like talking to. He was one of those people who always seemed to know the right thing to say.

Usually, if either of us needed to chat or had a problem, we'd walk through the park to the local coffee shop and talk everything through. By the time we got back to the office, we'd usually solved our problems, or at the very least felt better about them.

Not that I thought that a walk through the park, a coffee and a brownie could solve this particular problem, however it would certainly help me to talk things over with him. But Nick was off on a week long holiday with his two kids.

I rubbed my temples and let out a long breath. Maybe I'd just nip to the newsagents and get myself one of their pre-packaged sandwiches? Then I could get stuck back into work before I started to think too much about how my life had been turned upside down.

'Everything okay, Samantha?' I heard a voice ask.

I looked up to see our junior partner, Simon Hardaker standing in my doorway. He had only worked for us for six months, but he had settled in well. He was quiet and shy and had a nervous energy about him, but he was good at his job and he seemed to care about our clients.

Gabriel was always claiming that Simon fancied me, but I always dismissed him. He lived with a woman, and although he claimed she was his flatmate, the way he talked about her made me think he'd at least like something more, if there wasn't more already.

The memory about Gabriel blindsided me. If I wasn't completely distracted by something else, he filled my every waking thought.

I blinked back a tear. 'Yes, I'm fine, thanks, Si,' I lied.

He walked into my office and sat down in the chair opposite my desk. 'Are you sure?' he asked softly. 'You look a little ...'

'A little what? Like I've been dragged through a hedge backwards?' I asked with a faint laugh. I'd spent half the night crying and had about two hours sleep. All of the carefully applied make-up in the world couldn't hide that.

He looked down at his hands. 'I'm sorry, I didn't mean ...' he trailed off.

'No need to apologise. The truth is, I've had better days. But I'm fine.'

'I'm sorry for whatever it is that's bothering you anyway. Can I get you anything? I was just about to nip out to grab a sandwich.'

'Actually, do you mind if I come with you? I could so with some fresh air?' I said.

It would do me good to get out of this office for half an hour.

My back was starting to ache from sitting at my desk all morning.

Simon's cheeks flushed pink and I couldn't help but smile. He was so shy.

'Of course not. Are you ready to go now?' he asked.

'Yes. Let me grab my coat.'

Half an hour later, I was back at my desk with a chicken and avocado sandwich and a bottle of freshly squeezed orange juice. It had been nice chatting to Simon, but it wasn't the same as talking to Nick. I didn't know him well enough to talk about anything more personal than my favourite films, or work. It transpired that he loved the film, Pretty Woman, almost as much as I did.

I'd mentioned I was staying with my dad for a few days and then he'd told me all about how his own father had never been around when he was growing up. His mum had got pregnant at sixteen, and there had just been the two of them until she'd died a few years earlier.

I hadn't felt able to open up to him in the same way though. I still found it hard to trust people, despite the fact that he was such a nice guy. But a twelve year marriage to a sadistic sociopath who tried to kill me had left its scars, and they ran deep.

I was about to take a bite of my sandwich when my office phone rang. I glanced at the display and noticed it was Beth, my receptionist.

'Hi, Beth,' I answered.

'Hi, Samantha. There's a Mr Lewis on the phone asking for you. Are you free or shall I take a message?'

I put my sandwich down. I could wait another five minutes. 'No, I'm free. Put him through.'

'Thanks, will do,' she said and then I heard her put the phone down and the other line was transferred to me.

'Hello, Samantha Donovan speaking,' I said.

There was nothing but silence on the other end. I waited for a few seconds. 'Hello?' I repeated.

Nothing.

I put the phone back in its cradle. Mr Lewis must have been cut off. No doubt, he'd call back when he could.

I picked up my sandwich and the smell of avocado hit me suddenly. I felt a wave of nausea rush over me. I leaned back in my chair, closing my eyes and taking deep breaths until it passed. It seemed avocado was now another thing I would no longer be eating.

CHAPTER 5
GABRIEL

I walked up the steps of Sebastian's house and rang the doorbell. I hadn't slept all night wondering how I was going to fix this whole situation with Jennifer, and more importantly how I was going to explain what happened to Samantha. I had been the biggest dick on the face of the earth to jeopardise what we had together.

I couldn't lose her.

I wouldn't.

She belonged to me and she always would. If she would just let me explain, then she would see that she was the only woman I loved and no matter what happened, her and our baby would always come first.

A moment later, Sebastian answered the door. He glared at me, his face full of anger. 'She's not home,' he snarled. 'And even if she was, I wouldn't let you anywhere near her.'

My heart sank through my chest. I was desperate to speak to her. I'd tried phoning her dozens of times since last night and she had ignored every call.

I shook my head. 'I'm sorry, Seb. I fucked up. You have every right to be pissed off with me.'

He folded his arms across his chest and glared at me. 'Pissed off? I'm fucking beyond pissed off, mate. You promised me you would never hurt her. I trusted you to look after her.'

I nodded because he was right. 'I know, Seb. I've let you down. But even worse, I've let her down, and I will never forgive myself.'

'Jennifer though, Gabriel? What the fuck where you thinking?'

I looked at him. My best mate who had supported me through every stupid decision I had ever made in my life. It killed me that he couldn't through this. 'I wasn't thinking, mate. I was fucking destroyed. I was heartbroken – and she was just there.'

'You're a fucking idiot!' he barked at me and I just nodded again, because I couldn't disagree with a single word he was saying. 'Now, I appreciate the irony of me lecturing you about fucking about with other women, when I can't make it work with anyone, but, Gabriel, this is you and Sam. You were so fucking happy.'

'I know.'

'You had everything you ever wanted, and now my daughter is back home with me and I had to sit up with her for most of the night while she sobbed in my arms.'

That statement felt like a knife twisting in my heart. 'She was crying all night?'

'Of course she fucking was!'

I swallowed. I felt like shit. Deservedly so. 'If I could just talk to her. Has she gone to work?'

'Yeah. But, if you want my advice, give her a bit of space. You know how stubborn she is. She'll talk to you when she's ready and not before. If you keep pushing her, it will only take her longer to come around.'

I frowned at him. I was losing my mind here. I didn't have

the luxury of time.

'I know it's not what you want to hear. And I know it's not how you're used to doing things. But you know her as well as I do, and so you also know that what I'm saying is right.'

I stuffed my hands into my trouser pockets and kicked the step in frustration. He was right but that didn't make it any easier to deal with. 'Fine. I'll give her a few days to cool down. But you'll let me know how she is, won't you? Her and the baby? If there's anything at all she needs?'

'Of course I will. And despite you breaking my daughter's heart and being a complete fuckwit to go anywhere near your ex-wife, I'm rooting for you. I know how much you love her, and how much she loves you,' he said with a brief nod of his head.

'Thanks, mate. I really appreciate that.'

'But I can't let you in, because she'll kill me. So, piss off,' he said with a smirk.

'Duly noted,' I replied before turning around and walking back to my car.

As I was about to pull away from the kerb, my phone started ringing. I pulled it out of my pocket, hoping it would be Samantha. I sighed when I saw Scott Thomas's name flashing on the screen instead. He was one of my employees and I'd left him in charge of moving Jennifer into an apartment earlier that morning.

I answered the call. 'Everything okay?'

'Well, she's moved in,' he said as he blew out a long breath.

'Something wrong?' I asked.

'She's a bit demanding, isn't she?' he started to laugh.

'That's an understatement, mate,' I agreed.

'And I know you told the lads that she was an old friend ...'

'Yeah, so?' I asked. I'd had a team of my employees helping Jennifer move, but only Scott knew me well enough to know that she was actually my ex-wife.

'Well, she's told all of the lads that she's having your baby, and basically referring to herself as your wife.'

'What? For fuck's sake,' I seethed. I had specifically asked her to keep that shit to herself. Not to mention, that she hadn't been my wife for a long time.

'I told the lads she was your ex-wife, and that you were just helping her out. But I just thought you'd want to know what she's saying.'

'Thanks, Scott,' I said with a sigh. 'She's sorted now though? Is the electric and water and everything sorted?'

'Yep. She shouldn't need to bother you for anything like that, Boss.'

'Hmm. She shouldn't, but no doubt she will.'

Scott laughed. 'I'd better get back to it and make sure she doesn't need anything else before we leave.'

I hung up the phone and leaned my head back against the headrest. I closed my eyes and felt the weight of the past twenty-four hours sitting heavily on my chest. I was so fucking tired. My jaw ached and my head throbbed. But I couldn't go home to an empty house where all I would see was Samantha. The only other option was to go to work.

I hadn't worked as a bouncer for years, but the thought of doing that tonight suddenly seemed like a welcome one. It never hurt to have an extra body on the doors of some of our more troublesome establishments. Hopefully, someone would piss me off soon enough and I'd be able to take all of my anger and frustration out on them.

I knew that I needed to have a word with Jennifer and tell her to stop calling herself my fucking wife, but I couldn't face speaking to her. I couldn't even stand to think about her. I wanted nothing to do with her, but if she really was having my baby, I knew that was impossible.

CHAPTER 6
SAMANTHA

It had been two days since Jennifer had turned up at Gabriel's house and blown my world apart.

I hadn't spoken to him since. I couldn't. I was too angry and too emotional. I was too heartbroken to even look at him. He had called and texted me over and over, leaving voicemails begging me to speak to him. His betrayal had cut me deeper than anything else I had ever known. But I knew that I couldn't put him off much longer.

We needed to talk. I needed some answers. And also I needed him to know that it was over. That was why I'd invited him round to my dad's house.

My heart leapt into my throat when I heard the sound of the doorbell. I knew it would be him. Right on time.

A few moments later, we were sitting at the large wooden table in my father's kitchen, staring across at each other awkwardly. I didn't even know where to start.

'I'm sorry,' he started for us.

'How could you, Gabe? Jennifer?'

He put his head in his hands. 'I know,' he said as his shoulders slumped.

'When did this even happen? How?'

He looked up at me. 'It was a few weeks after we'd split up. I was in the club. I'd drank half a bottle of whisky. I was completely wasted. She was there,' he said with a shrug and then he looked down at his hands.

'And?'

'She asked me if there was anything I needed. We had sex in the disabled toilet.'

'Classy!' I sniped.

'It meant nothing to me, Sam.'

'Tell that to the baby you put inside her.'

He swallowed. 'Please come home. We can work through this.'

'How, Gabe? You screwed your ex-wife and she's having your baby. Tell me exactly how we're going to work through that?'

'We'll figure it out, Sam. You and me –'

'There is no you and me,' I interrupted him and I saw the hurt on his face but it was nothing compared to the hurt that I was feeling.

'Don't say that,' he growled at me.

'You fucked your ex-wife!' I shouted.

'When you and me were broken up, Sam. You told me you didn't love and me you didn't want to be with me. I thought we were over. I was all over the fucking place.'

'But her, Gabe? You could have screwed any woman you wanted.'

'Well, the one I wanted wouldn't give me the time of day!'

I took a deep breath. I deserved that. And as much as I felt betrayed, he was right about us being broken up. But that didn't change the fact that Jennifer was pregnant, and she was having his baby.

I veered between angry and devastated, and as the anger

subsided, I knew in my heart that Gabriel would be hurting as much as I was.

'I can't share you with her,' I said as I felt a hot tear running down my cheek.

'You don't have to share me, Sam,' he frowned.

'Really? You don't think that she'll need you? You don't think that she'll phone you every time she's worried that the baby hasn't moved, or when she thinks every twinge means there's something wrong? When she needs peanut M&M's in the middle of the night?' I stifled a sob.

He shook his head. 'You will always be my priority.'

'You can't say that, Gabe. Not when you have another child on the way. I know you. You will be the best dad you can be to both of your children, and I love that about you.'

He stared at me.

'But that's why I can't do this. I can't bear to be sitting at home while you're with her. I don't want to be the one who is always making you choose. Because I know you would choose me if I forced you, and I can't be that person. I love you too much to make you do that.'

He glared at me. 'You can't be serious. Please, Sam! Just let me figure this out. I can make this work but I need you by my side.'

I shook my head as the tears started to fall faster. 'You don't. You need to do this alone. You're about to be a father to two amazing children, and you need to focus your attention on that. Not me.'

'No, Sam! Don't tell me what I need. I need you,' he banged his fist on the table.

'Even if you think that, I can't do this, Gabe. I don't want to be the other woman.'

He scowled at me. 'You're not the other woman,' he snapped.

'It was one time, Sam. It was a mistake. Don't throw away everything we have because I made a mistake.'

I shook my head. 'I've made my decision. I want you to be in our child's life, but you and me are done. It's for the best, and one day you'll realise that too.'

He scowled at me. 'You don't get to just decide that we're done, Sam. And I will never agree that us being apart is for the best.'

I didn't argue back. He was angry and hurt. But then so was I. 'I think you should leave. There's nothing left to say.' I said as I wiped the tears from my cheeks.

He glared at me for a few moments and I wondered if he was going to refuse to leave and what I would do if he did. Then he stood quickly, pushing his chair back so hard it almost toppled over. 'We're not done. Not by a long shot,' he said, but then he turned around and walked out of the kitchen and out of the house.

I rested my forehead on the cool wooden table as the sobs convulsed through my body. I had lost the only man I'd ever loved and it hurt like hell.

CHAPTER 7
GABRIEL

I climbed into my car and punched the steering wheel. I felt a rage inside me so fierce that I could taste it in the back of my throat. I was angry at Samantha, and the fact that she seemed to have all the power to decide whether we were over or not.

I was angry with Jennifer for turning up and tossing a hand grenade into what had been my almost perfect life.

But mostly, I was angry with myself. How could I have been so fucking stupid to have gone anywhere near my ex-wife? How could I have jeopardised what I had with Samantha? And for nothing more than a quick, unenjoyable, and completely meaningless, fuck!

As much as I told myself that Samantha and I had been broken up at the time, I had known on some level how much screwing Jennifer would hurt her.

Perhaps I should have told her? But I had honestly thought there'd be nothing to tell. If she'd had a meaningless encounter while we were apart, I'd have rather not known about it. I had made sure I was careful. I'd used protection. So, why was Jennifer pregnant and claiming her kid was mine?

I didn't believe her. But I knew that my disbelief may have

been borne out of my desperate need for her to be lying. Whether Jennifer was lying or not, Samantha believed her, and even if it wasn't my child, I'd still fucked her. Until I could find out the truth for sure and have a DNA test done when the baby was born, I supposed I had to give Jennifer the benefit of the doubt.

I started the engine of my car and pulled away from the kerb. My pulse throbbed in my fingertips as I gripped the steering wheel. I needed to do something about all this tension and anger that was coursing through me. I looked at the clock and realised that it was about time for the night shift to start for our bouncers. It had been a long time since I'd worked on the doors of nightclubs, but I'd done it last night, and it had been a welcome distraction.

I wasn't sure my employees all saw it that way, given that I'd tried to pick a fight with any fucker who'd even looked at me the wrong way. But what else was I supposed to do? Go home to my empty house and think about Samantha not being there with me? I couldn't do that. It was fucking torturous.

I drove to the nightclub that Sebastian and I owned. I'd work for a few more hours until I was too exhausted to do anything more than sleep. And I'd do my best to keep my temper in check, whilst secretly hoping that some idiot might try and push my buttons anyway.

Four hours later, I was standing outside the nightclub with three other bouncers.

It had been quiet – too quiet for my liking. People just didn't kick off these days like they used to. My bouncers assured me it was because they did such a good job, and because our firm was too well respected for anyone to take the piss, which under any other circumstances, would have made me happy. But tonight, I just wanted to punch someone's face in.

I watched the couple walking out of the club a few moments later. The woman looked at least ten years younger than the man she was with. She was unsteady on her feet and stumbled towards him. He grabbed her roughly by the arm and leaned in towards her ear as they approached the entrance. Something about the way he touched her, and the look on her face when she heard whatever he said, made the hairs on the back of my neck stand on end.

But, I had promised to be on my best behaviour.

They walked past us. He nodded as he passed. 'Night, lads,' he said with a wink, as though we were his comrades. He still held onto her arm, his fingers pressing into her soft flesh, and she looked down at her feet, not making eye contact with any of us.

I stepped out of the doorway when they left, watching them walk up the street. They had walked a few hundred yards, and when they'd reached a distance away, one which he incorrectly assumed they were no longer being watched from, he did it. He turned his body and threw her against the wall, one of his large hands on her throat. She pulled at his arm but he only pressed his face closer to hers.

I ran down the street towards them, thinking about Samantha and all of the times she must have had to fight off her cunt of an ex-husband. I reached him quickly and he turned to me with a look of shock on his face. I heard footsteps behind me and knew that one of my bouncers would have followed me for back-up. Not that I needed it.

'Let go of her, or I will break every one of those fingers,' I snarled at him.

She looked at me, her eyes wide in fear and he glared at me. He was a big fella, and no doubt he thought he could handle himself. 'This is none of your business, mate. This is between me and her,' he snarled back.

I stepped closer to him. I considered giving him another warning given what was about to happen to him. After all, how was he to know who he was dealing with? A few days earlier, I might have.

But not tonight.

I grabbed hold of his wrist, the one he had her by the throat with, and squeezed hard. He looked at me, blinking as though he was shocked by the amount of pain you could feel from someone simply squeezing your wrist. As he released his grip on her, I twisted his arm backwards until I heard a satisfying pop and he screamed in agony.

The woman rubbed at her throat and stepped away from him, towards my bouncer, Scott, who was standing by us now. Scott put a protective arm around her as I brought her attacker to his knees. I had his wrist twisted and his fingers splayed in the air when I noticed his wedding ring.

'Is this your husband?' I asked her.

'No,' she sniffed. 'He's a photographer.'

'A photographer?' I snarled as I brought my boot up and used it to kick him in the jaw. He slumped to the floor and lay sprawled on the pavement, groaning in pain.

I turned to the woman again. 'What happened?'

Her lower lip trembled. 'He said he'd get me some modelling work if I went out for a drink with him. I didn't want to, but he wouldn't leave me alone. He took some topless pictures ...' she shook her head and started to cry and Scott pulled her closer to him.

I turned back to the man on the floor. Given the mood I was in, this guy would have got a kicking whatever happened, but hearing that he was a complete creep somehow made me feel vindicated for what I was about to do.

'I imagine your hands are pretty important for your job then?' I asked as I looked down at him.

He started to shake his head violently as tears streamed down his face. 'No, please. No!' he begged.

'I did warn you,' I said as I stood on the fingers of his right hand, crushing them under the heel of my boot as he howled in pain. 'Do you know there are twenty-seven bones in the human hand? That's fifty-four in total. I wonder how many I can break before you pass out?'

I shifted my weight towards his wrist and heard a satisfying crack. He screamed and I heard a yelp of fright, or maybe it was horror from the woman behind me. That was when I felt Scott's hand on my shoulder. 'Come on, Boss,' he said quietly. 'He's not worth it. Let's go.'

I lifted my boot, allowing the crying man on the floor to withdraw his hand, cradling it to his body.

I turned to Scott. 'Get her a cab and make sure this prick knows who he's fucking with,' I said as I gave him a parting kick to his feet. 'I'm going home.'

'Will do, Boss,' Scott said.

I walked around to the back of the club to my car. My temples throbbed and my blood thundered around my body. Unfortunately, I knew that there was only one thing that would make me feel better, but Samantha had made it clear she didn't want to see or speak to me.

I felt my phone vibrating in my jacket pocket and I pulled it out. Despite knowing that it wouldn't be, I still foolishly hoped that it was her. I frowned when I saw Jennifer's name flashing on the screen instead.

It was almost 1am. What the hell did she want?

'Hello,' I snapped.

'Gabriel,' she cried. 'I think there's someone trying to get into the flat. I heard a noise.'

I frowned. This was all I fucking needed. 'You're on the second floor of a building. There's a mortice lock on your front door. You're perfectly safe. It was probably just one of your neighbours walking past.'

'Please, Gabriel. I'm really scared. You know I hate living on my own. What if it was someone? Could you please just come and check for me?'

I sighed loudly. 'Fine. I'll be round there in twenty minutes.'

I walked around the back of the flats and down the alleyway and could see no-one hanging around and no sign of forced entry at the back door. Whatever Jennifer had heard, if she'd heard anything, had probably come from inside the building and was one of her neighbours.

Walking back around to the front, I pressed the buzzer and told her it was me. Two minutes later I was standing outside her door inspecting it for any signs of damage.

She smiled at she opened it. Her eyes were pink from crying and I groaned inwardly. Her drama was quite literally the last thing I wanted to deal with right now.

'Thank you for coming,' she said as she opened the door wider allowing me to step inside.

I walked into the living room and sat on the sofa. 'I couldn't see anyone hanging around. There's no-one in the corridors and your door doesn't look like anyone has tampered with it. I'm sure whatever you heard wasn't someone trying to get in.'

She nodded and sat on the sofa next to me. 'That's such a relief. I was convinced I heard something. And then I couldn't get back to sleep and I kept imagining all sorts of horrible things happening to me,' she shuddered.

'Well, like I said, these flats are really safe.'

'I'm sorry to have dragged you here at this hour of the night. Can I get you a drink or anything?'

I shook my head. 'No thanks, I'd better go.'

She bit her lip as though she had something else on her

mind. 'I haven't felt the baby move for a few hours,' she said. 'Do you think that's normal?'

I'd actually done a lot of reading up on pregnancy and movements. 'Maybe he or she is asleep? When was the last time you felt them move?'

She shrugged. 'I don't know. Maybe this morning?'

'You're only seventeen weeks, aren't you? I think it's unusual to feel loads of movement that early. But why don't you go and see your midwife tomorrow if you're worried?'

She nodded. 'Yes, I will. Thanks.'

'Want me to come with you?' I offered, suddenly feeling guilty that she might be genuinely worried and I was being little help.

'No, it's fine. I'm sure our little jelly-bean is just asleep, like you said.'

I nodded and stood up. 'If there's nothing else?'

She stood up too. 'You can stay if you like?'

'What?' I frowned at her. Was she being serious?

Her cheeks flushed pink. 'I mean on the sofa. You look tired, that's all.'

I was more than tired. I was fucking exhausted. I'd barely slept a wink since she'd walked back into my life and blown my world apart. 'I'm fine. But I need to get home,' I said instead.

She looked like she was about to cry again. 'I'm sorry, you know?' she sniffed. 'If I've messed things up for you. But, I didn't plan this,' she started sobbing then and she ran her hands over her stomach.

For fuck's sake! I hated to see women crying – especially because of me. If this baby was mine, then I was as much responsible for it as she was. She hadn't forced me to have sex with her – that had been my own choice – a stupid one, but it was still mine. It wasn't her fault that my life was falling apart. It was my own.

I felt a wave of guilt for being so short with her. I crossed the room and put my arms around her and she buried her head against my chest.

'Everything will be okay,' I said as I stroked her hair.

She looked up at me, tears streaming down her face. 'Everything feels better when you're here, Gabriel.'

Fuck!

I realised that was my cue to leave. I let my arms drop to my sides. 'Try and get some sleep. It's not good for you or the baby to be so upset. I'll give you a call tomorrow to see how you are.'

'Okay,' she said as wiped her tears with the sleeve of her pyjamas.

I looked at her and couldn't tell whether this was all an act or she was genuinely upset. Perhaps even a bit of both? But one thing I did know was that I didn't want her getting any ideas about what the two of us were to each other. I said my goodbyes and left, thankful to be out of there.

CHAPTER 8
SAMANTHA

I placed the phone back in its cradle and frowned. That was the fourth time this week the elusive Mr Lewis had called to speak to me before being mysteriously cut off. This time he'd given my receptionist his first name too, Edward.

It was so strange.

Being cut off once was an accident, twice a coincidence, but four times – well, that was just weird. I wracked my brain trying to think of an Edward Lewis that I might know to offer some clue as to who he was, but the only Edward Lewis I'd ever heard of was Richard Gere's character in Pretty Woman – and it obviously wasn't him.

Whoever he was, he never left any details, other than his name. Beth had tried to get a contact number or any further information from him but all he would say was his name and that I would know him when we spoke.

It was baffling and it was starting to bother me.

My thoughts were interrupted by a soft knocking at my open office door. I looked up to see Gabriel standing in the doorway. He was, as usual, wearing one of his finely tailored suits and looking good enough to be dipped in chocolate and licked clean. He was carrying a large package under his arm.

I hadn't seen him since I'd told him that we were over six days earlier. He had phoned me every day, to make sure that me and the baby were okay. And I supposed that I couldn't deny him the opportunity to do that – this child was as much his as it was mine.

'You okay?' he asked with a frown as he stepped inside the room. He must have sensed the tension in me, or perhaps my concern was written all over my face.

I forced a smile. It made me feel less anxious just having him around. His presence filled the room and I felt it in every part of my body. 'Yeah, work is just busy, that's all.'

He crossed the room and stood in front of my desk. I looked up at him. 'What's that?' I indicated the strange shaped package he still had tucked under his arm.

'This,' he said as he placed it on the desk in front of me, 'is a pregnancy pillow. I read that they can help pregnant women find more comfortable positions to sleep in. I know how much you like something to hold onto when you sleep.'

'Am I supposed to snuggle up to that and pretend it's you?' I asked.

'If it helps?' he said as he walked around to my side of the desk and perched himself on the edge, so his thighs were only inches from my forearm. 'Would it?' he said in that low growl of his that seemed to rumble through my bones, followed by a slow, sexy smile that I felt deep inside my core.

It was the killer combination and I squeezed my thighs together under my desk to quell the throbbing sensation that was building. Why did my body have such a visceral reaction to him? When he was around all I could think about was how good it would feel to have his hands on me.

Any contact between us was always fraught with sexual

tension, and now I had to make smart-ass comments that only made the situation worse.

I swallowed and looked up at him. 'The pillow will certainly help me get more comfortable, so thank you,' I stammered.

'You're welcome. Are you sure you're okay?' he said as he reached out and lightly dusted my cheek with the back of his hand.

I wanted to tell him that no, I wasn't okay at all. Not even a little bit. I missed him like crazy. I was still so angry with him for what he'd done, but that didn't make me love him any less. I wanted to tell him that these weird phone calls were making me paranoid and anxious. I wanted him to wrap me in those huge arms of his and tell me everything would be okay.

But I couldn't. I still couldn't get past what he'd done, and giving him such mixed signals was unfair to him.

'Yes. I'm fine. Promise,' I lied instead.

He nodded but I got the sense he didn't believe me. 'Do you need anything else?' he asked softly.

Yes! I need you to bend me over this desk and fuck me senseless.

'No. I'm good. I appreciate the pillow though. Did you buy Jennifer one too?'

He shoved his hands in his trouser pockets then licked his lower lip as he looked away from me. 'I suppose I deserved that,' he said with a sigh as he stood up.

Then he walked out of my office and didn't even say goodbye.

I placed my hands on the v-shaped pillow and took a deep breath. Had he deserved that? Or was I being a bitch? He'd hurt me so much that I couldn't tell any more. I wished that I could get past this, but it felt like an impossible task.

CHAPTER 9

SAMANTHA

I took a deep breath as I walked up the driveway to Gabriel's house and knocked on the front door. I still had a key but it didn't feel right to use it. I didn't live here any more.

I'd been putting off returning to collect the rest of my stuff for over a week now and I was fast running out of clothes. Not only that, I missed being surrounded by my own things.

I'd moved into my old childhood bedroom back at my Dad's house, and I wanted to make it feel like it belonged to Samantha, the woman rather than the stroppy teenager who had last occupied it.

I waited on the doorstep for what felt like an eternity until Gabriel opened the door. He'd phoned me earlier that morning and I'd taken the opportunity to arrange to call round, so, of course I knew he'd be there and he was expecting me, but it didn't make it any less awkward as we stood there staring at each other, wondering what was the right thing to say.

'Come in,' he finally said as he opened the door wider.

I stepped inside the hallway and swallowed the lump in my throat. I tried not to think too much about how, if only for a short time, this place had been my home - and it had been the happiest time of my life.

Now, it never would be again and that realisation hit me like a punch to the stomach.

I placed my hand on the bannister. 'Is it okay if I go upstairs and get my things?' I asked, the tremor in my voice clearly audible.

Gabriel glared at me for a few seconds, as though he was considering whether to approve my request.

'Of course,' he replied eventually with a sigh. 'Do you need me to do anything?'

I shook my head, afraid to speak in case I stayed crying. Then I walked up the stairs leaving him standing alone in the hallway.

Walking into the bedroom I had shared with him was even harder that stepping into the house a few moments earlier. Every memory of being in this room came flooding back to me in an overwhelming rush and I had to sit on the bed as my legs trembled beneath me.

I looked around the room and saw the pieces of myself scattered around. My perfume; my shoes – discarded near the wardrobe as though I'd simply taken them off after a long day of work and would be putting them back on the next day; the half empty packet of cotton wool pads I used to take off my make up each night still sitting on the dresser. It was as though the room was waiting for me to come back - and I realised that he was waiting for me to come back too.

I felt the sadness settling over me like a heavy shroud as I realised that Gabriel was hurting just as much as I was. He was still hoping that we'd work through this somehow and I wasn't sure how I felt about that. Part of me was glad that he hadn't given up on us, but the other part of me wondered if he was only prolonging the heartbreak for us both.

I was a complete mess. I didn't know what I wanted because it changed from day to day and moment to moment.

I wanted space, but I also wanted to be close to him. I wanted to make things easier for both of us but I didn't know how. The one thing I did know was that nothing had changed in the last week. If he'd been hoping that I'd calm down and reconsider my decision, then he was sadly mistaken.

I wished that I was able to reconsider, but I couldn't. I couldn't bear to share him with *her*. I couldn't stand to watch him leave me to go to her. And I knew that he'd have to, because she needed him as much as I did. Maybe more? She had no one, and I had my father, and Nick, and besides that, I was more than used to taking care of myself.

I stood up and opened the wardrobe and took the large suitcase from the bottom. Then I started removing some of my clothes, placing them carefully in the case.

I was zipping up the suitcase having filled it with as much as it would hold when I heard Gabriel walking up the stairs and along the hallway. He leaned against the doorframe, his hands in the pockets of his jeans. His green eyes were full of fire as he looked at me like he wanted to throw me down on the bed and tear my clothes off.

For a few seconds I wondered if he would - and whether I'd be able to resist him if he did. I looked away from him and swallowed as my insides turned to jelly. Damn the effect this man had on me!

'I think I've got everything I need,' I said quietly. 'I've left a few bits though. I couldn't fit it all in.'

'That's okay,' he said as he crossed the room. He stood in front of me. I was wearing flats and he towered over me. He leaned forward and I felt the breath catch in my throat. But he only leaned down and picked up my heavy suitcase.

Then he walked out of the door, carrying it downstairs and

out to my father who was waiting outside in his car. I took a deep breath and mentally checked myself. I'd known this was going to be hard. A few more minutes and it would all be over and I'd be in the safety of my dad's car.

I was walking down the stairs by the time Gabriel came back into the house. He closed the front door behind him and the sound of the latch clicking as he stood there glaring at me brought an unwanted memory to the surface.

A memory of a time when my ex-husband, Jackson had refused to let me leave the house because I'd said something he'd taken offence to. I couldn't even remember what I'd said. It was probably nothing at all knowing him, but I remembered all too well the feeling of terror. I swallowed it down.

Gabriel wasn't Jackson, and my dad was right outside in his car.

I was safe.

Still, Gabriel must have seen the tension in me. 'Are you okay?' He asked, his eyes so full of concern that it almost broke me.

'Yes. I'm fine. I'll get going and leave you in peace.' I said. It was just a turn of phrase, and I hadn't thought about the actual words.

I saw the pain flash across his face. 'There is no peace for me when you're not here,' he replied. Then he walked to the foot of the stairs, blocking my path to the bottom.

'I need to go,' I said to him, afraid that if I didn't get out of there soon, he might convince me to stay.

'And you will, but I need you to hear this first. And I don't mean just listen to the words, Sam. I need you to hear what I'm actually saying.'

I blinked at him. 'Okay.'

'I'm sorry that I had sex with Jennifer. If I could change it, I would.'

I opened my mouth to speak, but he glared at me so I didn't. I suppose it wouldn't hurt to let him finish what he had to say. He stared into my eyes, his green eyes almost black as they burned into my soul.

'I know you think that being apart is the best thing for us, but I know that it's not. And I'm going to do everything in my power to prove that to you too. So, although I'm going to let you walk out of that door, don't mistake that for my compliance. This thing between you and me is far from over. I love you, Sam. You are everything to me, and I refuse to spend the rest of my life without you by my side. But I know that I've let you down, and so I'm letting you go - for now. But know that you are mine and you always will be. And I'll be right here waiting for you as soon as you realise that too.'

He stepped out of my way then, but I stood rooted to the spot. What was I supposed to say to that? I felt the power of his words deep in my core.

He was claiming me.

I felt my legs tremble as I looked at him. He radiated power – fierce and strong and protective. He was everything I had sworn I didn't want after my nightmare of a marriage had ended. But he was everything I needed. I closed my eyes and willed my heart to stop racing.

This was for the best.

It had to be done.

'Bye, Gabriel,' I said softly.

'Bye, Sam,' he replied as I walked to the door and opened it. I walked out without looking back, afraid of what I might see on his face if I did.

CHAPTER 10
GABRIEL

It had been two weeks since Samantha had walked out on me and I felt like I was slowly losing my mind. I'd seen her three times and spoken to her almost every day and it wasn't nearly enough. I missed her so much that my heart physically ached.

At least Sebastian and I had managed to sort our differences out. I knew that he was angry and disappointed in me, but he also knew that I loved his daughter more than anything else in the world, and there was no greater punishment he could dish out to me than the one I was already suffering. He also knew that nobody hated what I'd done more than I did.

We'd been in meetings about some potential takeovers of smaller firms all day, and it had been a good distraction. But, whereas his working day would soon be over, mine would last at least another ten hours. Working sixteen to eighteen hour days was the only way to numb myself to the pain of losing her.

Sebastian had some signed paperwork at his house for me to drop at our solicitors and I decided I had nothing better to do than go home with him and pick it up.

I walked up the steps to his house with him and waited

while he opened the door. I pushed my hands into my trousers pockets and licked my lips.

'Don't worry. She'll be in work,' he said as he turned to me.

'I know,' I nodded. He'd obviously mistaken my edginess for nervousness that she would be there, when in fact the opposite was true. I was on edge because I wanted her to be there. I wanted to see her. I wanted to touch her.

I followed Sebastian into the house and we walked into the kitchen.

'Hello, love. What are you doing home from work so early?' Sebastian said.

I felt my heart start pounding as I looked past him and saw her sitting there at the kitchen table with her laptop. I felt the tightness in my chest. She looked tired and it made me worried that she wasn't looking after herself properly. She used work as a distraction too, just like me – but I wasn't almost five months pregnant.

'I decided to work from home for the afternoon. I was feeling a bit ropey,' she said as she rubbed her temples.

'Gabriel just called in to pick up some papers from me,' Sebastian mumbled apologetically.

'Of course,' she replied softly.

'I'll just go and get them,' he said as he placed a hand on my shoulder. I gave a small nod of thanks. He was giving me some time alone with her and I was eternally grateful.

I walked into the room as Sebastian walked out and sat at the table opposite her. 'You not feeling too good?' I asked.

She looked up at me and I was sure I could see the tears in her eyes, but she blinked them away. Still, I felt the weight of the guilt crushing me.

'Just a bit of a headache and some morning sickness. Nothing serious,' she replied.

'Are you sleeping okay?'

She shrugged. 'As well as can be expected, I suppose. I like the pillow though.'

I looked at her and wanted to pull her into my arms and make everything okay. Her hand rested on the table and I reached out to take it. My fingertips only brushed hers for a second, but she pulled her hand back as though mine was made of fire. So now, she couldn't even stand to have me touch her.

'For fuck's sake, Sam!' I growled. I couldn't help it. Only a few weeks earlier, she couldn't keep her hands off me, and she would have happily begged me to touch her.

She looked up at me, tears in her eyes again and I felt like shit. I sat back in my chair and ran a hand through my hair.

'Do you want a cup of peppermint tea?' I asked her, desperate to do something useful for her. The peppermint was one of the few things that eased her nausea.

'Yeah, okay,' she nodded.

I walked over to the cabinet where Sebastian kept the tea, but when I opened it there were none in there. 'Where's the teabags?'

'Oh, my dad moved them,' Samantha replied as she stood up. 'He didn't want me stretching for them,' she said with a roll of her eyes. 'He's even worse than you for wrapping me in cotton wool.'

I smiled at her. I was glad that he was looking after her while I couldn't. She opened a low cupboard and took out the box of peppermint tea. Her fingers brushed mine as she handed it to me, but she didn't flinch this time. I stepped closer to her and heard her breath catch in her throat. I placed my hand on her arm and she looked up at me, her pupils dilated and her skin flushed pink.

'Sam,' I breathed.

'Don't, Gabe,' she shook her head but she didn't pull back from me. I took my chance and slipped my other arm around her waist, pulling her closer to me. She buried her head in my chest and I buried my face in her hair. She smelled so fucking good. I felt my dick twitching to life and cursed the fact that she made me constantly hard.

'I'm sorry,' I said against her hair.

She nodded and I felt her hot tears on my shirt. I cupped her chin, tilting her face up towards mine. I brushed the tears from her cheek with the pad of my thumb. It broke my heart to see her crying, especially knowing that I was the cause.

'Please tell me what I can do to make this better, Sam. I hate seeing you like this. I hate not being with you.'

She shook her head. 'There's nothing you can do, Gabe,' she sniffed. 'I wish there was.'

I swallowed and had to fight my instinct to lift her onto the kitchen counter and slide my fingers and my cock inside her.

'I need you, Sam.'

She stepped back from me. 'You don't need me. You want me. That's different.'

The muscles in my jaw tensed. 'Don't tell me what I need, Sam. You have no idea what it's like ...'

'Oh, really? I don't? Tell me then, Gabe. Tell me how hard this is for you,' she glared at me.

'Okay,' I snarled. 'Shall I tell you how I think about you and our baby every single second of every single day, wondering what you're doing and whether you're okay. How I can't sleep at night without you lying next to me. How I can't bear to be in our house because everywhere I look, I see you.' I pulled her back to me, one hand in her hair and the other on her backside. 'How it takes every ounce of willpower I have not to carry you back home and fuck some sense into you.'

She looked up at me and took a deep breath. I could feel her heart hammering against my chest.

'Gabe,' she whispered and my cock stiffened. I was about five seconds away from lifting her onto the kitchen counter top and burying myself in her.

Then with the most annoying timing in the history of the world, Sebastian walked back into the room, clocked that I had my hands all over his daughter and frowned at me.

'Am I interrupting something?' he asked.

I released her from my embrace and took a step back.

'No. Of course not, Dad,' Samantha replied. 'I was just going to take my laptop upstairs and give you both some space.'

Then she was gone and all I could do was watch her walk out of the room and know that there wasn't a thing I could do about it.

CHAPTER 11

SAMANTHA

I was lying on my bed scrolling through the internet and looking at baby clothes on my phone when it rang in my hand, startling me. I saw Gabriel's name flashing on the screen and my heart lurched in my chest.

I contemplated not answering, but he'd only call back until I did. I hadn't spoken to him since that awkward moment in my dad's kitchen yesterday when it had seemed we'd been moments away from tearing each other's clothes off.

'Hi, Gabe,' I said.

'Hi, Sam. I was just wondering how you're doing? Any sickness today?'

I checked the time on my watch. It was 9pm and I usually had an intense bout of nausea at this time of night. He would usually make me a cup of peppermint tea and hold my hand until it passed. The memory made me want to smile and cry at the same time.

'Actually, it's not been too bad today. I think it's finally starting to ease.'

'Good,' he said and then there was an awkward silence.

'Are you working?' I asked. He'd stopped working nights while we'd been together, but I knew from my father that he had started up again. In fact, it seemed he was working sixteen hour days, and I couldn't help but worry about him.

'Yeah. I've just finished checking on one of the clubs and I thought I'd call you before I headed to the next one. Where are you?'

'Just lying in bed, watching telly and scrolling through my phone.'

'In bed? What are you wearing?' he laughed softly and I couldn't help smile.

'Nothing exciting actually. The grey t-shirt with the little bird on the arm.'

'My t-shirt?' he asked.

'Yes. I brought it with me. It's so comfy. I didn't think. Sorry.' I didn't tell him that I hadn't washed it yet either, and it still smelled of him.

'I love that you're wearing my t-shirt,' he growled and I felt my insides clench and contract. 'Fuck, Sam! This is so hard.'

'I know. It's hard for me too,' I said as I blinked away the tears.

'Then let me make it better. I can be there in twenty minutes,' he offered.

I seriously considered it for a second. I missed him so much and his almost daily phone calls, during which he was funny and caring and charming, really weren't helping matters. 'Don't, Gabe,' I said with a sigh instead.

'Okay,' he said. 'I'll speak to you tomorrow. Get some sleep, Sam.'

'I will. You need to sleep too though, you know?'

'I can't sleep without you,' he said softly. 'Bye, baby,' he finished and then he hung up the phone.

I pressed my head against the pillow and closed my eyes. I

contemplated phoning him back and telling him that I struggled to sleep without him too. I never slept as well as I did when I was nestled against his body.

But I couldn't do that. Nothing had changed. There was still another woman out there carrying his baby.

CHAPTER 12

SAMANTHA

I rubbed a hand over my bump and smiled. These past few weeks had been tough, but whenever I thought about my baby it made me realise how much I had to be thankful for. Gabriel was trying his best to give me space, although that included phoning me almost every day.

I supposed I couldn't blame him, he wanted to know how the baby was doing too. I had to admit it was nice to hear his voice. I missed him so much, but I couldn't stop thinking about him and Jennifer. Every time I closed my eyes, I imagined the two of them together and it made me feel sick.

My thoughts were interrupted by my office phone ringing.

'Hi Beth,' I answered.

'Hi, Samantha. I've got Mr Lewis on the line again,' she said with a sigh.

'Okay. Put him through. Maybe I'll actually get to speak to him this time?' I laughed.

He had called me again every day this week, and still each time he seemed to get cut off before he spoke to me. Given that Beth managed to put every other call I got through to me successfully, I knew there was no problem our end.

I waited as Beth put him through. 'Hello?' I said.

No answer.

'Hello? Mr Lewis?'

Nothing.

Sighing, I put the phone down and walked out into the reception.

'Did he cut off again?' Beth asked, her mouth open in surprise.

'Yes. Is there ever a problem when you speak to him? Does he sound like he has a poor line or connection issues?'

She shook her head 'None at all. He's as clear as day.'

'Then what the hell is going on? That's about the tenth time now that's happened.'

'Maybe I should refuse to put him through next time and insist on taking a number from him? Then maybe you can call him back and finally get to speak to him?' she suggested.

I nodded. 'Yes. I think that's for the best.'

'Do you think it's anything to worry about?' she asked me.

'No,' I replied a little too quickly, trying to convince myself as much as her that there was absolutely nothing to the spate of lost connections.

CHAPTER 13
GABRIEL

I sat at my desk, trying to make sense of the new staff rota when I felt my mobile phone ringing in my pocket. 'For fuck's sake,' I mumbled to myself.

Taking it out, I intended to press the end call button until I saw Samantha's name flashing on the screen. She hadn't called me once since she'd walked out on me almost six weeks earlier. It was always me who called her. I answered it immediately.

'Hi, Sam. Is everything okay?'

'Yes. I just ... I got my appointment for my twenty week scan through. It's on Thursday at half past ten. I know you said you wanted to come with me.'

The sound of her voice made my heart hammer in my chest.

I swallowed.

The fact she was phoning me and telling me about this was something – wasn't it? 'Of course I do. I'll pick you up and we can drive together.'

'I can make my own way. You can meet me there if you like?'

'Sam,' I sighed as I ran a hand through my hair. 'Please, just let me drive you.'

There was a moment's pause before she answered. 'Okay. Pick me up from my office about quarter to ten then?'

'I'll be there.'

'Okay,' she said quietly.

'How are you doing?' I asked her.

She sniffed and I wondered if she was crying. It seemed all I did lately was make her cry. 'Fine,' she eventually replied.

'Do you need anything?' I asked, hoping that she would need something, anything, from me.

'No. I have to go. I'll see you Thursday.'

My heart constricted. I was desperate for any contact with her but she could barely even stand to talk to me, and I supposed I couldn't blame her. 'Okay. Bye, Sam.'

The line went dead and I leaned back in my chair. Just six weeks earlier my life had been completely different. I'd had a future with Sam all planned out. We were going to be a family.

We were happy.

Now I had two kids on the way instead, and the woman I adored couldn't stand me.

I scrolled through the contacts of my phone and dialled Jennifer's number.

'Hey, Gabriel,' she answered. 'It's so lovely to hear from you.' I winced at the tone of her voice. Now, this was a woman desperate to speak to me – how fucking ironic.

'Have you had you twenty week scan?' I asked.

'What?'

'Your twenty week scan? You haven't had it yet, have you? Shouldn't you have by now though.'

'Oh, yeah, I had it a couple of weeks ago.'

'A couple of weeks ago? Why didn't you tell me?'

'I didn't want to bother you with it,' she replied sweetly. 'I know how busy you are.'

I frowned. She was happy to call me at 1am to tell me she

thought she'd heard someone outside her flat, or to tell me she had a cramp, but she didn't want to bother me with our child's scan? That didn't make sense to me.

'Did you get any pictures?' I asked, recalling the fuzzy black and white photograph from Samantha's last scan that I kept on my refrigerator.

'What?' she asked.

'Pictures? Of the baby?'

'Oh, yes. Of course I did.'

'Well, can I have one?'

'I'm sorry. They only gave me one. I'll take a photo of it and send it to you if you like?'

'Yeah, that would be good. I have to go.'

'Okay. I'll speak to you soon?' she said expectantly.

'Yeah. Bye.'

I ended the call and a few moments later the photograph appeared on my screen. I stared at it and couldn't help but smile. It actually looked like a baby. My baby? I sent her a quick text message of thanks in response.

CHAPTER 14

SAMANTHA

I climbed into the passenger seat of Gabriel's car and gave him a faint smile. My stomach was churning and I was a bundle of nervous energy. I couldn't wait to see our baby on the screen and find out if he or she was okay, but I was also terrified that something might be wrong.

'I brought you something,' Gabriel said as he pulled a packet of peanut M&M's from the door panel.

My favourite.

I took them from him and a sob caught in my throat. Why did he have to be so bloody thoughtful?

'What's wrong?' he asked.

'I wish you wouldn't be so bloody nice. You're not making this easy, you know?'

'Sam,' he said with a sigh. 'I would do anything for you, but please don't ask me to make it easier for you to be away from me.'

I turned away and looked out of the window, placing the packet of M&M's in my handbag. The sooner we got this over with, the better. Being in such close proximity to him and not touching him was torturous.

I looked up at the sonographer and smiled nervously as she squirted the clear gel onto my stomach.

I felt sick. This was it. She would tell me whether our baby was healthy and well. I had never felt so anxious in my entire life.

I reached for Gabriel's hand and he squeezed it tightly. 'It's going to be fine,' he mouthed.

I nodded at him while the sonographer readied her equipment. She turned to me and pointed to the large screen beside us. 'This is where you'll get to see your beautiful baby,' she said with a smile as she placed the small device on my stomach.

She rolled it over my gel covered skin, down towards my abdomen. I looked at the grainy image on the screen but I couldn't make anything out and I swallowed. Was everything okay?

A few seconds later, she gave me a huge smile. 'There's your little one,' she said as the head came into focus. 'Woah, okay,' she laughed as she moved the machine around. 'Did you want to know the sex?'

'Yes!' I blurted out before Gabriel even had a chance to answer.

The sonographer looked at him and he laughed. 'Whatever the lady wants,' he said with a shrug.

'Great. In that case, you're having a boy,' she beamed at us both.

'A boy!' I breathed. 'And is he okay?'

'I just need to take a few measurements, and some pictures, but he's looking good so far. He's very photogenic.'

'Handsome like his Daddy,' I found myself saying without thinking.

She carried on viewing the images, taking pictures and pointing out our boy's heart and limbs. As she worked, I squeezed Gabriel's hand tighter with each passing second. My heart was in my mouth. He smiled at me, before lifting my hand to his mouth and kissing it gently.

The touch of his lips sent shockwaves up my arm – right to that place between my thighs that had missed him endlessly.

'So, your boy is perfectly healthy. He's measuring a little smaller than average, but that's fine.'

I almost cried with relief. 'Really? He's okay?'

She nodded. 'Perfect.'

'Thank you so much,' I said and then I did start crying.

Gabriel stood up and handed me a tissue from his pocket. I dabbed at my eyes and the sonographer smiled at us both – no doubt thinking what a happy couple we seemed.

'I'll just print you some pictures,' she said and then she walked to the other side of the room.

'He's okay, Gabe,' I said to him when she walked away. 'She said he's perfect.'

'Of course he is,' he smiled at me.

I was so happy I felt like I would burst. The whole emotion of the day washed over me and I pulled him to me, kissing his beautiful soft lips. He brushed my lips with his, gently at first, but then he slipped his tongue inside my mouth and I melted into him.

It was brief and passionate – and in that kiss, we told each other all that we weren't able to say.

We heard a cough beside us and we broke apart. The sonographer stood, smiling at us, her hand outstretched, holding out a roll of photographs. 'Here you go. I printed the best ones,' she said.

'Thank you,' Gabriel said as he took them from her and looked at them, his eyes shining.

'Thank you,' I added.

'I'll leave you to get cleaned up,' she said as she handed me some blue paper towels.

She left the room and I started to wipe the gel from my stomach. Gabriel took the towels from me when I'd finished and put them into the waste paper bin. Then he walked back over to me and took my hand, helping me down from the bed. 'You okay?' he asked.

I nodded. 'Yes. Can I see the photos?'

He handed them to me and I looked at the perfect pictures of our perfect baby boy. 'I want one of them, you know,' he said.

'Of course. But we'll need scissors. I'll cut one off when I get home.'

'I want the top one,' he said with a grin.

I studied them. They were all great shots. Our baby really was photogenic. 'Okay,' I agreed.

Then he held out his arm and I linked mine through it. For just a little while longer, I could ride this wave of happiness, and pretend that we were the perfect couple.

The drive back from the hospital was unbearably tense. We drove in silence and the sexual tension crackled in the air between us.

I drummed my fingers on the door panel. 'I'm sorry about kissing you,' I said when I could bear the silence no longer.

Gabriel turned to me and frowned. 'Don't be. I'm not.'

'I shouldn't have ... It was just ...'

'You were in the moment. You were happy. I like that your first instinct was to kiss me,' he grinned and I felt my stomach do a little somersault.

It suddenly felt very hot in his car and I wound down the window for some air.

When we pulled up outside my dad's house, Gabriel switched off the engine. I noticed that my dad's car wasn't outside meaning he wasn't home. The house was empty.

'So, can I come in while you find the scissors?' Gabriel asked.

'What?' I blinked at him.

'The scissors? I want my picture.'

'Oh, of course,' I said. 'The picture. Yes, of course you can come in,' I agreed, even though I knew if he came into the house, there was likely to be only one inevitable outcome.

After letting us in, I walked into the kitchen towards the counter with Gabriel close behind me. My body, as always, was acutely aware of his presence and all of my nerve endings were on edge.

'Why don't you sit down and I'll find those scissors,' I said as I turned to face him.

He continued walking towards me and I held out a hand to stop him. 'I really think it's better if you sit down.'

He frowned at me. 'Why?'

'For both of our sakes, I think you should keep at least a metre distance between us at all times.'

His frown turned to a scowl. 'What? Why?'

'Because this pregnancy has got my hormones raging, Gabe. I feel like I'm on heat. And this,' I waved my hand in his direction. 'Isn't helping at all. My body just kind of gravitates towards you. It's like it knows there's a part of you inside it.'

He sucked in a breath and I saw his eyes blazing with fire. I swallowed as I realised I had just handed him the keys to the cookie jar.

He ignored my request and took another step towards me. I stepped backwards. Distance was my only defence. But then I found myself backed up against the large refrigerator. He kept walking towards me until our bodies were just inches apart. I felt the heat searing my skin. God, I wanted him so much.

He placed his hands either side of my head and leaned his face towards mine. 'I bet your body would like another part of me inside it, wouldn't it?' he growled.

I swallowed. There was no point in denying that fact. I was

practically panting with lust. There were several parts of him I'd like inside me, and he knew it.

'I think we both know that's true,' I breathed. 'Which is why you should go and sit on the other side of the kitchen.'

'Why? We're both adults. Let me take care of you, baby,' he said as he ran a fingertip down my cheek.

His touch was like an electric current on my skin. 'No. We can't,' I insisted.

'Why can't we? We both want this.'

I shook my head. 'That doesn't mean we should do it. It will only make things more complicated.'

'I don't think things between us could get any more complicated, Sam, do you?' he said as he edged ever closer to me.

My heart was pounding so hard in my ears, I could barely think straight. My skin burned and that space between my thighs throbbed painfully, and I knew he could make it all go away in an instant.

But we couldn't. 'It's not like we can have no strings sex, is it?' I said.

'Well, I'm not suggesting no strings sex,' he replied with a scowl. 'We could never have that.'

'So, what are you suggesting?' I breathed as he pressed even closer to me.

'We will always have strings, Sam. But that doesn't mean we can't have sex just because we need to.'

'Do we need to?' I panted.

'I do,' he growled. 'I can hardly think straight without you. I think about fucking you almost every minute of every day. And when I'm not doing that, I'm thinking about eating your delicious pussy.'

I felt my insides melting like warm butter. I loved his filthy mouth. I couldn't answer him though. I couldn't lie and tell him that I didn't need this when my body was so brazenly betraying me.

'You don't have to answer me, Sam, because I already know you need this. I can tell by the way your breathing has changed. The skin on your neck is turning pink the way it does when you're turned on. You're already thinking about how, very soon, I'm going to fuck you, and your legs are trembling in anticipation of it. So, tell me, baby, why is it such a bad idea?'

'We don't have any condoms,' I offered feebly, grasping at any excuse as even my voice trembled now.

'Why the fuck would we need them?' he said with a frown.

'We wouldn't,' I whispered.

'So? Any other poor excuses for why we shouldn't do this?'

'We're not together,' I reminded him. 'It's hard enough being apart as it is ...'

'Do you think denying this will make it any easier to be apart? Do you remember how good we are together?'

I couldn't help but gasp as my insides contracted. Of course, I remembered every delicious way this man could make me feel. 'Yes.'

'When you get yourself off, you pretend that it's my fingers on you instead of your own, don't you?' he growled and my pussy clenched in response.

'You're pretty sure of yourself,' I mumbled.

'Tell me I'm wrong,' he glared at me and I wanted to look away but I couldn't. He held me captive with those incredible green eyes.

'You're not,' I whispered.

'So, what's the problem?'

'It won't change anything, Gabe.'

'I know that,' he said. Then he pressed his body against mine and I felt his erection pressing against my stomach. He bent his head to my neck and planted a soft kiss on my throat and it was my undoing. I almost came on the spot.

'Not here, in my dad's kitchen,' I panted.

He nodded and took my hand before leading me upstairs to my bedroom.

Once we were inside the room, Gabriel pulled at the belt on my wrap dress and opened it before sliding it over my shoulders. He slipped his warm hands over my hips and onto my behind, pressing me into him.

I groaned as he started to trail soft kisses up my neck. I started undoing the buttons on his shirt but he stopped me and pushed me back onto the bed. 'Not yet, baby,' he growled. 'Let me take care of you first.'

He crawled over me and planted soft kisses on my stomach as he slid my underwear down my legs. His hands ran back up my thighs, pulling them apart until I was completely open to him. He started to trail soft kisses up from my knees and all the way up to the top of my thighs, driving me crazy. He had been right in the kitchen, I needed him inside me just as much as he needed me. So, why was he being so hesitant?

'You don't have to hold back, Gabe,' I breathed.

'I won't,' he growled against my skin. 'But I've gone six long weeks without fucking you, baby. I want to take my time. I want to taste every part of you.'

And he did just that. Lazily exploring my body with his hands and his mouth, until I was begging him to let me come.

'Soon, baby,' he groaned. 'Let me taste you.'

When he finally took pity on me, I almost passed out. My orgasm exploded through that point in my body where he had his fingers and his hot mouth on me.

As I lay, breathless and in an orgasm induced stupor, he stood up and undressed. Then he walked over to me, and took hold of my hand.

'On your knees, Sam,' he ordered.

I allowed him to pull me up until I was kneeling on the bed, facing the large, mirrored wardrobe. He slipped onto the bed behind me, until he was kneeling too and we were both facing the mirror. He pressed his body against mine, his erection nudging against the seam of my behind. Then he pulled my hair to one side and planted a soft kiss on my neck.

'Do you see how beautiful you are, Sam? Do you see how good we look together?'

I felt the skin on my cheeks flush pink as I looked at the two of us in the mirror. I watched as his left arm snaked around my body until his forearm was pressed against my breasts and he began teasing my right nipple, rolling it around between his finger and thumb. I moaned loudly as I leaned back against him, enjoying the feel of his hard body against mine.

God, I had missed him so much.

When his right hand slipped over my hip and between my thighs, I whimpered in response. He found my swollen clit and began to rub slowly as he continued nuzzling my neck and tugging at my nipples.

'Is that good?' he whispered in my ear.

'Yes,' I just about managed to get the word out.

'Look in the mirror and spread your legs,' he ordered. 'I want you to watch when I slide my cock into you.'

I felt his words deep in my core as I felt another orgasm building. I looked in the mirror, at our bodies melded together as I spread my legs further apart. My cheeks flamed with desire and longing as I watched him slide his huge cock into me.

'Gabe,' I cried out as he slowly started to thrust into me. My senses were completely overloaded. He continued his assault on all my favourite pleasure points and I suddenly felt like I was falling. The pressure was intense and incredible. I was about to completely lose myself to him.

'Gabe, stop!' I panted.

He stopped moving, but he stayed inside me and kept his hands where they were.

'What's wrong, baby?' he asked, his voice full of concern.

'I just need a minute. It's so intense.'

'In a good way or a bad way?' he asked.

I smiled at him in the mirror. 'Good.'

'So, why am I stopping then?' he said as he planted a soft kiss on my shoulder blade.

'Because I feel overwhelmed.'

'Well, that's kind of the point, baby. You feel overwhelmed because I'm doing all of your favourite things at the same time. Because I'm kissing your neck, and you love that. You love having your nipples played with. You can hardly control yourself when I rub your clit, but most of all, you love being filled by my cock, don't you?'

Not to mention the dirty talk! 'Yes. But I feel like I'm going to completely lose control.'

'And why is that a bad thing, Sam?' he whispered. 'Let go. I've got you. I've always got you.'

I tipped my head back against him. My breath caught in my throat as I tried to speak. 'I know,' I whispered hoarsely.

'So, shall I carry on?'

'Yes.'

He kissed my neck as he drove further into me, and his hands continued their previous endeavours.

Every single part of my body felt like it was on fire. My blood thundered around my body. My heart hammered in my chest. The tightening in my core was so intense, I thought I might pass out at any minute.

'Do you see how good you look when you're full of my cock, baby?' he growled and his filthy talk was my undoing.

I felt the orgasm tearing through my body, trying to burst out of every place where he had his hands on me, before funnelling back through my core and rolling through my abdomen and legs in wave after wave. My legs trembled violently and he had to hold me upright as he gave a few final thrusts before he found his own release.

He pulled out of me and lay me gently down on the bed, lying beside me and wrapping an arm around my waist.

'You're the devil,' I hissed.

'The devil?' he flashed an eyebrow at me. 'You used to call me your angel.'

'Angels don't torture people like that.'

'That was torture?'

'Delicious torture,' I said with a smile. 'I'm not sure I'm going to be able to stand up for at least an hour.'

'Good. Because I'm happy to stay right here for as long as you need to,' he said as he pulled me closer. 'And I'll be ready for round two in about ten minutes.'

I rested my head under his chin. I should tell him to go. This closeness between us wasn't helping matters.

But I couldn't. I ran my hand over the tattoos on his chest. I loved his body. But more than that, I loved his soul. He was the missing part of me.

So, why did he have to go and fuck it all up? And why couldn't I let him go?

I needed his touch like I needed air. I railed against the feeling of being owned, but I couldn't escape that fact that my body was completely his.

A few hours later, I was lying with my head on Gabriel's chest and his strong arms wrapped around me. I could feel his heart hammering in his chest as we both recovered from our exertions.

He had spent the entire afternoon reminding me of how

good we were together. He had fucked me over and over again. It had been hot and passionate and intense – but it didn't change the fact that he had screwed his ex-wife when we'd been apart and she was having his baby. I could never get past that, no matter how much I wanted to.

'Did I tell you that one of our bouncer's wives has just set up her own business doing those 4D scans?' Gabriel asked me.

'Has she? I've seen those, they're really good.'

'What do you think? Shall we book one?'

I looked up at him. 'I don't know. Have you seen how detailed they are? I'd kind of feel like I'd seen our baby's face properly, and I'm not sure I want to – not until he's born. Does that make sense?'

He smiled. 'Whatever you decide.'

'I'll think about it though. And it's handy to know if we ever change our minds?' I said and suddenly realised I'd said we. As though we were still a unit – a couple. And we weren't. Not any more.

Gabriel planted a kiss on my head and hugged me tighter. As I was wondering how best to extricate myself from his embrace, I heard the front door opening.

'Crap. It's my dad,' I said as I sat up straight. 'Quick, you need to get out of here.'

'Shit!' Gabriel muttered as we both jumped out of bed and started dressing.

'You need to go now,' I hissed to him.

'What are you suggesting? That I climb out of the window?' he asked with a smile.

'My dad can't know about this.'

He stopped dressing and stared at me. 'Sam! You're carrying my child. I think he knows that we have sex.'

'He knows we used to. But we're not supposed to any more.'

He scowled at me and then he bent and picked something up off the floor. 'Here,' he said as he threw my bra to me.

'Thanks.'

'I'm missing a sock?' he said.

'Under there,' I replied as I saw the tip of it peeking out beneath the bed.

A moment later, we were both dressed and headed down the stairs as my father was standing in the hallway shouting my name.

'Hi, Dad,' I said as I jogged down the stairs.

He looked up at me and smiled, and then he noticed Gabriel walking behind me and flashed his eyebrows.

'I was just showing Gabriel something I bought for the baby,' I said quickly.

'Oh, is that what you call it?' my dad said with a grin.

'Hi, Seb,' Gabriel said.

'You staying for a brew, mate?' my dad asked him.

Gabriel looked at me and then he shook his head. 'No, I think I'd better go.'

'Okay. I'll see you at work later?' my dad replied, then he walked down the hallway and into the kitchen.

We reached the bottom of the stairs and Gabriel slipped his arms around my waist. I tried to shrug him off, but he held me firmly in place.

'Gabe,' I said with a sigh.

'I know. Nothing's changed,' he said as he leaned his head towards me. 'But thank you for this afternoon,' he smiled before leaning closer.

His lips brushed mine softly and my treacherous body melted into him. He pulled back and looked into my eyes. 'I love to hear you moaning my name, Sam.'

My insides clenched at his words. I put my hands on his chest. 'You need to leave. This can't happen again.'

He stepped back from me. 'But you already know that it will, right?' he said in that low growl of his. Then he turned on his heel and left.

I leaned against the wall and let out a long, slow breath. That had been incredibly stupid. But it had also been incredibly worth it.

CHAPTER 15

GABRIEL

I climbed into my car and leaned my head against the headrest. My heart had only just stopped pounding. I could fuck Samantha Donovan every hour of every day and it would never be enough.

I could still taste her on me. I could smell her on me, and it made my dick twitch. I couldn't get enough of her. I couldn't live without her. I needed her back by my side and the sooner I made that happen, the better for everyone.

I slipped the scan photograph out of my jacket pocket and stared at it.

Our beautiful, strong boy.

The picture was perfect. The sonographer had said he was posing to have his photograph taken. I looked at the name on the top. Samantha Donovan. Along with the date of the scan and our boy's gestation – twenty weeks and one day.

I took out my phone and looked at the similar photograph Jennifer had sent me. She had cropped it in such a way that only the image was showing. None of the information was visible.

Maybe it was just the way she'd taken the photo? Or maybe there was something more to it?

CHAPTER 16

GABRIEL

I walked into my office at Archangel Securities and was surprised to see Sebastian still there. I checked my watch and noticed it was almost eight o'clock. He rarely worked late, and since Samantha had moved back home with him, he ate dinner with her every night. He loved cooking, and he loved cooking for her. It was one of the ways he showed his love and affection.

'What are you still doing here?' I asked him. 'I thought you'd be at home with Samantha?'

He looked up at me and blinked. 'What?'

'I said what are you doing here?' I stared at him. Something was off.

'Just catching up on a bit of paperwork,' he said.

I nodded. That wasn't unusual, but not eating dinner with his daughter was. 'Samantha eating alone then?' I asked him.

He just stared at me.

'What is it?' I frowned. 'Where is she?'

'Don't freak out,' he started and that statement obviously had the exact opposite effect.

'Freak out about what?'

'She's gone out for dinner.'

'Who with?' I snarled.

'I don't know. Some bloke. But I'm sure it's not a date,' he offered.

'What the fuck!' I growled as my hands balled into fists. Samantha and my unborn baby were on a fucking date!

'Where?' I snarled.

'I don't know, mate,' he said. 'Why don't you calm down –'

'I don't want to fucking calm down, Seb. She's out having dinner with some geezer and I'm supposed to be calm about that?'

'It won't be like that,' he said with a sigh. 'She's in love with you, you fucking plant-pot. She's just having dinner.'

'If it's just dinner, then tell me where she's gone.'

'She honestly never said. All she mentioned was pizza.'

'Pizza?'

'Pizza,' he nodded.

I turned around and walked out of the office. Samantha loved the pizza at the Italian restaurant around the corner from her office. If she was out on a date with another man, I would fucking carry her out of there and take her straight home.

Half an hour later, I walked into Vincenzo's. The place was busy and I was approached by the maître d.

'I'm meeting a friend,' I said as I brushed past her and into the crowded restaurant.

I stood by the bar and looked around, and then I saw her. She had her back to me but it was undeniably her. I had a good view of the man sitting opposite her though.

He was older than her. Late-forties. He wore a dark shirt, open at the collar. Dark hair, peppered with grey. He was smiling as he looked at her.

Well, of course he was. She was fucking beautiful and he was probably thinking about getting laid later. It had only been two days since we'd spent the whole afternoon in bed together, and now she was out with another man. I wanted to walk over there and ask her what the fuck she was playing at, but she was just sitting there having dinner and I was going to look like a raving lunatic in this restaurant full of unsuspecting diners.

Suddenly, I felt someone walk up beside me and lean towards my ear. 'If she sees you spying on her, she will go fucking ape-shit,' he said with a soft chuckle.

I turned to see the smiling face of Samantha's business partner, Nick. 'What are you doing here?' I frowned at him.

'Having dinner with Samantha and Russell. What are you doing here?' he asked with a cock of one eyebrow.

'You're with them too?'

'Yes.'

'So her and Russell aren't ...'

'God, no!' he started to laugh. 'He's our old uni professor. Very happily married with three kids.'

'Fucking hell,' I hissed and Nick gave me a sympathetic smile. 'I'm going fucking crazy here, Nick.'

He nodded. 'I get it. But she wouldn't do that to you. I know you're worried, mate, especially with the phone calls, but you can't go around spying on her.'

'What phone calls?' I asked. Had I misheard him?

He swallowed and the colour drained from his face. 'Shit! She didn't tell you?' he shook his head.

'What phone calls, Nick?' I demanded.

He looked over at their table and then back at me. 'She's been getting some weird calls, that's all. Nothing threatening, just weird. I told her she needed to tell you and her dad about them and she promised she would.'

'This is the first I've heard about them,' I snapped.

'Yeah? And now I feel like crap for telling you. You can't say anything. She'll kill me.'

'But ...' I started as I ran a hand through my hair in exasperation.

'Look, I need to get back to the table. I was only nipping to the toilet. I'll have another word with her and convince her she needs to tell you, okay? But please don't ambush her now.'

I nodded. 'If she doesn't tell me by tomorrow, I'm going to have to tell her I know, Nick.'

He rolled his eyes. 'I'll talk to her. Now you should leave before she sees you.'

I sucked in a breath. 'Okay.'

As I was turning to leave, Nick put a hand on my shoulder. 'She'll come round, mate. She's just hurting right now.'

I nodded. 'I fucking hope so.'

One hour later, I was sitting in Sebastian's kitchen with a mug of coffee. I'd told him all about my visit to the restaurant and Nick's revelation about the phone calls. We agreed that we'd give Samantha a chance to tell us herself, but then we'd have to ask about them.

I'd apologise to Nick for dropping him in it, but I couldn't sit on information like that and do nothing about it. I needed to know more. I needed to know what was going on, or I couldn't protect her from any of it.

My mind was already racing wondering what this new phone call situation was about. More specifically, I was worried whether it was linked to the events of a few months earlier, when Samantha had been the target of a spate of threatening letters and an attempted assault at the hands of the ex-husband of one of her clients, Anthony Garvey.

Samantha had been worried that someone else was behind it after something Garvey had said to her. Sebastian and I were convinced that if anyone was, it could only have been her ex-husband, Jackson Carver. However, Samantha hadn't been so sure.

Now Carver and Garvey were dead, and I had assumed that would be the end of it. But now there were phone calls and I had a terrible feeling Samantha might have been right all along.

All we could do now was sit and wait for her to come home and hope that Nick had persuaded her she should tell us what was going on.

CHAPTER 17

SAMANTHA

I kicked off my heels and walked down the hallway of my dad's house to the kitchen where I could see a light on.

'Are you home, Dad?' I shouted.

'In here, love,' he called back.

Walking into the room, I was met by the sight of him and Gabriel sitting at the kitchen table with a mug of tea each. The sight took me back almost sixteen years.

My eyes were drawn to Gabriel. He was wearing one of his finely tailored suits, his shirt open at the collar, a glimpse of one of his tattoos peeking out. I took a deep breath and willed my heart to stop racing. The two of them stared at me, as though they were waiting for something from me.

'What are you two doing in here? I feel like I'm sixteen years old and I'm in trouble,' I said, thinking of the many nights I had arrived home after my curfew to find the two of them waiting for me, and how I'd try and pretend to be completely sober, but eventually end up breaking into fits of giggles.

'Gabriel just stopped by. We had some business to discuss,' my father said. But Gabriel continued to stare at me and I had the feeling there was something I was missing.

'Then why do I still feel like I've done something wrong?' I asked as I walked to the refrigerator and took out the jug of filtered water.

'Have you?' Gabriel asked with a cock of his eyebrow.

I frowned at him but the area between my thighs started to thrum with energy and anticipation. There was something about the low rumble of his voice that reverberated throughout my whole body. 'No.'

'How was your dinner, love?' my dad interrupted our awkward exchange.

'Lovely, thanks, Dad. It was nice to get out.' Was that why Gabriel was here and scowling at me? Did he think I'd gone on a date?

'Dinner?' Gabriel asked and my dad shot him a look.

'Yes. With Nick and an old friend of ours,' I snapped as I walked to the cupboard and took out a glass before pouring myself a drink of cold water. I took a large gulp and then held the cool glass to my cheek.

'Everything okay, Sam?' Gabriel asked me.

I wanted to say that no, it wasn't. That having him sitting there in my kitchen, looking good enough to eat, and glaring at me with those incredible green eyes, was making me feel hot and faint – and horny! 'Yes, why?' I lied instead.

He shrugged. 'You look a bit flustered, that's all.'

I walked over to the table and took a seat. Nick had been right about them needing to know about the phone calls. 'Actually, there's something I should probably mention,' I said as I ran my finger around the rim of my glass. 'It's probably nothing at all. But, well after everything that happened earlier this year ...'

'What is it?' my dad asked.

'There have been a few strange calls to the office. They come through reception, and it's a man who calls himself Edward

Lewis asking for me. But then when they get put through, the line goes dead.'

'How long has this been going on?' my dad snapped.

'Five or six weeks.'

'What?' he shouted. 'Then why haven't you said anything before now?'

I sat back against my chair and groaned inwardly. My father's temper was legendary and I didn't feel like dealing with it right now.

'Seb!' Gabriel snapped. 'Let her explain, mate.'

I smiled at him, thankful for his interruption, although I could see his hands balled into fists and knew he was feeling just as angry as my father.

'Well, at first, it didn't seem like anything at all. The first couple of times it happened, I thought that maybe he'd just been cut off or something. But then it started happening every day. Now, none of my calls are put through to me and Beth takes a message instead, which is a pain in the arse. He still calls a few times a week but he never leaves a message.'

'Have you contacted the police?' Gabriel asked.

'Yes, although not officially. That Sergeant who dealt with the letters came and spoke to me. They don't think it's connected though. There are no threats made or anything like that. No heavy breathing. The line just goes dead. We've just got to monitor it. But, like I said, I don't take any calls now. And there could well be a perfectly innocent explanation for it all.'

'Or it could be much more sinister?' Gabriel suggested. 'I know you always thought there was someone else behind Garvey's threatening letters, Sam?'

'But that was Jackson, wasn't it?' my dad interrupted.

'Sam didn't think so,' Gabriel said. 'And I'm sorry I didn't look into it more at the time.'

'Who knows what it's about. But, it doesn't feel threatening.

Just a bit weird. I feel fine about it. I only mentioned it to that Sergeant because he called in to discuss a domestic abuse case that I'm working on.'

'He didn't ask you out again, did he?' Gabriel frowned.

I looked down at my bump. 'I think this kind of put him off.'

He looked down at the table but I didn't miss the flicker of a smile on his face.

Suddenly, the sound of my dad's phone was filling the kitchen. '

It's Kayleigh,' he said, referring to his soon to be ex-girl-friend. They were engaged to be married but it seemed like their honeymoon period was already over and my dad was doing his best to let her down gently. She'd been trying to get him to commit to setting a wedding date, or at the very least moving in together, but he'd been dodging her for weeks now.

Annoyingly, it seemed he was using my return to the family home as his excuse, when in fact, it was just the fact that he didn't know how to tell her that he wanted to end things. Despite being engaged five times, my father was actually a massive commitment phobe, and he seemed to have an innate inability to remain monogamous.

'I promised I'd pick her up. I've decided to tell her that it's time for us both to move on. But we still need to talk about this more when I get back, Sam. I'm not happy,' he said as he answered his phone and walked out of the kitchen.

Then there was just Gabriel and I. 'You sure you're okay?' he asked.

I nodded. 'Yeah.'

'I know I let you down, Sam. But please don't keep stuff like this from me. Don't shut me out.'

I felt the lump in my throat. 'It's hard to talk to you, Gabe.'

'Why?'

'Why? Because when I look at you, all I can think about is

how much you've hurt me.' I saw the pain in his face and I felt the tears springing to my eyes. 'And I know that you're hurting too. I know that you feel just as shit as I do, and then that makes me feel guilty.'

'You have nothing to feel guilty for, Sam,' he said as he reached out and squeezed my hand. 'I'm the one who fucked up. I hate that I've hurt you like this. If there was some way I could make it better, I would. But please don't cut me out of your life. I couldn't handle that,' he said softly and as much as I hated what he had done, I was reminded of all the reasons why I loved him so much. I hated to see him in pain.

'I wouldn't ever cut you out of my life,' I admitted as I wiped a tear from my cheek. 'I couldn't.'

'Your dad is going to insist on you being driven to and from work again, you know that?'

I rolled my eyes. 'I know. I suppose it might not be so bad. Standing on the tube in the heat was getting a bit uncomfortable anyway. I think I've got too soft being chauffeured around everywhere. Besides, my last bodyguard turned out to be plenty of fun,' I smirked at him.

'Well, don't be getting any similar ideas with your new one,' he growled.

I smiled at him. 'Don't worry. I'm still completely hung up on the last one,' I said and then wondered why I'd said that. I needed to change the subject – and fast. 'I don't feel like talking to my dad when he gets back. I'd rather leave it until tomorrow when he's calmed down. I think I'm going to go to bed,' I said as I stood up.

Gabriel nodded and stood up too. As I walked around the table, he reached out and grabbed my hand, pulling me towards him. He wrapped his arms around me and I responded in kind. 'If anything ever happened to you ...' he breathed.

I pressed my face against his chest. God, he smelled so good. My heart pounded as I stood there, breathing him in.

'Don't make me go, Sam,' he whispered and my insides melted into hot liquid. I seriously considered letting him stay. There was nothing I would like more than to have him take me to bed. I wanted to fall asleep in his arms and wake up with his body against mine.

'We can't, Gabe. I can't do this.'

'Just give me tonight. No sex. Just sleep. Just me and you.'

I looked up at him. He looked so tired, there were dark circles under his eyes and lines on his face that I was sure hadn't been there a few weeks before. I wondered if he'd been sleeping at all these past six weeks.

'Just sleep,' I agreed.

I stepped back from him and took hold of his hand before leading him up the stairs.

CHAPTER 18

GABRIEL

I followed Samantha upstairs and into her bedroom with my heart hammering in my chest and my cock straining at the seam of my trousers. I closed the door behind us and watched as she started to peel off her clothes.

I had never felt so out of my comfort zone. I was in charge, especially when it came to her body. But tonight wasn't about fucking. It was just about being with her, and I didn't know how to do that when we were hardly even speaking.

'You coming to bed in your suit?' she asked me as she took off her bra. Then she slipped under the covers, wearing just the tiniest scrap of black lace and I felt my dick twitch uncontrollably. I readjusted myself and then shrugged off my jacket.

A minute later, I'd removed the rest of my clothes and shoes and slipped into bed beside her wearing just my boxers. I usually slept naked but my massive erection was getting in the way of my attempt to behave like a gentleman.

I held up my arm and Samantha nestled against my chest. I pulled her close to me and closed my eyes. I was so fucking tired. She planted a soft kiss on my chest and I groaned. Then she draped her leg over me, her knee nudging at my groin.

'Are you always hard?' she purred.

'Around you? Yes,' I planted a kiss on her forehead. 'But don't think I don't know the feeling is mutual, Sam. I know you're desperate for it just as much as I am.'

'Oh, really?'

'You think I don't know that you're dripping wet?'

'Well, you might suspect that I am, but you can't know, because you promised no sex, remember?'

I placed my hand under her chin and tilted her head up so I could whisper in her ear. 'I don't need to touch you to know that you're ready, baby,' I growled. 'You smell so fucking good, you're lucky I'm exhausted or I'd have my face buried in your delicious pussy.'

She flushed pink and punched me lightly on the chest. 'Has anyone ever told you, you have a filthy mouth,' she laughed.

'Only you,' I said as I hugged her tighter. 'Now, let me get some sleep before you make me break our no sex agreement.'

I woke the following morning just as it started to get light. I hadn't slept this well in weeks. Samantha's warm body was still pressed against me. She murmured in her sleep and pushed her body closer to mine.

I sucked in a breath and tried not to think about how good it would feel to be inside her. The promise I'd made about eight hours earlier now seemed impossible to keep. But, a promise was a promise and I had taken her trust for granted before and got my fingers well and truly burned.

I kissed the top of her head and tucked her hair behind her ear. Her hair always smelled so beautiful. I considered untangling myself from her soft body as my erection was becoming increasingly painful. I wasn't sure if it had subsided at all in the night. But it was worth the discomfort to hold her a while longer.

Although we'd spent almost the entire day in bed together a few days earlier, and despite some part of my body being inside for most of that time, this between us now felt somehow more intimate. And I wanted to hold onto it for as long as I could.

Soon she'd wake up and things would be awkward. We'd both get up and go back to our separate lives and I didn't know when I'd even get to touch her again.

I wanted to push her to make a decision about us. I couldn't stand living in this limbo, but I knew that wasn't how she worked. If I pressed her now, there was every chance I could lose her for good.

I don't know how long we lay there like that, except to say that it wasn't long enough. Eventually, her eyes fluttered open and she smiled at me.

'Morning,' she said sleepily.

'Morning, beautiful.'

'Did you sleep well?' she asked as she stretched out her limbs.

'Like a log,' I replied.

'Well, that would explain the morning wood,' she grinned.

'No, that's all down to you,' I said as ran a hand up her arm.

She nestled back into me and I stifled a groan. I had to get out of this bed while I still could. Then her hand slid down my chest towards my cock and that's when I realised all bets were off. There was no way I was leaving this bed yet.

I groaned as she wrapped a hand around my cock. 'Fuck, Sam!' I hissed. 'I thought we agreed no sex?'

'That was last night. This morning I need to be taken care of. I'd do it myself, but as you're here?'

I wanted to ask her what had changed. Was this just a quick fuck to satisfy a carnal need that we both had? Or was it something more?

After spending the night with her again, it felt like more. I wanted answers, but she was staring at me with those beautiful brown eyes, and then she started grinding herself on me and I thought I might lose my mind if I didn't fuck her soon.

I flipped her onto her back and pulled her underwear down her legs. She spread her thighs wide apart and I could see how ready she was for me. Her whole pussy glistening with her arousal. I dipped my head and ran my tongue the length of her slit.

'Fuck, Sam!' I growled. 'You taste so fucking good, baby.'

'Fuck me, Gabe,' she panted and I was more than happy to oblige.

I hooked her legs under my forearms and drove my cock into her. The relief at being inside her calmed my racing heart. This was exactly where I belonged.

She arched her back in pleasure as she took me to the hilt.

'You want it soft and slow or hard and fast, baby?' I asked her. I wanted to nail her to the fucking bed, but her pregnancy had made me more cautious of how rough I was with her.

'Every way, Gabe. I just want you,' she said as she reached for my neck, clawing at my skin as she pulled me closer to her. I slipped my tongue into her open mouth and let her taste herself on me. She rewarded me with a groan and a clench of her pussy muscles.

Then I gave it to her just how she'd asked for. Soft and slow at first, gently easing my cock in and out of her dripping wet opening. Until neither of us could stand it any longer and she was begging me to fuck her harder.

Then I fucked her like I really wanted to, like I might never get the chance to again.

She screamed my name when she climaxed and I had to put my hand over her mouth to keep her quiet. Sebastian was only down the hallway and I didn't want him thinking about what I was doing to his daughter.

When we were done, I lay on my back and pulled her to me. 'I love you, Sam,' I panted. 'Please tell me that meant something more to you than just the need to scratch an itch.'

'Of course it did. It always does,' she said quietly. 'But can we talk about this later? I still have to face my dad and talk about the phone calls.'

I kissed the top of her head. 'Of course we can. Maybe if you just agree to let him have someone driving you for a while, it won't be such a battle with him? Would it really be such a bad thing to let him look after you?'

'I suppose not.'

'It would make me feel a whole lot better too,' I added.

'Okay,' she said with a sigh. 'If it will make you both feel better.'

I left Samantha's house before Sebastian got up. I'd been tempted to hang around for as long as I could and drive Samantha to work myself, but it was better to leave and let her have some space.

She had said that we'd talk later, and I felt hopeful for the first time in weeks. It felt like something had shifted between us last night.

My night with Samantha had almost made me forget about Jennifer and my plan for later that afternoon. I took my phone out of my pocket and dialled her number. She answered on the second ring, as though she'd been waiting on my call.

'Hey, Gabriel,' she said sweetly.

'Hey,' I replied. 'Are you busy this afternoon?'

'Not especially. Why?'

'I have a surprise for you. Can you be ready if I pick you up at two?'

'Yes,' she squealed and I felt a pang of guilt. She was so eager to spend time with me and she didn't even attempt to disguise it.

'Great. I'll pick you up then.'

'Great. See you then,' she said and I hung up the phone.

I'd go home and shower and then do a bit more digging into these calls Samantha was getting before meeting Jennifer later. Who the fuck was this Edward Lewis and what the hell was he playing at?

CHAPTER 19

SAMANTHA

I sat at my desk, staring into space as I thought about the previous night – and earlier that morning. Although Gabriel and I had ended up spending the afternoon in bed together a few days earlier, what had happened last night felt different. It made me even more confused.

It seemed like I couldn't be near him without wanting him – and my willpower was currently non-existent. The only way to resist him was to stay away from him completely, and I couldn't bear to not see him at all. Not to mention how difficult that would be given that I was having his baby.

I sighed and put my forehead on the desk.

What the hell was I going to do?

My head told me to stop this. Keep my distance before I got hurt again. But my heart, and the rest of my body, were screaming at me to find a way to make this work.

I lifted my head and the business card on my desk caught my eye. I picked it up and turned it over in my hands. Gabriel had dropped it off a couple of days before.

Sneaky Peeks 4D scanning.

I took my mobile phone out and dialled the number. The phone was answered after a few rings.

'Hi, I was just wanting a bit more information about the 4D scans you offer,' I said.

'Yes, of course. Can I ask where you heard about us?'

'Yes. I think your husband works for Gabriel. He's my baby's dad.'

'Oh, is this Jennifer?' she asked. 'I've got the two of you booked in for three o'clock this afternoon.'

My heart almost leapt out of my throat and I felt the urge to be sick. I ended the call without saying anything else, slamming the phone down onto my desk as though it was on fire.

She thought I was Jennifer!

The tears sprang to my eyes and I didn't even try and stop them. Why shouldn't he be taking Jennifer for a scan? He'd offered to take me for one, and she was having his baby too. Of course he would do that.

I had obviously been wandering around in an orgasm induced stupor all morning and now the reality of the situation hit me again. Gabriel had fathered another child with his ex-wife. And every special moment that he shared with me, he was sharing with her too.

I was completely naive to think that I could handle that. Completely blinded by love and lust to think that Gabriel and I could be anything more to each other than co-parents. I had to let him go, because the alternative was to share him with his ex-wife, and I couldn't do that.

CHAPTER 20
GABRIEL

Jennifer was standing on the doorstep when my car pulled up outside her flat. She smiled widely as she saw me and waved before jogging over to the car, her designer handbag bouncing along at her side.

'Hi,' she said breathlessly when she got into the car.

'Hi,' I smiled and waited for her to fasten her seatbelt.

'So, where are we going?' she asked me, her eyes wide as her smile.

'A surprise,' I said. 'Don't worry though. You'll love it.'

Forty five minutes later, I pulled my car into the street and parked up. Jennifer looked around. It was a high street with a few shops and cafes dotted along the road. 'Where are we, Gabriel?' she laughed.

'You'll see,' I said as I climbed out of the car. I walked around and opened her door for her and she stepped out.

'This way,' I said and we walked along the street for a few yards before stopping outside Sneaky Peeks clinic.

'Surprise,' I said to her.

I watched the colour drain from her cheeks until they turned from pink to white.

'What's this?' she asked.

'It's one of those 4D scanning places,' I said with a forced smile. 'I thought it would be great to see the baby together. Especially as I missed your last scan?'

She looked at the building and then back at me. 'Oh, I wish you'd told me, Gabriel. You need a full bladder for one of these scans, and I ... well, I peed before we left,' she shrugged apologetically.

I walked to the door and opened it. 'Actually, you don't need a full bladder as the baby gets bigger. That helps when they're tiny but it's not as important at almost six months. Let's go and see what they can see, eh? I don't mind if the picture's not great.'

She swallowed as she stared at me. Then, realising she had no choice, she plastered a smile on her face. 'Great,' she said and walked through the open doorway with me close on her heels.

I waited until we were in Jennifer's apartment before I confronted her. I'd hoped that she'd have a crisis of conscience on the drive home and explain what we'd just seen on that screen.

'Do you honestly think I'm stupid?' I asked her as she put her handbag down on the counter.

She blinked at me. 'What?'

Did she really think I hadn't noticed? 'Who is the real father?' I asked her.

She blinked again. 'What?'

I slammed my fist onto the breakfast bar. 'I said who is your baby's fucking father?'

'You are,' she stammered. 'You know you are.'

I stepped towards her. 'Stop fucking lying to me. Do you think I can't fucking read a screen, Jennifer? Tell me how the hell your baby is due six weeks before mine and Samantha's when it should be two weeks before? We had sex once! Two weeks before me and Sam! Which means there is no way in hell that baby is mine. So, why the fuck have you been lying to me?'

She shook her head. 'I haven't, Gabriel. I haven't. How do you even know when yours and Samantha's baby was conceived? It could have been any time.'

I shook my head. 'So, you didn't even know? You came to my house to blow my whole world apart, thinking that I'd cheated on Samantha with you? I would never fucking cheat on her. I had sex with you because me and Sam had broken up. We got together again on the night of Seb's engagement party. That's how I know the exact date our child was conceived.'

'Maybe Samantha is lying?' she said. 'Maybe she slept with someone else? Have you considered that?'

I stalked towards her. 'No I haven't, because unlike you, she's not a lying slut!'

'Then the sonographer must have got the dates wrong,' she stammered.

'Are you fucking kidding me with this? Those things are as accurate as hell and you know it.'

I felt the anger coursing through my veins as though it was the iron in my blood. I had never hurt a woman in my life, but Jennifer Sloane was pushing every single boundary I had. 'So, I'll ask you again. Who is the father and why the fuck have you tried to ruin my life by making me believe you were carrying my fucking child?'

She continued shaking her head and then she started to cry. It had always been a tactic of hers. Crying when she wanted to shut a conversation down. Well, it wouldn't work this time.

'That's why you didn't let me go to your twenty week scan. That's why you almost shit a brick when I took you to that place today, because you wanted to cover up this little fantasy of yours for as long as you could?'

She looked up at me, tears streaming down her face, but I didn't feel an ounce of pity for her.

'Tell me the fucking truth, right now, Jennifer,' I snarled at her. 'Or you will be out of this apartment by the end of the day and I couldn't give a fuck if you end up sleeping in a cardboard box. Who is the fucking father?'

'Steve,' she snivelled.

'Steve? Your sister's husband?' I snorted. 'Is that why she really threw you out?'

'Yes,' she sniffed.

'So, you thought you'd pin it on some other poor fucker instead then?' I snarled.

'It wasn't like that. I didn't know I was pregnant when you and me had sex.'

'Stop fucking lying to me. You must have known. How else do you explain that fact that I don't see you for four years, and you just happen to show up at that particular time? You have always known I wasn't the father. We used a condom for fuck's sake! I knew you were fucking lying to me. I shouldn't have even considered giving you the benefit of the doubt.'

'I wanted this baby to be yours, Gabriel. I love you.'

'Oh, fuck off! You wanted someone to look after you and you didn't give a fuck who that was. I'm just the unfortunate bastard who was desperate enough to have sex with you.'

'No, Gabe. I love you,' she pleaded.

I stepped back from her before I did something I regretted.

'You don't fucking know what love is. You care about no-one but yourself. You slept with your own sister's husband and when he knocked you up, you came looking for me to take the fall for it. You are the most selfish, spoiled bitch I have ever met in my life.'

She started sobbing again but I didn't buy a second of it.

'The rent is paid on this place until the end of the month. After that, I want you out of here and I never want to see you anywhere near me, Samantha, or our child ever again. Do you fucking understand me?' I growled at her.

She nodded and I walked out of there before I completely lost my temper and threw a chair through the window.

CHAPTER 21

SAMANTHA

I was sitting at my desk when I saw Gabriel's name and face flashing on the screen of my mobile phone. I sighed. If I didn't answer then he would just keep calling, or worse still, he would turn up here or at my dad's place later. I took a deep breath. I felt like bursting into tears but I needed to hold it together, at least for the next few minutes.

'Hi, Gabe,' I said.

'Hi, Sam. Can I pick you up from work? I need to talk to you.'

'If this is about last night –'

'It's not just about last night,' he interrupted me. 'I need to tell you something.'

'Gabe, last night, and this morning, it was a mistake.'

'What?' he growled.

'It was a mistake. It should never have happened. This morning when I said we could talk, I wasn't thinking straight. But this has to stop.'

'Sam! What the fuck has changed since this morning?' he snapped.

'What has changed is that I can think clearly when you're not around. Whenever I'm with you, you bamboozle me.'

'So, what are you saying?'

'I'm saying that I need space. And this time I mean it. So, no more late night phone calls. No more stopping by to see how I am. And definitely no more sleepovers.'

'Sam! Why are you doing this? This morning we were –'

'I told you, that was a mistake. One that won't happen again. Bye, Gabriel,' I said and then I hung up the phone before I started to cry.

As soon as I put the phone on my desk, I couldn't stop the tears from falling down my cheeks. If it was the right thing to do, why did it hurt so damn much?

CHAPTER 22
GABRIEL

I put my phone back in my pocket. What the fuck had just happened? Samantha Donovan was the most infuriating woman I had ever met in my life. She drove me fucking crazy. This morning we had been on the verge of working everything out. I'd thought we were finding a way through things, and now she'd changed her fucking mind again.

I punched the wall in my hallway and the plaster cracked beneath my fist.

'Fuck!' I shouted.

I grabbed my car keys from the sideboard. Samantha might not want to talk to me, but I'd damn well make sure she listened to me. I needed to tell her that Jennifer had lied about the baby. I needed to make her understand that we belonged together and her fucking me about was starting to piss me off. I let my rage take over because it was an emotion I was used to. It was one I knew how to control. And if I didn't have that, then I would only feel the pain of losing her.

I walked out of my house and down the path towards my car. I had a meeting to go to, but then as soon as that was done, I'd go to Samantha.

I was distracted. My mind filled with thoughts of her. That was why I didn't see the two men approaching until they were standing directly either side of me.

'Mr Sullivan,' one of them said.

I turned and glared at him. They had picked the wrong fucking day. As I turned my body ready to strike, one of them opened his jacket, revealing a concealed handgun. I looked back at the other one and he did the same.

'Our employer would like a word with you,' the other one said.

I looked the two of them over. They were ex-special forces. There was no denying it. We had a few of them working for us and they were ruthless and professional.

A car approached and I realised I had no choice but to get into it. I climbed into the back seat and they sat either side of me. The driver and the man in the passenger seat looked like ex-forces too. I sat and wondered who the hell I had pissed off enough for this.

'Phone?' the one on my left said.

I took it out of my pocket and handed it to him and watched as he wound down the window and threw it onto the pavement.

'What the fuck is this about?' I asked.

'I told you, our employer wants to talk to you,' the one on my right answered.

'And who is your employer?' I asked as I shifted in my seat. This car was not made for three large men to sit in the back.

The one to my right laughed. 'You'll find out soon enough.'

CHAPTER 23

SAMANTHA

I sat on the sofa and flicked through the glossy magazine but I couldn't take anything in. I kept replaying the day over and over in my head. This morning when I'd woken up next to Gabriel and we had made love, I'd thought that somehow we could get past this whole business with Jennifer.

Then later on, when I'd discovered he was taking her for a private scan appointment, I had been heartbroken all over again. And finally, I relived our argument a short while ago. I'd hurt him so badly. I'd heard it in his voice. And now I was wondering if I had overreacted to the whole 4D scan situation.

My dad walked into the room and broke my train of thought. 'I have to go out, love,' he said as he rubbed a hand over his beard. 'I'll be back soon.'

'Is everything okay, Dad?'

'What? Yes. Everything's fine,' he answered distractedly.

'Are you sure?'

He smiled at me. 'Yes. Don't wait up for me, love.'

'I won't. In fact, I'm going to have an early night.'

Suddenly, he walked over to me and kissed the top of my head. 'Night, love,' he said and then he walked out of the living room and I heard the front door close behind him a few seconds later.

What was going on? He'd seemed anxious. Was it something to do with Gabriel?

All I knew was that something felt off.

I rang Gabriel's number but it went straight to his voicemail. That was unusual for him. I didn't leave a message. I felt like such a hypocrite. Just a few hours earlier I'd told him that I needed space, and now I was phoning him because I was worried about him.

CHAPTER 24

GABRIEL

We had driven for two hours, out of the city and towards Kent. Ninety minutes into our journey, one of my kidnappers had blindfolded me. I hadn't resisted. I'd expected it. It was what I would have done.

When the car stopped, I was marched a few hundred yards with an armed guard at each arm. I could smell the sea air and realised we were near the coast. We walked into a room and I heard a heavy metal door close behind us. That was when the blindfold was removed and I was forced to sit on a chair while my wrists and ankles were bound with cable ties.

'Just a precaution, Mr Sullivan,' one of them said with a smile.

I didn't speak. I seriously considered making a run for it. I could have broken one of their noses and possibly another one's jaw, but there were four armed men and one of them would put a bullet in me before I got out of the door.

Who the hell had I pissed off enough to do this? As soon as I was securely bound, the four of them nodded to each other and walked towards the open doorway, turning off the light switch as they did, until I was alone in the room.

I sat still for a few moments, my eyes adjusting to the darkness, and my ears straining to hear something – anything, to give me a clue as to where I was and why I was here. I was sure there was no-one else in the room as I couldn't hear any breathing other than my own. I scanned the dark room. It looked like I was in a cellar. There were no windows but one small vent near the top of the room. The walls were bare brick.

I sat and waited. Whoever wanted to speak to me was playing with me. Psychological torture was often more effective that physical pain. But I had been in plenty of worse situations than this.

CHAPTER 25

SAMANTHA

I woke with a start and looked at my phone. It was just past midnight. I could hear my father downstairs. I got up to go to the bathroom and heard him talking.

I walked downstairs and heard part of his telephone conversation.

'I have no fucking idea. He's been pissing people off left, right and centre lately. But I don't know why anyone would do this. No, he wouldn't do that to Sam. Just in case something happened with the baby.'

I felt my stomach starting to churn as I realised he was talking about Gabriel. I jogged down the few remaining stairs and walked into the kitchen just as my dad was ending his phone call. He was pacing up and down the room.

'What's happened, Dad? Is Gabriel okay?'

He looked at me, his face pale and drawn. 'Sam! What are you doing up?'

'Please, Dad. What's going on? Who were you talking to?' I heard my voice wobbling.

'Sit down, love,' he said as he pulled out a chair for me.

I sat down with shaky legs.

'Gabriel has gone missing. He never showed up to a meeting earlier and nobody can find him.'

'What?' I felt my blood running cold. 'Maybe he's just ...' I couldn't finish the sentence as I didn't know what to say. 'Maybe his phone ran out of battery or he has no signal?'

My dad shook his head. 'No, that's not it. Why don't you go to bed and let me sort this out, love?' he said quietly.

'How can I go to bed when Gabriel is missing, Dad? Please don't treat me like a child. Tell me what you know.'

He stared at me for a moment, as though he was considering whether to tell me the truth. He sighed softly before he spoke. 'When he didn't show up for the meeting, I tried to call him and his phone kept going to voicemail. I knew he wouldn't leave his phone off in case you ever needed him. I went to his house to see if he was there, but he wasn't home. His car was outside, so he hasn't driven anywhere. And then I found his phone on the pavement outside, smashed to pieces.'

'What?' I gasped as my hand flew to my mouth. 'What does that mean?' I asked although I feared I already knew the answer.

'I think someone has taken him, Sam,' he said and my heart constricted in my chest. I felt like I might pass out.

The room started to spin.

My dad put his hand over mine, grounding me. 'But I have got every single man out there looking for him, love. And we will find him. I promise you.'

I nodded but his words had started to sound far away. I watched his mouth moving but couldn't focus on what he was saying. The next thing I knew, he was wrapping his arms around me as I sobbed into his chest. He stroked my hair. 'I'll find him, love. I swear.'

It was almost 6 a.m. and my dad had spent most of the night on the phone. I'd listened and waited patiently, hoping that each phone call might bring us news of Gabriel, but none did.

I replayed my last conversation with him over and over in my head and wished I could take back what I'd said.

What if they were the last words I ever spoke to him?

What if I never got the chance to tell him how much I loved him?

I felt the sob catch in my throat and I swallowed it down. I had cried more tears in the past few weeks, than I'd done in my whole life. And tears were not going to do anyone any good right now.

'I'm going to go out and drive around some of our old haunts. I need to do something,' my dad said as he picked up his car keys. 'Will you be okay, love?'

I nodded. 'I'll be fine, Dad. Go out and bring him back for me,' I sniffed.

He put his arms around me. 'We'll find him. He'll be back here before we know it.'

I nodded. 'Yeah, I know.'

My father left and I sat and stared out of the window. I checked my phone again to see if Gabriel had called or texted, but of course he hadn't.

I went on checking my phone at least ten times a minute. If Gabriel came back, I would tell him how sorry I was. I would tell him how much I loved him. I would find a way to get over this thing with Jennifer. If only he would come back to me and our baby. If only he would be okay.

CHAPTER 26
GABRIEL

My head snapped up as I heard the door behind me opening. I must have fallen asleep. I had no idea how long I'd been sitting in that room, but it had at least been eight hours. It had been dark the last time I'd looked at the slivers of moonlight coming through the vent, and now it was morning.

I heard the sound of footsteps walking into the room and turned my head. The light was switched on, temporarily blinding me and obscuring my vision. I blinked to adjust my eyes and the four men from the previous day walked into the room.

'Apologies for the delay in getting to you. I was held up unexpectedly,' I heard a man's voice say.

I didn't recognise it. He had a strange accent. It was almost cut glass English, but with an American lilt. I looked ahead, and as my eyes adjusted, I saw a man who looked far too much like Jackson Carver for my liking. He was lying about being sorry for keeping me waiting, but I would hear what he had to say before I spoke.

'Strong, silent type, are we?' he said with a sharp laugh.

Then he pulled up a chair and let out a long, exaggerated

sigh. 'I suppose you want to know who I am and why I've brought you here?'

I knew exactly who we was, but I wouldn't let him know that.

He was Milton Carver, the disgraced younger brother of Samantha's ex-husband, Jackson. That explained the accent. Educated at Eton, but banished to the States for the past ten years. I wondered how fucked up a man had to be, to be disowned by the Carver family. I glared at him instead of answering.

'Well, let's just stay we have a mutual friend in common, and she happens to have all of my family's money,' his voice was light and even cheerful up until this point. But then he leaned in close to me. 'And I want it back!' he hissed.

I stared at him. If I inched forward I could bite his nose clean off his face.

'What does that have to do with me?' I asked, feigning my ignorance. So, it was the most obvious motive in the world – money. That was good. I could work with that.

'Because, she's your little fuck-toy, isn't she? Samantha? You do know her, yes?'

I pulled at my restraints instinctively. My whole body was tense with rage.

He started to laugh. 'Hit a nerve, have I?'

I took a deep breath. 'Why don't you tell me exactly what it is you want, and then let me fucking go,' I snarled at him.

He stopped laughing and stared at me, his mood changing again in an instant.

'For some reason, my pathetic brother left every penny of our family's money and assets to that whore of a wife of his. I tried to get her to back off when Jackson was in prison, but well, that didn't quite work out to plan,' he said, to himself more than me.

So, he had been the one who had paid Anthony Garvey to

threaten Samantha? That didn't make any sense. 'Why?' I asked. 'While Jackson was still alive, Samantha had no claim to your money?'

'Ah, well, she did. After Jackson disgraced our family's good name and ended up getting himself thrown in prison, I was entitled to make a claim on the family assets. But, with Samantha still married to him, they were technically hers too, so I needed her out of the way.'

'So, you intended to kill her?'

He shrugged. 'It was nothing personal. It's worked out infinitely better for her that Jackson died instead, and now I need her alive. If she dies, I assume her money will go to her father. But, now she has the opportunity to do the right thing and hand it over to me.'

'And you'll just walk away then, will you?' I snorted.

He nodded. 'All I'm interested in is my family's legacy. I want you to advise her that it would be in her best interests to sign everything over to me. That house in Knightsbridge has been in my mother's family for generations. Samantha has no right to it.'

'And it's not about the fact that it's worth millions then?' I asked.

He scowled at me. 'Of course it is. That money belongs to me.'

As I understood it, Milton had also been left half of the family money when his father had died, but the assets had been left to Jackson. Still, he'd inherited a few million quid himself. Greedy fucker!

'Fortunately for you, Samantha wouldn't touch a penny of your family's fucking money. She'd be happy to relinquish any claim on it, leaving you the sole heir. She doesn't even know he's left it to her. So, all of this could have been saved by a phone call, couldn't it?' I snarled.

He rolled his eyes. 'Well, she might say that now, but wait

until she has that little bastard of hers and she sees how expensive good private schools are.'

I was really struggling to keep a lid on my temper now, and I lunged myself forward at him but was held back by two of his hired guns. 'You watch your fucking mouth when you're talking about her and our baby,' I growled at him.

I wanted to rip his fucking head off.

He smirked at me. 'I'd heard you had a bit of a temper, Mr Sullivan. I bet it really pisses you off that a posh boy like me has the better of you, doesn't it?'

I frowned at him. 'You have the better of me, do you? Why don't you untie me and send your boys outside and we'll see who has the better of who, eh?'

He didn't like that. He drew his fist back and punched me in the mouth. It stung, but I'd had far, far worse. I ran my tongue across my lip and tasted blood.

'One day, I'll make you regret that,' I said.

He shook his head. 'You're a Neanderthal, Mr Sullivan. People like you, will never best people like me. I will always come out on top. That's just the way this world works. You have no idea who I really am and what I'm capable of. You should consider yourself lucky that this is just a friendly warning. My solicitor will be in touch with you. One of my employees will provide you with his business card. I'd suggest you encourage Samantha to draw up some paperwork to relinquish any claim she has on my family's money as soon as possible.'

Then Milton stood up and looked at his hired guns. 'Take him back to whatever gutter you found him in. Feel free to give him a good kicking on the way,' he said and then he walked out of the room.

A moment later, I was blindfolded again and my ties were cut.

'This way, Mr Sullivan,' I heard someone say and then I was

frogmarched back to the car. None of them laid another hand on me though and I wondered what that was about. Their boss had just given them free rein to do me over and they hadn't. Either they didn't like violence, or they didn't like him. Given their job roles, I assumed it was the latter.

As we joined the motorway again, my blindfold was removed and we continued the rest of the drive in uncomfortable silence. Twelve hours after they'd picked me up, the four armed men dropped me back outside my house.

CHAPTER 27
SAMANTHA

I was boiling the kettle for my millionth mug of peppermint tea when I heard the doorbell ringing. I rushed out into the hallway with a mixture of anticipation and terror churning in my stomach. I looked through the spyhole and my legs almost gave way when I saw him standing on the doorstep in one piece.

I scrambled to open the door as quickly as possible. 'Gabe!' I stammered.

He stepped into the hallway and I flung my arms around his neck. He wrapped his huge arms around me and I started sobbing onto his shoulder. He stroked my hair and we must have stayed like that for at least five minutes before I stepped back to take a good look at him. He had a cut on his lip, but other than that he looked fine.

'Where have you been? What happened?' I asked.

'Is your dad not home?' he asked as he looked past me and down the hallway.

'He's out looking for you. We need to phone him and tell him you're okay.' I held his face in my hands. 'You are okay, aren't you?'

He smiled at me. 'I'm fine. I didn't know if you'd even realise I was missing.'

'You missed a meeting, and my dad went to your house and found your phone,' I sniffed as I wiped my eyes. God, why couldn't I stop crying lately? 'He's had people looking for you all night.'

'I'm sorry if I worried you,' he said as he smoothed my hair from my face.

'Where were you? What happened?'

'Let's phone your dad and I'll tell you both when he gets here. Can I get a drink?' he said as he rubbed his throat.

'Of course,' I said and we walked into the kitchen. I handed him a bottle of water from the fridge and watched as he downed the whole bottle.

I could hardly believe he was standing there in front of me. I'd been convinced that I would never see him again.

'I'm sorry, Gabe,' I said. 'I'm so sorry about what I said,' to my annoyance I started to cry again and he crossed the kitchen and pulled me into his arms.

'Shush, baby. I'm here now. It's okay,' he soothed in my ear.

'It's not okay. I love you, Gabe. I love you so much and I thought I'd never get to tell you.'

He tilted my face to his and smiled. 'I know you love me, Sam. I love you too.'

'I know,' I breathed and then he bent his head low and pressed his lips to mine, lightly at first as though he was seeking permission. Then his hands were in my hair and he crushed my face to his and kissed me so deeply I thought I might pass out.

I kissed him back with as much need as he had for me. He pushed me back against the kitchen counter and I slipped my hands under the jacket of his suit and onto his muscular back.

'God, I need you, Sam,' he groaned.

'I need you too, Gabe, but we should phone my dad. He's still looking for you and he's out of his mind with worry.'

Gabriel stepped back and nodded. 'Yeah, of course. Let's ring him.'

I hadn't even dialled my father's number when I heard the front door opening. 'Dad! We're in here,' I shouted.

I heard him running down the hallway and his face broke into the biggest smile I had ever seen when he walked into the kitchen and saw his best mate standing there as large as life.

'Where the fuck have you been?' he said as he bounded across the kitchen and wrapped Gabriel in one of his famous bear hugs.

'Sit down, and I'll tell you,' Gabriel said when my father finally released him.

A moment later the three of us were sitting at the table and Gabriel looked anxiously between my father and me.

'I was on my way to meet Graham Johnson last night, when two men stopped me. I could tell they were ex-special forces straight away. They told me their boss wanted a word with me. There was a car waiting for me with another two of them in the front. I didn't have much choice but to go. They kept me there until this morning, when their boss finally made an appearance.'

'So who was he? And what the fuck did he want you for?' my father snapped.

Gabriel's tongue darted out of his mouth and he licked the dried blood on his lip. Then he looked at me and I felt a churning in my stomach. I didn't know what he was going to say next, but I knew I wasn't going to like it.

'Milton Carver,' he said and I almost passed out from shock. I felt the tea I'd been drinking half an hour earlier threatening to make a reappearance.

'What?' was all I could gasp.

Milton Carver was the disgraced brother of my ex-husband, Jackson. He'd been cut off from the family twelve years earlier, at the age of thirty-two after a series of scandalous and embarrassing exploits. The Carvers were a sick and twisted lot, but they generally liked to keep their vile tendencies private. To the outside world, they were a respectable and incredibly wealthy family, dripping in privilege and old money. Behind closed doors, however, was an entirely different matter. They were a family of narcissists, psychopaths and cruel individuals. To be disowned by that lot, meant you were a special kind of fucked up.

I'd only met Milton a handful of times when I'd been married to Jackson. Each of those times had been thoroughly unpleasant. The last I'd heard of him, he was living in L.A.

What the hell was he doing back here and what did he want with Gabriel?

'He was the one who paid Garvey to threaten you, Sam. You were right all along. There was someone else behind it.'

'But why?' I shook my head. 'Milton is a vile excuse for a human being, but I've never done anything to make him come after me. And it couldn't be about Jackson. The two of them hated each other. So what does he want from me? And why has he come after you?'

'Money,' Gabriel replied. 'Nothing more complicated than that.'

'Money? I don't have any money.'

Gabriel reached out and squeezed my hand. 'Actually, Sam, you have fuckloads of it. Apparently, Jackson left everything to you in the will. Didn't you know that?'

I shook my head in horror. 'I was invited to the will reading, but I didn't go. And then I've had a few calls from his family solicitors, but I've been so busy, I didn't call them back. Jesus! Why would he leave it to me?'

'Because you were his wife,' my dad interrupted. 'That's kind of how it works, isn't it? Who else did he have except his brother who he hated?'

'Still, he would have hated me to have it too, I'm sure. He mustn't have had the chance to change it after we separated. But we were divorced when he died. Milton has legal grounds to contest the will anyway.' I sat back against the chair. 'And what was the whole thing with Garvey about? That was before Jackson was even killed? What the hell was Milton trying to achieve?'

'With Jackson serving life in prison, he wanted to make a claim on the family's assets. And with you as Jackson's beneficiary, he needed you out of the way to do that,' Gabriel replied.

'Wow!' I blew out a slow breath and rubbed the back of my neck with my hand.

'Are you okay?' Gabriel asked.

'No. No, I'm not okay. Milton Carver has just had you kidnapped because he thinks I want his family's money. Why didn't he just speak to me? I'd be happy to sign the lot over to him. I don't want a penny of it,' I shuddered.

'Well, he thought he'd speak to me instead of you.'

'Why?' I snapped.

'You'd rather he kidnapped you then?' he frowned at me. 'Because I fucking wouldn't.'

My father nodded his agreement. 'I second that.'

'No. But I don't see why there was a need to kidnap anyone. He can have every single penny of his rotten family's money. I'll have some papers drawn up as soon as possible relinquishing my claim to it. How do we get in contact with him?'

'I have his solicitor's details. I'll deal with them,' Gabriel replied.

'No you won't. I can deal with this myself. I'm not helpless.'

Gabriel rolled his eyes and my father sighed.

'What?' I snapped at them. 'You know how I feel about being mollycoddled by you both. I can handle Milton Carver. If all he wants is money, then I'll give it to him.'

Gabriel and my father shared a look that I couldn't quite work out. Even from the grave, it seemed that my ex-husband was still trying to ruin my life. All of my old survival instincts were kicking in. Pushing people away, convincing everyone I was invincible, handling everything myself and not having to rely on anyone. They were instincts that had served me well in the past, and they were hard habits to break.

'What is it?' I demanded. I was on edge. I was nervous and scared. My anxieties about feeling weak and needing to be protected were playing out and it felt like there was nothing I could do to stop them. I had to let my subconscious do its thing and recognise it for what it was.

'Tell her what you're thinking,' my father said.

'Tell me what?' I snapped.

'Sam, he had four ex-special forces bodyguards working for him. You already said he's so crazy even the Carvers disowned him. I'm not sure paying him off is going to get rid of him. Men like that don't just stop,' Gabriel said.

'So, what are you saying?' I asked.

'I'm saying, that let us think through what we're going to do first. Please let us handle this. This is what we do.'

I shook my head. 'All he wants is the money. All he's inter-ested in is the money. And I definitely don't want it, so I'll sign it over and he can be out of our lives.'

My father opened his mouth to speak, but Gabriel gave him a subtle shake of his head. It annoyed me. They were going to do what they liked anyway. They would discuss it when I wasn't in the room and decide what they were going to do whether I liked it or not.

I looked at the clock. 'Shit! I have to get to work. I have a meeting with a Judge at nine o'clock.'

'Let me drive you,' Gabriel said.

'No. There's no need. Simon is picking me up this morning. He's in this meeting too.' I stood up from the table.

I was angry and annoyed – not at Gabriel or my father, but I just wanted out of the room. I needed some time and space to think and breathe. 'I'll talk to you both later. I need to get ready for work.'

I walked out of the kitchen and left Gabriel and my father sitting there in silence. I showered and dressed and all I could think about was how much I wished I'd never laid eyes on Jackson Carver. And now Gabriel was at risk – and probably my father too. And it was because of me. The sooner I relinquished my right to the Carver family money and left it open for Milton to claim, the better.

CHAPTER 28
GABRIEL

I'd wanted to drive Samantha to work. I wanted to be near her. I was worried about her safety now that Milton had made his intentions clear, and I still needed to tell her about Jennifer. But, she'd understandably not taken the news well that Milton was back and that he'd been the man behind the attacks on her earlier this year.

I'd known she'd revert to her defence mode of pushing anyone who wanted to protect or care for her away. It was the way she functioned – the way she'd to learn to survive her twelve year marriage to a psychopath.

I knew that I had to let her push me away before she'd let me back in. It was infuriating, but it was the only way to handle her. So, I'd let her go. I'd let her get into Simon Hardaker's car and drive away.

I didn't trust him. There was something about him that set my teeth on edge, and my instincts were rarely wrong. But I had nothing on him – yet.

Now it was just Sebastian and I sitting in his kitchen.

Sebastian was seething with rage. 'I can't believe that fucker was behind the threats to Sam. I can't believe he had the fucking brass neck to kidnap you.'

'Yeah, well, like I said, better me than her,' I replied.

Sebastian nodded in agreement. 'What are we going to do about him?' he snarled.

'Well, we both know there is no way he's going to back off just because she signs over that money to him.'

Sebastian nodded and slammed his fist on the table. 'I know. Haven't that family of cunts taken enough from her?'

'You'd think,' I said with a sigh. 'We can't take any chances, Seb. We need to plan this carefully, but we need to remove the threat of Milton Carver for good.'

Sebastian nodded. 'I couldn't agree more. So when?'

'I think we should let Sam sign over the money first. That will buy us some time and placate him for a while. It will give me time to look into him a bit more.'

'Why do we need to look into him?' Sebastian asked. 'Let's just bury him.'

'Knowledge is power, my friend, you know that. Besides, he's got four ex-special forces as his personal bodyguards. He's not going to be that easy to get to.'

'We have a few ex-special forces working for us.'

I nodded. 'I know. I've already sent one of them a message asking him to meet us at the office later. He might be able to find out who is working for Milton. I got the impression they didn't particularly like him, and if that's the case, we can definitely use it to our advantage.'

'Yeah. Good.'

'Now, I need to get home and have a shower before I go and see Sam and try and persuade her to let me handle Milton.'

'Yeah? Well, good luck with that, mate,' he said with a grin and a shake of his head. 'She loves you though, you know. She was so worried last night. We both were.'

'I know,' I said. 'It's not her loving me that's the problem, it's whether she can forgive me.'

'She will,' Sebastian nodded. 'Just give her time.'

I stood up and cracked my neck. My limbs ached from being tied to a chair all night. I could do with a long bath and an even longer sleep. But, that would have to wait.

CHAPTER 29

GABRIEL

I walked into the offices of Donovan Cook and nodded a greeting to Beth, the receptionist.

'Good morning, Gabriel,' she said.

Samantha's business partner, Nick Cook was coming out of his office and we almost bumped into each other.

'Gabriel,' he said with a smile. 'How are you, mate?'

'Losing my fucking mind, Nick. You?'

Nick gave me a sympathetic nod. 'I hope you two sort this out. I've never seen her so bloody miserable, and it's making her unbearable to work with. I hope you've got your tin hat with you if you're planning on going in there,' he nodded towards Samantha's office. 'She's like a bear with a sore head today.'

'Better wish me luck then,' I replied as I patted Nick on the shoulder.

I knocked before pushing open the door to Samantha's office and stepping inside. God, she was even more fucking beautiful now than she'd been earlier that morning. Pregnancy looked good on her.

'I'm not in the mood for a lecture, Gabe,' she said with a shake of her head.

I held up my hands in surrender. 'Then I promise not to lecture you. I just wanted to say how sorry I am for worrying you.'

She blinked at me. 'Well, you don't have to apologise for that. It wasn't exactly your fault, was it? I'm sorry that my psychopathic ex-husband and his family are still trying to ruin my life and you got caught up in that.'

'You have nothing to apologise for, Sam. And like I said, I'm glad that they came to me and not you.'

'Well, I'm really happy you're okay. But, I can't really talk right now. I'm busy. Can you go and we can talk later?'

I ignored her request and sat on the chair opposite her. She blanked me for a few moments, but I sat and waited, watching her as she pretended to work. But she had been scanning the same page for the past five minutes.

'We should probably talk about Milton, and what we're going to do next.'

She shook her head. 'There's nothing to do. I'm going to have some papers drawn up that will make it clear I have no right to a current or future claim on the Carver family fortune. Then he can have it all. The sooner, the better.'

'Let me help.'

'I don't need your help. I can handle it,' she snapped.

I frowned at her. 'God, you are in a bad mood today, aren't you?'

Her head snapped back up. 'Of course I'm in a bad mood. I'm fat. None of my clothes fit me any more. I have indigestion almost permanently. My ex-husband and his crazy family are still trying to ruin my life. I spent most of the night worrying that the father of my baby was dead in some ditch and I'd never see him again. But now that you're back, there's still no escaping the fact that you knocked up your bloody ex-wife too. And to top it all off, this pregnancy has turned me into the horniest woman alive.' She blew a strand of hair out of her eyes and glared at me.

I felt my dick standing to attention at her last revelation and I shifted in my seat to relieve the pressure.

I looked at her calmly and smiled. 'You're not fat. You're five and a half months pregnant. Your clothes are uncomfortable because you won't buy any maternity clothes and insist on continuing to wear those sexy little pencil skirts. Stop eating ice cream for dinner and the indigestion might ease a little. I will deal with Milton Carver and I'm sorry that I worried you. I did *not* in fact knock up my lying, cheating ex-wife. And as for being the horniest woman alive, I'm not sure you can blame your pregnancy for that. But, give me five minutes and I'll take the edge off for you. Give me a few hours and I'll make sure you can still feel me inside you until the baby is born.'

She continued to stare at me and I saw the blush creeping up her neck. She bit her bottom lip and her hands gripped the arms of her chair. I knew that she would be thinking about that offer and it turned the twitch in my cock into a throb.

'Wait. What?' she said, suddenly.

'I said, give me five –'

'Not that, you sex pest. I meant what about you not knocking your ex-wife up?'

'Oh, that? I wondered if you'd heard me or were too distracted by your raging hormones. It turns out Jennifer is still a lying, cheating bitch and she lied about her due date. Her baby is due six weeks before ours.'

She sat back in her chair and gasped. 'So, it's not yours?'

'Not a chance. I had sex with her once and that was two weeks before your dad's engagement party. So, I was definitely nowhere near the scene of that crime.'

'God. How did you find out?'

'I took her to one of those 4D scans. The due date was there on the screen.'

'Of course. The scan?' she nodded.

'Wait. Did you know about that?'

'Yes. I phoned there yesterday morning and spoke to someone to find out more about them. When I said you were my baby's father, she assumed I was Jennifer.'

'Fuck! I'm sorry, Sam,' I sighed. 'Is that why you were so pissed off with me yesterday?'

She nodded.

'So, when she asked who I was to you, you said I was your baby's father and nothing more?' I frowned at her.

No wonder they'd thought she was Jennifer. I knew the woman who owned the clinic well, and she knew that Samantha was so much more to me than that.

'Well, what else was I supposed to say, Gabe? That you were the man I'd thought I'd spend the rest of my life with but you'd knocked up your ex-wife too and I didn't know what I was to you any more? I wasn't sure she needed that level of detail.'

I didn't answer her. I rubbed a hand over my jaw and wondered what the fuck I was to Samantha any more too.

'Anyway. Tell me about Jennifer. Did she know her dates, or did she think …?'

'Oh, she knew exactly what she was doing,' I said

She shook her head. 'Jesus Christ. What a bitch!'

'I know.'

'Imagine if you'd never found out. Imagine if …'

'I know,' I said softly. 'And I know it doesn't change the fact that I had sex with her, Sam. But I only did that because I thought you and me were over.'

She closed her eyes. 'It's a lot to take in,' she said as she let out a long breath and lifted her hand to her forehead.

I picked up the bottle of water from her desk and handed it to her. 'Are you okay?'

She nodded. 'I'm just hot. And tired.'

I looked at her. What had I been hoping for? That she'd run into my arms and realise it had all been one huge mistake? That wasn't the Samantha I knew. She was the most stubborn woman I had ever met in my life. I would have to give her space to make a decision in her own time, as much as it killed me to walk away from her.

'I wanted you to know, Sam. I wanted to tell you yesterday but then things didn't work out as planned, did they? I know that you're still hurt, but I hope that we can talk about it when you're ready.'

I stood up to leave and she looked up at me with tears in her eyes.

'I don't ...' she started and then she shook her head. 'I'll talk to you later. I have a client due in half an hour.'

'Okay,' I nodded. 'Bye Sam.'

CHAPTER 30

SAMANTHA

I watched as Gabriel walked out of my office and blinked back the tears. I felt so many emotions I wasn't sure which one to deal with first.

I was angry that Jennifer had lied to us – she had tried to tear us apart, and had almost succeeded – and for what? I felt relieved that Gabriel wasn't the father of his ex-wife's baby. But, I was still annoyed with him for having sex with her and putting us in this predicament.

I was confused too. I loved him so much and last night had proven that I couldn't bear to live without him. I'd just needed a few hours of space to get my head around the last twenty-four hours. Then he'd walked into my office and sat there, looking damn near edible in that tailored suit, while my hormones rampaged around my body. I found the most innocuous things arousing these days, and he had the nerve to sit there, literally oozing sex appeal, wearing my favourite suit and that bloody aftershave. I'd had to make him leave so I could think straight.

I tried to tell myself that I still had some thinking to do and that I still had a decision to make – but I didn't. I'd known earlier that morning when I'd thought I may never see him again, that I was going back home to him. Even if Jennifer had been pregnant with his baby, I would have still gone back to him.

I hated that he'd screwed his ex-wife, but he was right about the two of us being broken up at the time. I'd told him that I'd never loved him and that I never wanted to see him again. It was really none of my business what he'd done in the interim.

Except that it stung like hell that it had been Jennifer whose arms he'd run into – the only other woman he'd ever loved. But even that wouldn't be enough to keep me away from him. I had still wondered how I would live with the guilt that I would be keeping him from his other child – that I would always be making him choose if he and I were together. But now it seemed there were no more choices left for either of us to make.

I leaned over and gave my dad a kiss on the cheek as he pulled up outside Gabriel's house – our house.

'His car's not here. You want me to come in and wait with you?' he asked.

'No. I'm sure he'll be home soon. I'll fine on my own. You get home. It will be nice for you to have the house to yourself for a change, won't it?'

'I have loved having you back home, sweetheart,' he said with a smile. 'But I'm glad you're working things out with Gabriel.'

'You think I'm doing the right thing then?' I asked him.

'Not that it matters what I think. But, yes. You're both miserable without each other. He's been torturing himself over this whole Jennifer thing. As he should be,' he added with a grin. 'But he adores you.'

'I know,' I said. 'Thanks for dropping me off, Dad. I love you.'

'Love you too, Sam,' he said.

I decided to shower and change once I got into the house. Gabriel and I had plenty to talk about when he got home. But that could wait, because I had had an itch of the kind that only Gabriel could scratch.

Freshly showered, I dried myself off and pulled one of Gabriel's t-shirts over my head, flicking my damp hair over my shoulder. I went downstairs and sat on the sofa.

My stomach growled but I was too nervous to eat. What if Gabriel didn't want me back here? I pushed the thought away immediately. I knew that he did.

Stifling a yawn, I looked at the clock. It was just before six. I hoped he'd be home soon. I was so tired I felt like I could sleep for a week. Laying my head on one of the soft cushions, I closed my eyes and listened to the soft ticking of the clock.

CHAPTER 31
GABRIEL

I walked into my office to see Jacob Cavanagh and Alex Brodie already sitting waiting for me. Sebastian and I had met with Jacob earlier that afternoon and told him about Milton Carver and his ex-forces bodyguards. He'd promised to reach out to his contacts and see what he could find out. I'd been impressed and surprised when he'd called me two hours later to tell me he had some information.

Alex was ex-special forces too, but he hadn't worked for me for as long as Jacob. If Jacob vouched for him though, that was good enough for me.

I'd saved Jacob's life six years earlier when he'd managed to find himself on the wrong side of a Russian gangster who happened to owe me a favour. Jacob had worked for me ever since, and proven himself to be loyal and trustworthy.

'Hello, gentlemen,' I said as I took a seat behind my desk. 'You have something for me?'

'I found out who is working for Carver,' Jacob replied.

'That was fast,' I said.

'Well, Alex here, served with one of them.'

'Really?' I looked at Alex.

'Yeah. Leroy Cain. He's a ruthless cunt. Not the kind of guy you want to make an enemy of. But he's a mercenary. He works for money and nothing else. He's fucking good at his job, but he has no real loyalty to his clients. He is however, loyal to his old regiment. I could try and reach out and see if he'd be up for a meeting if you want?' Alex said.

'What if I wanted to put a bullet in his head? Where would your loyalty lie?' I asked him.

'Well, I'm not going to lie, I'd rather you didn't. But I work for you now and I aim to keep doing so for a very long time. I'd put a bullet in his head myself if it was necessary. Leroy knew what he was getting into working for Carver. He'll know who you are when I set up a meeting and if he chooses to take that meeting, he'll do so in full knowledge of the facts. If he does something to get his head blown off, that's on him, not me.'

I looked at Alex. I considered myself a good reader of people, and I had a good feeling about him.

'What about the other three?' I asked.

'Kelvin Cain is Leroy's cousin. He'll follow Leroy anywhere. The other two are ex forces, as you suspected. Former marines. They've worked for Carver for about nine months as far as I can tell,' Jacob replied.

I nodded. 'He was in the States for years. He's only been back here about a year. He must have recruited them soon after he got back.'

'Do you need us to look into Carver too?' Jacob asked me.

I shook my head. 'No. I can do that myself.'

Carver's hired guns were one thing. They had no particular axe to grind with me or Samantha. Like Alex said, they worked for money. But Carver – that was personal, and I wouldn't let anyone else deal with that cunt. He was all mine.

'Shall I set up a meeting with Leroy, Boss?' Alex asked.

'Yeah. As soon as possible.'

Alex nodded. 'Will do. He's not an easy man to get hold of. I'll have to reach out to some old contacts, but I'll do my best.'

'Good. And I appreciate you getting me this information so quickly.'

'Anything else we can do?' Jacob asked.

'No. That's it for now. Let me know when Leroy has agreed to a meeting.'

They both nodded and stood up. I watched them walk out of my office and leaned back in my chair. Milton Carver had just become my new pet project.

I suspected that Samantha signing over the money to him would keep him sweet for a little while and give us some breathing room. But as soon as I found out a way to get to the horrible little fucker, I would make sure he never bothered me or Samantha ever again.

I stepped through my front door and into the hallway of my house and my skin bristled.

There was someone here.

The kitchen and lounge doors were open and I always closed them before I left the house. Then I looked down and saw her shoes in the hallway and my heart started to hammer in my chest.

'Sam?' I called as I walked into the lounge.

Then I saw her there, fast asleep in one of my t-shirts. Her hair damp from a shower, her long legs stretched out and her perfect, peach of an arse half on display.

I felt my cock harden as I looked at her. But she looked so peaceful, I couldn't bear to disturb her – not yet.

Sebastian had told me she wasn't eating properly and

although she had a small baby bump, I noticed that that her arms were looking thin. I'd make us both some dinner first and then we could talk about our future – without my dick getting in the way.

CHAPTER 32

SAMANTHA

I felt soft fingers brushing my cheek and my eyes flickered open. I smiled as I saw Gabriel's handsome face.

'Hey, you,' I said sleepily.

'Hello,' he said as he returned my smile. 'Welcome home, baby.'

Reaching out, I took hold of his collar and pulled him towards me for a kiss. He parted my lips gently with his tongue and I groaned into his mouth.

God, I had missed him so much!

He placed his warm hand on my thigh as he deepened our kiss, before running his hand over my hip and underneath the fabric of my t-shirt. I shivered in anticipation as his hand warmed my skin.

Suddenly he broke our kiss, pulling back and leaving me panting for more.

'Have you eaten?' he asked.

I shook my head. 'Have you?' I said with a wicked grin.

'No. I've made some pasta,' he replied as he grabbed hold of my hand. 'Let's eat.'

'Not yet,' I breathed. 'Dinner can wait.'

'Sam,' he said sharply. 'You need to start eating properly.'

'I do,' I frowned.

'Ice cream in one hand and M&M's in the other doesn't constitute a balanced diet,' he said with a flash of his eyebrows.

Damn my father! The traitor. 'I'll eat later,' I said as I pulled his hand back towards my body.

'Sam,' he sighed, 'you need to start taking better care of yourself.'

'I've mostly been taking care of myself for the past eight weeks. Now it's your turn,' I said as I opened my legs wider and placed his hand between them.

His eyes darkened as he stared at me and for a second I thought he was going to cave. 'Dinner! I'll take care of you all night long if you like. But first we eat.'

'Later.' I insisted as I pulled him back to me, sealing his mouth with a kiss before he could refuse.

He rubbed his hand over the skin on my stomach and I writhed beneath him, angling my body so that I could feel him where I was so desperate to.

He broke our kiss and started to pull his hand away, but I grabbed hold of it. 'Please Gabe, I need you now,' I breathed. My body was on fire and I felt like I'd implode if I didn't get some relief soon - the type that only he could provide.

'After we eat,' he said as he pulled his hand from mine.

'I'm going on hunger strike then. I refuse to eat until you take care of me.'

He glared at me as he leaned in close. 'Can't you ever just do as you're told?' he growled.

I shook my head. 'No. You already know that. I'm going crazy here, Gabe. Take pity on a girl, would you?'

I saw the flicker of a smile cross his face and he bent down to kiss me. How the hell could he maintain such self-control while I behaved like a dog in heat? But then his hand slid up the inside of my thigh and inside the seam of my underwear. I gasped as he slid his fingers through my cleft and he responded with a growl of pleasure as he felt how ready I was for him.

'I'll get you off if you promise to eat some dinner with me,' he said with a flash of his eyebrows.

'Yes,' I panted as he slipped a finger inside me. I'd have agreed to anything for the promise of what he was about to do.

He bent his head to kiss me again as he pushed a second finger inside me and started to pump in and out of me. He was fast and rough and I struggled to kiss him and breathe at the same time. When his thumb started to brush over my swollen clit, I couldn't hold on any longer and my orgasm hit like a truck, crashing over me and knocking me for six. It was the quickest climax I'd ever experienced in my life.

The bastard!

He sat back on his haunches with a triumphant grin on his face before holding up his two fingers and sucking them clean. Then he held out his hand to me.

'Dinner.' He ordered.

I took hold of his hand and stood on shaky legs.

A deal was a deal.

Walking into the kitchen, I saw the table was set with a single rose and a candle in the centre.

'Wow,' I said with a grin. 'Were you planning to seduce me, Gabe?'

He started to laugh. 'Seduce you? Are you serious? You've just been begging me to fuck you,' he said as he guided me to my chair and planted a kiss on my head.

'No I wasn't.'

He raised an eyebrow at me.

'I asked you to take care of me,' I said with a grin. 'Like wash my hair, cook me dinner, tuck me up in bed. It's not my fault you interpreted that as a demand for sex.'

He bent down and kissed me, nipping my lower lip before he pulled away. 'Oh, right? My mistake.'

I put my knife and fork down and sat back in my chair. 'That was delicious, thank you,' I said with a smile. It was the first proper meal I'd eaten in days.

'You're welcome,' he said as he continued eating his larger portion. 'It's good to see you eating something decent.'

I rolled my eyes. 'How do you know how I've been eating?'

'Your dad told me about your newfound relationship with Ben & Jerry,' he said as he looked at me, his eyes twinkling with amusement.

'Are you worried I'll get fat?' I smirked at him.

'No,' he laughed. 'Not at all. But I am worried about you and our baby being as healthy and well as you can be.'

'But the baby loves ice cream,' I said as I rubbed a hand over my bump.

Gabriel continued eating and I stared at him until he'd finished.

'It wasn't just the baby. And it wasn't that you slept with someone else,' I said eventually. 'It was that you slept with her.'

He looked up at me and nodded. 'I know.'

'Do you still love her?'

'No,' he said firmly. 'I haven't had those feelings for her for a very long time.'

'Then why, Gabe?'

'I told you. She was there. She was a warm body and I was hurting, Sam. I just wanted someone to take my mind off you. It could have been anyone, and I'm sorry that it was her.'

'Did you choose her to punish me?'

He ran a hand across his stubble. 'She found me. I didn't choose her, but if I'm honest, fucking her did fulfil some kind of need for revenge, no matter how petty that sounds. Maybe, subconsciously, it was a way to stick it to the two women who had ripped my heart out. All I can say is it seemed like a good idea at the time.'

I nodded at him. 'I want to know what happened?'

'I told you,' he started.

'No,' I interrupted. 'I want to know the details. What did you do together?'

He frowned at me. 'What? No.'

'I need to know, Gabe.'

'Why?'

'Did you make her come?' I asked.

His eyes darkened as he glared at me. 'No,' he snapped.

'So, you just fucked her?'

'I didn't intend to. We were in the nightclub. We went into the toilets. I was planning on letting her suck my cock! She was always pretty good at that,' he snapped.

I got the sense he was trying to push my buttons now, but I didn't bite and he went on. 'But there was a condom machine. She had change. So, we fucked instead.'

'In the nightclub toilet?'

'Yes.'

'Did you think about me?' I asked.

He continued to glare at me, his dark eyes burning into mine. 'Every fucking second.'

I suppressed a smile. I was glad he'd thought about me when he'd been screwing his ex-wife.

I stood and started to clear the dishes, taking them over to the sink. I was running hot water into the bowl when I felt Gabriel walking up behind me. He slipped his warm hands around my hips and under my t-shirt, pressing his body into mine so I could feel the full length of his rock hard cock against my back.

'I'll do those later,' he said against my neck as he slid his hands over my rounded stomach.

'That's okay. I can do them now,' I said. Let him see how it felt to be kept waiting for a change.

'But I thought you wanted me to look after you,' he said as he started to trail soft kisses up my neck. Then his hands found my breasts. He cupped them and gave a gentle squeeze and I rocked back against him.

Who was I kidding? I couldn't resist him for even a moment. He played me like a fiddle and I loved it. When he started to circle my nipples with his fingers I moaned loudly. My breasts were heavy and tender but he knew just the right amount of pressure to apply. I felt the wetness pooling between my thighs and was contemplating begging him to fuck me against the sink when he started to whisper in my ear.

'So, I've fed you. Your hair is already washed. Would you like me to take you up to bed now, tuck you in and give you a kiss goodnight? Is that really the kind of looking after you meant?' He kissed my ear as he continued gently kneading my sensitive breasts.

I pressed my behind into him, rubbing myself up and down his cock as much as I could, struggling to gain any momentum as his large frame held me in place.

'Or,' he growled. 'Did you mean you'd like me to fuck you all night and make you come so hard you'll forget your own name?'

'You know what I meant,' I panted.

He chuckled against my neck. 'Yes I do. But I want you to tell me. What do you want?'

'You know. You always know, Gabe,' I pleaded.

'Say it anyway, Sam,' he growled as he slid one hand south-wards, under the band of my underwear and down to my throbbing clit. He rubbed slowly. 'Say it. Tell me what you want, baby.'

God, he was a fiend. 'Fuck me, for God's sake, fuck me,' I gasped.

He removed his hand from between my thighs and I whimpered at the loss of his touch.

'Let's go to bed,' he whispered as he took my hand in his and led me up the stairs.

Standing in the bedroom, Gabriel peeled his t-shirt from my body and threw it onto the floor. Then he hooked his fingers into the band of my lace underwear and slid them slowly down my legs, kissing each of my thighs in turn as he stood back up.

He was about to push me onto the bed when I placed a hand on his chest.

'No,' I said with a smile. 'I want you naked first.'

He glared at me. He was in charge in the bedroom, he always had been. Despite that, he started to undo the buttons on his shirt. I sat on the edge of the bed and watched him. He peeled off his shirt and dropped it beside us. Then he went for his belt, and I felt a shiver running down the length of my spine as I remembered all the fun that we'd had with it in the past.

'Not tonight, baby,' he said with a smile and a glint in his eyes.

I watched him continue undressing until he was standing before me in all his naked glory. I felt faint as my heart started to pound in my chest and my clit throbbed to the same steady rhythm. His body should come with a health warning.

I looked over every inch of his rock hard body, glistening with a thin sheen of perspiration. It was only that and his huge erection which betrayed his cool facade. He was desperate for it as much I was.

Before he could push me back against the bed, I leaned forwards, taking his cock in my hand and kissing the tip. I looked up at him and saw the fire in his eyes before I wrapped my mouth around his shaft. Licking and sucking as I cupped his balls and fisted him at the root with my other hand.

I listened to the guttural noises he made as I sucked him hard. Soon his hands were in my hair and he was fucking my mouth like he'd never get enough of me. Then he was pulling me away.

'Fuck, Sam. Stop,' he ordered but I ignored him and continued to pump and suck until he exploded hot and sticky into my mouth and down my throat.

I looked up at him. 'So, pretty good?' I asked as I licked my lips, recalling what he'd said about his ex-wife earlier.

'No,' he groaned. 'That was fucking incredible.'

He pulled me up into a standing position and dragged his thumb across my lip before placing one of his hands on the back of my head. He crushed my face to his, kissing me greedily. 'You taste so good with my cum in your mouth,' he said when we came up for air.

I smiled at him and that was when I noticed the look in his eyes. 'But I told you to stop and you ignored me,' he growled.

I shrugged. 'Seemed like you were enjoying yourself?'

He ran a hand down my cheek, along my neck until it was resting around the base of my throat. 'I was, but I've hardly fucked you at all in eight long weeks. I should be buried deep inside your hot, tight little pussy right now instead of standing here with a limp dick.'

'Sorry,' I said with a flash of my eyebrows. 'I'm sure it won't stay limp for long. It never does.'

'That's not the point though, is it?' he said.

'Does this mean you're not going to fuck me after all?' I ran a hand down his muscular chest and towards his cock, which was already twitching back to life.

'Oh you're getting fucked,' he said as started to caress my neck. 'Hard.'

I swallowed as my abdomen contracted. I smiled at him but he continued to glower at me. Then he pushed me back onto the bed.

Crawling over me, he held me down by my wrists. Bending his head, he sucked one of my hypersensitive nipples into his warm, wet mouth. He nipped me lightly before moving to the other one and I yelped in pleasure.

'Gabe,' I panted. I wanted his head lower. Or his hands lower. Anything as long as he was there, easing the intense throbbing between my thighs. I lifted my hips to find some friction and relief on any part of his body, but he raised his hips too and I groaned in frustration.

'You're a devil,' I snapped.

He chuckled as he continued suckling my nipples. 'No, I'm patient – unlike you.'

'You're a monster. We've been apart for so long. Is it any wonder I'm impatient? I wonder if you've even missed me at all,' I hissed.

It was unfair and I knew I was acting like a spoilt child, but I was desperate to feel him inside me. The events of the last two days were messing with my emotions too, and coupled with his constant torment, it was making me crazy.

His head snapped up and he stared at me. 'You really think I haven't missed you?'

I glared back at him defiantly. 'Who knows?'

'You're a little firecracker tonight, aren't you?'

I felt his erection pressing against my stomach but I turned my head away from him.

'You just want me to fuck you then?' He asked. 'That will prove how much I missed you, will it? Not the fact that I have phoned you almost every single fucking day since you walked out on me. That I have made some pathetic excuse to see you as often as I could. I've put up with your smart-arse remarks, and mood swings and your constant refusal to have a grown up conversation about our future. You left me fucking swinging in the wind never knowing if I would ever get to even touch you again. Then you walk back in here tonight like nothing has happened and have the fucking cheek to suggest I haven't missed you!'

I blinked back the tears. 'Get off me,' I hissed.

'My fucking pleasure,' he snapped and rolled off me. I jumped out of the bed and stalked out of the room, grabbing his T-shirt from the floor before I slammed the door.

CHAPTER 33
GABRIEL

I lay with my hands behind my head as I listened to the door to the spare bedroom slam shut.

At least she hadn't left altogether. Running was what Samantha did best.

I lay there for a few moments, listening to the sound of my heartbeat thumping in my ears. How had it all gone so wrong in a matter of minutes?

Samantha Donovan was the most frustrating woman I had ever met in my life. I should have just given her what she wanted. My need to be in control was greater than ever tonight and I wasn't sure why. Maybe, I needed to prove that she was mine? Maybe, I needed to remind her that she was?

I sighed and wondered how long I'd have to leave her stewing in her own juice – quite literally – before I went after her. Because I would. I always did.

She had me by the balls. She never backed down. She didn't have to because she knew I always would. That was the pattern we had become locked into and I wondered how, or if, we would ever break it. It was fucking exhausting. How could she even dare to suggest that I hadn't missed her?

I looked up as the door opened, creaking softly in the quiet house. I watched as Samantha crept back inside the room. My heart contracted in my chest.

Here it was. Now she was about to tell me she was leaving – again, and I wasn't sure what I was going to do this time to make her stay.

She walked over to the bed and lifted the cover, taking me completely by surprise as she slipped underneath the duvet beside me. She pressed her naked body against mine and I let out the breath I'd been holding in.

'I'm sorry,' she whispered. 'I swear these pregnancy hormones make me crazy.'

'You've always been crazy,' I said with a grin and she nudged me in the ribs. I rolled on top of her. 'Me too.'

'You too? Crazy or sorry?'

'Both.'

'I love you, Gabe. I've been so miserable without you. I know it was my choice, but that didn't make it hurt any less. Every single time I saw you or spoke to you a part of me wanted you to pull me into your arms and carry me back home. If I was a bitch to you it was because I had to push you away, because you have so much power over me. It terrifies me how much I need you.'

I tucked a strand of hair behind her ear. 'I will always be anything you need, Sam. You don't ever have to be scared of your feelings for me. I will never do anything to hurt you again. I promise.'

She placed her hands on my face and nodded as she blinked back tears. 'I know,' she whispered before she pulled my face to hers.

Soon I was kissing her so hard I thought I might run out of breath. The throbbing in my cock which had been present since I'd first got home and saw her asleep on the couch, intensified to dangerous levels.

She opened her legs wide for me and I shifted between them until I was nudging at her opening. She gasped as I pressed against her.

She was so fucking wet. I loved how easy she made it for me to slide into her. She always took all I could give her without complaint or resistance, even when I knew she was tender. I knew that she loved to be fucked by me just as much as I loved to fuck her and I revelled in it. I would never get enough of her.

She wrapped her legs around my waist and pulled me towards her.

'Please, Gabe?' she whimpered and this time I didn't deny her. Thrusting myself deep inside her until there wasn't a millimetre of space between us. We were two pieces of a puzzle that fit together perfectly. She arched her back in pleasure as she took me to the hilt.

'Jesus, Gabe,' she breathed.

I drove into her over and over again, hitting at the sweet spot inside her that made her cry out my name. 'I'm sorry, Sam. This is exactly what you needed, wasn't it? A good fucking,' I breathed in her ear. 'It's what we both needed.'

'Yes,' she whimpered.

'You feel so fucking good, Sam. I'm not sure how long I can hold on.'

'That's okay, I'm almost there,' she panted.

I kissed her neck and she dug her fingernails into my shoulders as she came apart around me, milking my cock with her hungry squeezes until I found my own relief.

CHAPTER 34
SAMANTHA

I woke up tangled in Gabriel's embrace and smiled to myself. This was where I belonged and it felt good to be back here. I listened to his soft breathing and stretched my arms gently, trying not to disturb him.

I failed miserably – he was such a light sleeper.

He opened one eye and grinned at me. 'Where do you think you're going?' he growled as he wrapped an arm around me and pulled me back to him.

'Nowhere. I just needed to stretch,' I laughed. 'My legs are aching. I'm not used to such late night exertions any more.'

He nipped at my neck with his teeth. 'Well, you're going to get used to them again pretty quickly, baby. Because I am going to fuck you senseless every single chance I get.'

My insides clenched at his words. I couldn't get enough of him.

His hand travelled southwards, settling between my thighs. His fingers slipped easily through my wet folds and he groaned in pleasure. 'Fuck, Sam. I love how you're always soaking wet for me.'

I whimpered as he taunted me with his fingers.

'Spread your legs wider for me, baby,' he ordered and I did as I was told.

My body obeyed his every command without question. He slipped his fingers inside me and I moaned loudly as he pumped them slowly, his thumb brushing over my clit and sending shockwaves of pleasure rocketing through my body.

'You want fucking, baby?' he growled.

'Yes,' I breathed.

'Yes, what?' he teased me.

'Yes, Sir?' I offered, lost on the brink of an orgasm.

He laughed out loud. 'I was thinking of please, but I like sir much better.' He rolled onto his back, pulling me on top of him. 'Slide onto my cock, baby, and show me how you want it.'

I took his hot, stiff length in my hand and squeezed, making him smile at me. Then I slid down onto him, as far as I could go, taking every inch of him and I watched in pleasure as his eyes rolled back in his head.

'Fuck, Sam! You feel so fucking good,' he groaned.

I lifted myself up before sliding back down onto him and he growled. Then his hands were on my hips and I realised that my momentary control was over. He was back in charge now, exactly how we both liked it.

He guided my hips, angling himself for just the right amount of friction and to make sure he hit that spot inside that made me completely come apart. His fingertips dug into the flesh on my waist and backside as he rolled my hips over his cock and I tipped my head back. My orgasm was about to crash over me and I felt it building deep in my core.

'Come for me, baby,' he ordered and I could do nothing but obey him. I cried out his name and with a few final thrusts, he ground out his own release until he spurted hot and heavy inside me.

I collapsed on top of him when we were both spent and he pulled my hair back from my face and kissed my forehead.

He was still inside me when he spoke again. 'Will you let me deal with Milton, Sam?' he asked.

I looked up at him. 'Why?'

He frowned at me. 'Why? Apart from him being a crazed psychopath?'

'He only wants the money, and I can sort that out. It's kind of my job,' I reminded him as I slid off him and rolled onto my side.

He turned on his side so he was facing me. He dragged his knuckles across my cheek. 'I know that. But we can have Nick draw up the papers. Why won't you let me handle this for you?'

'Because I can handle it myself.'

'But that doesn't mean you should. It doesn't mean you have to. What would be so bad about letting me deal with this cunt and leaving you out of it? You don't need the stress.'

'I don't know,' I admitted. 'I just ...'

'Sam, like it or not, you're having my baby, and that means that I will do everything in my power to protect you both. I know that you can look after yourself, but I can look after you too. Please let me.'

I bit my lip as I stared at him. He was right, but it was hard to let go of that need to do everything for myself. It had been a part of me for so long, that it was almost like instinct.

'Okay,' I agreed. 'I'll let you and Nick draw up the papers and deal with Milton's solicitors. But I want to be kept in the loop with everything. I don't want to be shut out of decisions that are made about my life.'

He smiled at me. 'You won't be. And thank you.'

I snuggled my head against his chest. 'You're welcome.'

CHAPTER 35

SAMANTHA

I walked into my office and put my briefcase down on the desk. Then I remembered I had forgotten my lunch. Gabriel had saved me a portion of his delicious chicken and chorizo pasta and I'd left it in the fridge.

Damn! I loved that stuff.

I took my phone out of my pocket and called him.

'Hey, baby. Miss me already?' he asked.

'Yes. But not as much as I miss my lunch. I've forgotten it. Are you going back home this morning?'

'I am. Would you like me to drop it off for you?'

'Would you mind? I was really looking forward to it.'

'Of course I don't mind. I'll swing by in an hour or so.'

'Thank you,' I purred.

'Anything for you, baby,' he said with a soft laugh. 'I'll see you soon.'

It was just over an hour later when Gabriel walked into my office, closing the door behind him before he placed the clear Tupperware container on my desk.

'Thank you so much. You're a lifesaver,' I smiled at him.

'Any time,' he said, but he didn't smile. He glowered at me. His green eyes full of fire as they burned into my skin.

He stalked towards me and I took a step backwards, bumping into my desk until I was perched on the edge of it.

'Do you have any appointments this morning?' he asked in that low gravelly growl that sent shivers down my spine.

'No. Why? Are you okay?'

'No, I'm not,' he shook his head.

'What's wrong?' I looked up at him. God, he was so intense sometimes.

His tongue darted out and he licked his lower lip as he edged ever closer to me, invading every inch of my personal space.

He bent his head low, so his mouth was resting against my ear. 'I *really* need to fuck you,' he breathed as he started undoing his belt.

My knees buckled at his words. 'What? Now? In my office?'

'Right now,' he growled.

I swallowed. *Wow!*

He unzipped his trousers and his huge, beautiful cock sprung free. 'I was driving over here and I thought about all of the times in the past eight weeks when I have been desperate to fuck you senseless and I couldn't even touch you. It made me so fucking hard, baby. And then I realised that you belong to me, and that means I get to fuck you any time I want.'

Dear God!

He tugged at the belt on my wrap dress until it fell open. 'Have I told you how much I love these dresses?' he said as he slipped his hands inside and ran them over my hips. 'They're fucking perfect.'

'Perfect how?' I panted.

'For easy access,' he grinned. 'And for my plan to fuck you everywhere and anywhere that takes my fancy.'

'You're a sex maniac,' I hissed.

He slipped his hand between my thighs, tugging my underwear to one side and slipping two of his thick fingers inside me, making me groan out loud. 'You're the one whose dripping wet for me, baby.'

I ground myself against his fingers as he pressed his cock against me. 'Fuck my fingers, baby. Show me how much you've missed me too.'

I wrapped my arms around his neck and buried my head against his shoulder as I ground my hips against his fingers.

'Gabe!' I panted. Even though he'd made me come twice that morning, I couldn't get enough of him. If he was a drug, then I was most definitely an addict.

He stroked his cock with his free hand before sliding his fingers out of me. 'You're going to come on my cock, not my hand,' he growled as he pushed me back against the desk.

He lifted my left thigh with one hand for easier access and wrapped the other arm around me as he impaled me with his thick length.

'Jesus, Gabe!' I groaned in his ear.

'I'm going to make up for all the time we were apart, baby. I'm never letting you go again,' he said as he pounded into me.

I clawed at his suit jacket as my climax washed over me. 'Oh, God,' I breathed.

'Fuck, Sam,' he hissed as he came inside me with a few final thrusts.

He let my thigh fall gently back onto the desk and then he wrapped his other arm around my waist. Pulling me closer to him as he nuzzled my neck. 'I love you,' he panted.

'I love you too. And I'm so glad I forgot my lunch.'

'So am I, baby,' he chuckled against my neck. 'I'm sorry I was quick and rough with you, but I have to get to a meeting, and I couldn't have lasted the rest of the day without burying my cock in that sweet pussy.'

I felt my insides clench around him. 'Have I ever told you how much I love your filthy mouth.'

'Yes, although you don't have to. I can feel your tight cunt milking me when I talk dirty to you,' he grinned.

My cheeks flushed pink.

'I have to go or I'll be late,' he said as he pulled out of me and started to fasten his trousers and belt.

I fastened my dress and watched him fix himself back in place. A moment later, he was back to looking like a respectable businessman again.

He looked up and smiled at me. 'I'll pick you up at five?' he asked.

'There's no need. I'm in court with Simon this afternoon. He already said he'd give me a lift home.'

Gabriel frowned. 'I'd rather pick you up myself.'

'Oh, Gabe. You're not jealous, are you?' I teased him.

'No,' he snapped. 'But there's something about that guy.'

'Simon?' I laughed. 'He's a sweetie. I promise you, I'm in safe hands. He'll bring me straight home after court.'

He stared at me for a moment. No doubt considering whether it was worth an argument. 'Okay. I'll meet you at home then.'

'Good. I'll see you tonight. Enjoy your meeting, handsome.'

He pulled me to him and gave me a deep kiss. 'I'll be thinking about you the whole day,' he said as he brushed the hair from my face. 'And every single way I'm going to make you come later.'

My insides trembled at the thought. 'Sex maniac,' I whispered.

'It's the only way to keep you satisfied, baby. I'll see you tonight.'

I smiled at him and then watched as he walked out of my office. As soon as he'd left, I sank into my chair and blew out a long breath. Gabriel Sullivan was a sex god and he was all mine!

CHAPTER 36
SAMANTHA

I glanced at the text as it flashed up on my phone. It was from Gabriel telling me he was outside in the car. He usually came in, but he was running a little late and I'd already told him I was ready to leave.

My afternoon court session with Simon had been cancelled so I'd accepted Gabriel's earlier offer to pick me up at five. I shouted goodbye to Nick and left the office for the evening. Climbing into Gabriel's warm car, I smiled at him and he leaned over and gave me a lingering kiss on the lips.

I felt the heat searing between my legs and had to pull back from him.

'Sorry, I'm late, baby. I was getting some supplies,' he said with a grin.

'Supplies?'

'Yep,' he indicated the back seat and I looked behind me to see a large paper bag from my favourite deli, with what looked like a bottle of champagne poking out of the top. 'I picked up all of your favourite foods from Hawthorn's.'

I turned back to face him. 'The huge green olives?'

He laughed. 'Yes.'

'And the lemon and coriander chicken?'

'Yep. And the tiny stuffed peppers.'

'Sounds delicious. And for dessert?' I grinned.

'For you, a chocolate brownie.'

'And for you?' I flashed an eyebrow at him.

'I think we both know what I'll be eating for dessert,' he said with a wink before he pulled the car away from the kerb, and my insides turned to jelly.

'And the champagne?' I asked. 'Who is that for?'

'Well, that's for later. Strawberries and alcohol-free champagne.'

'Alcohol free champagne? I didn't even know they did that.'

'They certainly do, baby.'

'And here was me thinking you were trying to get me drunk so you could have your wicked way with me,' I laughed.

'Well, firstly, I wouldn't be giving you, or our baby real champagne, would I? And secondly, I cannot recall a time when I have *ever* had to ply you with alcohol,' he started to laugh. 'You're pretty much always ready to go, baby.'

I opened my mouth and feigned my horror. 'How dare you? I think you'll find it's you who's always ready for action.'

He laughed out loud, throwing his head back and I felt a rush of love for him. I hadn't heard him laugh like that for a long time. 'Well, I can hardly argue with that,' he agreed. 'Seems we're a match made in heaven, then?'

'Seems so,' I agreed. 'Anyway, what's with the food and fake champers. Is there a special occasion I'm missing?'

He turned to me. 'Yes. A very special occasion. You are back home and I've missed eight weeks of looking after you and our baby. So, when we get home, I'm going to run you a nice warm bubble bath and then you can have a soak while I get dinner ready. Then I've got Pretty Woman ready to go on the Sky Q box.'

I loved that he knew how to take care of me so well, like how he knew pregnant women shouldn't soak in a hot bath and how he was prepared to sit through my absolute favourite film ever. 'You hate Pretty Woman,' I reminded him.

'Yes. But I love you,' he said.

I felt my heart swell in my chest. 'You'd better be careful, I could get used to this,' I said with a sigh as I closed my eyes and leaned my head back against the seat.

'Well, that's kind of the idea, Sam,' he said softly.

Three hours later, we had eaten the delicious food and I was sitting on the sofa with my legs draped over Gabriel's lap and my head on his chest while the credits to Pretty Woman rolled over the screen. He had an arm wrapped around me and was holding the remote control in his other hand.

'I love that film,' I said with a sigh. 'Although I think it set me up to have very unrealistic expectations of relationships.'

'You want the fairy tale?' Gabriel asked, mimicking the line from the film as he cupped my chin and tilted my face up to his.

'Well, I kind of have it ... now,' I said with a smile.

'Kind of?'

'Okay, I do have it,' I said as I wrapped my arms around his neck. 'You're my knight in shining armour, Gabriel Sullivan.'

He nuzzled my neck and switched off the television. 'Actually, baby I think you might be mine,' he breathed against my skin. 'So, if we're done with the cheesy movie, can we go to bed? Because there's plenty more things I've missed doing with you.'

'Really?' I panted as he slipped his warm hand under the t-shirt of his I was wearing, and gently squeezed my breast. 'Like what?'

'Hmm, I could tell you, but I'd rather show you,' he grinned. 'And I just remembered I never got my dessert.' Then he slid his hand out from under the t-shirt and hooked his arm under my legs before standing up from the sofa with me in his arms.

Gabriel kicked open the bedroom door and walked into the room, placing me down onto the bed. The way he was looking at me suggested that he wasn't going to be so gentle with whatever he had planned next.

'Take off the t-shirt,' he ordered and I did as I was told until I was lying on the bed in only my white cotton briefs.

He peeled his own t-shirt over his head and tossed it onto the floor. 'Are those things supposed to be some kind of turn off?' he nodded towards the white cotton underwear. I usually wore black or colourful lace affairs, but they weren't as accommodating for my ever increasing proportions. 'Because they're having the completely opposite effect, baby,' he growled.

I grinned up at him. 'They're not supposed to be a turn off, no. But I'm glad you like them, because they're much more comfortable now that my ass is getting so fat!'

'Your arse is not getting fat. It's fucking beautiful,' he said as he unbuttoned his jeans and slid them down his strong thighs. He was naked underneath and his beautiful cock was standing tall and firm, the head glistening with pre-cum. 'And those little white panties you've got on are driving me fucking crazy.'

'I can see that,' I smiled.

He stalked towards the bed and leaned down towards me. Hooking his fingers under the band of white cotton, he pulled them slowly down my legs and over my ankles. Then he held them to his nose and inhaled deeply before tossing them onto the floor too.

'Do you know what I missed most when we were apart, Sam?' he growled as he crawled over me.

'My sparkling personality?' I grinned at him.

He glared at me and placed his hands on my knees,

spreading my thighs far apart. 'No,' he said as he bent his head low and blew cold air onto my wet folds. 'Try again.'

'My cooking?' I giggled and he nipped at my thigh.

'Nope. You've got one more try, baby, and if you want to come tonight, I'd suggest you put some thought into your next answer.'

I chewed on my lower lip. I could feel his warm breath close to my skin and then he started planting soft kisses at the top of my thighs while I writhed beneath him.

'So,' he growled against me.

'My pussy,' I panted.

'Nope,' he murmured. 'But, that was a good try. Because I *have* missed this sweet, hot pussy, baby.' I was rewarded for my better effort by his tongue swirling over my clit and I cried out. 'I missed burying my cock in it, but not as much as I've missed eating it every single day.'

I groaned in pleasure as he sucked the sensitive bud into his mouth and then he licked and sucked me to a long, rolling orgasm.

When he'd finished, he crawled up the bed. 'Turn onto your side, Sam,' he ordered.

I rolled over onto my left side and he lay behind me, pressing his body against mine. He lifted my right leg into the air until I was stretched wide open, before sliding his cock deep inside me until there was no space left between us.

'What have you missed most about me?' he growled in my ear.

'Your chorizo pasta,' I groaned. 'No-one makes it quite like you.'

He pressed deeper into me, pushing his cock a few extra millimetres until there was literally nowhere left for him to go. 'Really? That's what you missed most, is it?'

I bit my lip to stifle a moan. How could he have me on the edge again so quickly? 'Hmm,' was all I could manage.

He stayed still and I could feel his cock throbbing inside me. I squeezed my pussy muscles around him and he groaned loudly.

'Stop teasing me with those hungry little squeezes, and answer my question,' he said as he nipped at my earlobe.

I felt the blood thundering around my body. I tried to grind against him but he held me in place with his powerful arms.

I was desperate.

All I could think about was the impending orgasm that was threatening to overwhelm me at any minute. 'I missed you,' I panted, 'and how much you make me feel loved.'

I sensed that wasn't the answer he was expecting and he sucked in a breath. Then he turned my head towards his and sealed my mouth with a kiss, pushing his tongue inside as he started to fuck me. I felt the pressure building in my core as he fucked me relentlessly, his pace unchanging as he devoured my mouth. As my orgasm crashed over me, I wrenched my lips away from his and gasped for air.

'Jesus, Sam! You make me feel like a fucking animal,' he hissed in my ear. 'I can't get enough of you,' he said before picking up his pace and finding his own climax.

He rolled onto his back and I turned to face him while we both caught our breath. 'So, what did you miss most then?' I asked with a flash of my eyebrow. Apparently, I hadn't given him the right answer earlier.

He smiled. 'The way you say my name when you come.'

I pushed him in the chest. 'That's it? I thought it was going to be something a bit more meaningful than that.'

'What?' he protested. 'It is meaningful to me. It's when you're at your most vulnerable. I love the way you let yourself go completely and the only word you can utter is my name.'

I rolled my eyes. 'Well, when you put it like that, it doesn't sound so shallow after all.'

He slipped his arm around my waist and pulled me closer to him. 'Nothing about my feelings for you could be described as shallow. But, you know that, don't you?'

I blinked at him. 'Yes,' I said as a tear rolled down my cheek.

He brushed it away with the pad of his thumb. 'What's wrong?'

'Nothing. Everything is perfect,' I whispered. 'I love you, Gabe.'

He smiled at me, making his beautiful green eyes twinkle and I nestled my head against his chest.

CHAPTER 37
SAMANTHA

The following morning, Gabriel and I pulled up outside my office in his car, just in time to see Nick arrive on his bike. Even from the comfort of Gabriel's car, it was clear to see the graffiti daubed all over the windows of our offices.

Whore. Homewrecker.

And underneath my name on our Donovan Cook sign, someone had crudely sprayed the words *'is a slut.'*

I stayed frozen to my seat as I read the words over and over again. I felt a familiar ball of anxiety settling in my stomach. What fresh hell was this now? Was this something to do with Milton?

'What the fuck?' Gabriel hissed as he leaned over me to get a better look.

Nick stood in front of the windows, looking at the graffiti with his mouth hanging open. Then he turned to the car and stared at me with a look of horror on his face before dismounting from his bike and leaning it against the wall. He jogged over to the car and the electric window was wound down in front of my eyes as I remained rooted to the spot in shock.

'Samantha,' Nick said and then he shook his head. It wasn't

often he was lost for words, but he opened and closed his mouth like a fish a few times before he spoke again. 'Why don't you go home and I'll deal with all of this,' he said softly.

I was aware of Gabriel's warm hand on my arm. 'That sounds like a good idea. I'll take you home, Sam.'

That seemed to snap me out of my daze. 'No!' I shook my head. 'After everything I've been through, you think a bit of nasty graffiti is going to stop me doing my job. I've got clients counting on me.'

I unclipped my seatbelt and picked up my handbag from the footwell of the car.

'Sam ...' Gabriel started but I turned and gave him my best glare.

'I want to know who did this. I'm going inside to check the CCTV.'

Gabriel sighed and unclipped his own seatbelt as he turned off the engine. 'Come on then. I'll call some of the lads and get them to come down and clean this up.'

Just as we were approaching the door to our office, it opened and we were greeted by our receptionist, Beth.

'Beth? What are you doing here this early?' Nick asked.

She looked at the three of us and blushed to the roots of her hair. A few seconds later, a young man appeared behind her, looking startled by our presence. '

I was just showing, Kenny where I work,' she stammered. 'But when I got here, I saw the paint, so I called the police. They're on their way.'

'You called the police?' Gabriel scowled. It was fair to say he wasn't their biggest fan.

'Relax, Gabe,' I said as I squeezed his arm. 'That's what most people do when something like this happens.'

'But she should have spoken to you and Nick first,' he snapped.

'Why didn't you call us first?' Nick asked her and I couldn't help feel sorry for our young receptionist. Couldn't these two read the situation at all? Her friend was obviously not there to see where she worked – her job wasn't *that* interesting.

'I didn't know what else to do,' Beth stammered.

'Look. Maybe your friend should leave, and we'll discuss this inside, eh?' I suggested.

Beth nodded and forced a smile. 'Yes,' she said as she stepped aside to let her friend out and us in.

The four of us walked along the corridor.

'Did you see anyone when you got here, Beth?' Gabriel asked.

'No. I only got here about fifteen minutes ago. There was no-one around.'

'How about you make us some coffee while we check the CCTV?' I suggested to Beth. 'And in future, don't be bringing your friends here out of hours – for any reason.'

Together, Gabriel, Nick and I walked into the conference room and Nick fired up the monitor so we could watch the CCTV.

Nick rewound until we found what we were looking for at 6am that morning. I looked at Gabriel and saw him glaring so hard at the screen, I thought he might give himself a nosebleed.

'Is that ...' I started

'Jennifer!' he snarled.

'Your ex-wife?' Nick added.

Gabriel nodded.

'Jesus Christ,' I breathed as I sat back in my chair.

Nick glanced between us both with an anxious look on his face. 'I'll go and see where Beth is up to with that coffee,' he said before clearing his throat and walking out of the room, closing the door behind him.

'Why would she paint those things?' I asked.

Gabriel shook his head. 'I don't know.'

'Homewrecker? Did you and her … again?'

He glared at me. 'No! Of course we didn't.'

'Then why would she do that? Does she think that you and her are together or something? Why would she think that, Gabe? Did you make her promises? Lead her on?' I heard my voice getting higher with each question and knew that I was firing questions at him faster than he could answer, but the fact that Jennifer had written those horrible things had me completely rattled.

Why would she do such a thing?

'Well?' I demanded.

He leaned forward in his chair and took hold of my hands. 'Sam! I don't know why she's done this, but I swear to you I have done nothing to make her think that there is anything between us. Even before I found out the truth about the baby, I didn't give her even the tiniest hint that she would ever be anything to me. I love you. You know that. She knows that. That can be the only reason she's done this. Because she's hurt. She's angry and she's jealous and she just wants to cause more shit between us.'

I stared up at him and wanted to believe him.

'For fuck's sake, Sam,' he snapped as he tried to keep a lid on his already frayed temper. 'I know that I kept something from you, and I know that I hurt you, but I have never lied to you. There is no-one but you. How can you doubt that?'

I was saved from answering by a knock at the door. A few seconds later, Nick popped his head in. 'The police want to speak to you,' he said apologetically.

I'd forgotten Beth had contacted the police. But they'd responded quickly to a bit of graffiti.

'Of course,' I said. 'Show them in.'

Nick opened the door wider and two police officers, one male and one female, walked into the room.

'Miss Donovan,' the woman said. 'I'm Constable Mallory and this is Constable Edwards. We're here about the graffiti.'

I nodded. 'Of course. Have a seat.'

They both sat down and Constable Edwards took out his notepad. 'Have you checked the CCTV?' he asked, nodding his head towards the monitor.

'Yes. We know who's responsible. And we don't want to press charges,' I said. I had no desire to drag the whole thing out further with a possible court case. 'But perhaps you could have a word with her and warn her off? If she does anything like this again, I'll pursue a restraining order.'

'Oh?' Constable Mallory asked with one raised eyebrow. 'Who is this *her* you're referring to?'

'My ex-wife,' Gabriel answered.

'This is my boyfriend, Gabriel,' I said.

The two officers nodded. 'Has she done something like this before?' Constable Edwards asked.

'No,' I replied. 'Not to me anyway.'

'Any reason why she'd do this now?'

'She's pregnant,' I started to say and was about to explain the situation when I caught the look of disdain on Constable Mallory's face. She rolled her eyes and looked at my own bump, and I felt my cheeks flush pink – both in embarrassment and anger.

'So your wife is also pregnant?' she said to Gabriel.

'No, I haven't had a wife for some time. My *ex*-wife is also pregnant with someone else's baby,' he snarled at her and she at least had the good grace to look contrite.

We answered some further questions and the two police officers left and promised they would speak to Jennifer as soon as they could.

Gabriel showed them out and then closed the door behind them before walking back over to me. He sat beside me and put an arm around my shoulder. I leaned against him and he kissed the top of my head.

'I'm sorry, baby,' he breathed against my hair. 'Are you okay?'

'I'll be fine. And your ex-wife writing some nasty stuff on my windows kind of pales in comparison to what my crazy ex-husband's brother did to you, doesn't it?'

'That's really not the point,' he said. 'I could fucking kill her.'

'Just let the police deal with her. Hopefully, she'll get the message and we can forget about her,' I said as I sat up and checked my watch. 'Anyway, I need to get a move on, I have a meeting to prep for.'

I stood up and Gabriel stood with me, fastening the buttons on his jacket as he did. We stood awkwardly and it felt like our world was off kilter once again.

Damn Jennifer! I could happily kill her myself.

'I'll see you later then,' Gabriel said and gave me a kiss on the cheek.

'See you later,' I said and watched him walk out of the room.

CHAPTER 38
GABRIEL

I climbed into my car and took a deep breath to try and calm my hammering heart. Just when things with me and Samantha were getting back on track, Jennifer goes and pulls a stunt like this.

What the hell was she thinking? As if she hadn't caused me enough fucking misery these past weeks. I could hardly believe she'd written those things about Samantha. She clearly didn't appreciate irony if she believed that it was Samantha who was the homewrecking whore.

I took out my phone and rang Scott Thomas. He answered on the second ring.

'Hiya, Boss.'

'Hi Scott. I'm going to need you and a few lads at my Oak Road flat.'

'The place where your ex-wife is staying?'

'Yeah. Give me an hour and then I'll text you the details of what I need you to do.'

'Okay, Boss,' he said.

I ended the call and started the engine. It was time to pay

Jennifer a visit and remind her exactly who she was fucking with.

Thirty minutes later, I was standing outside the door of my Oak Road apartment waiting for the door to be answered. I had a key and I'd use it if I needed to, but I'd prefer to give her the opportunity to open the door herself. She did a few seconds later and took a step back when she saw me. Her face paled as she stared at me.

She opened her mouth to speak, but I pushed my way into the flat, barging past her and into the sitting room. Seeing her handbag on the sofa, I picked it up and handed it to her. 'Let's go,' I snapped.

'What? Where?' she asked, her mouth hanging open in shock and horror.

'Just fucking move, or I swear to God, I'll carry you out of here,' I said.

She blinked at me, no doubt weighing up whether I would follow through with my threat. She knew me well enough to know that I would, and she started to walk out of the flat.

I followed her, locking the door behind me and leaving the key under the mat for Scott. We walked silently down the stairs and out of the building. I pressed the key fob to unlock my car and opened the door for her. She looked up at me, her eyes full of fear. A part of me wanted her to suffer, but the other part of me remembered that she was pregnant, and while she was a bitch, her baby was completely innocent.

'I'm not going to hurt you,' I sighed. 'Just get in the fucking car.'

I saw the relief wash over her face and she climbed into the passenger seat.

We drove along in silence for a few minutes while I tried to get my anger under control. My hands gripped the steering wheel and she sat tapping her foot on the floor. I could see her handbag jostling up and down on her lap out of the corner of my eye.

'What the fuck were you thinking going to Samantha's office and scrawling that shit all over her windows?' I snapped.

'I didn't ..' she started.

'You're on fucking CCTV, Jennifer. Is lying just your fucking default mode?' She started to cry and I rolled my eyes. 'Oh, give it a rest. The tears don't fucking wash with me any more.'

'I'm sorry. I don't know what came over me. I went for a walk because I couldn't sleep, and I was walking past, and I just ...' she sobbed.

'You just happened to be walking past with a can of spray paint?' I snarled.

'Actually, I was. I bought it yesterday. I was going to spray some wooden picture frames and it was in my handbag.'

'The police were called. They'll be wanting a word with you, it worked out quite well that you're still registered as living with your sister. And fortunately for you, Samantha didn't want to press charges. Unlike you, she's not a vindictive bitch!' I snarled.

She continued crying and I kept driving.

'Please tell Samantha I'm sorry,' she sniffed as she rummaged around in her handbag. I pulled a tissue from my inside pocket and handed it to her. I had taken to carrying them around in recent months, since I always seemed to be making someone cry.

'Thank you,' she said as she took it from me and dabbed her eyes.

'Why did you do it?' I asked, feeling slightly calmer.

'I don't know,' she shook her head.

'Yes you do. For once, can you stop lying and give me the

truth? Don't you think I deserve that after all the shit you've pulled?'

She was quiet for a few seconds. 'I was jealous,' she finally admitted. 'I am jealous. Samantha has everything I want. She has this perfect life, while it feels like I struggle for everything.'

I bit the inside of my cheek to stop myself from correcting her. The truth was that it was Samantha who'd had to struggle in life. Jennifer had always had everything handed to her and she'd never had to work for anything. She was entitled and spoiled and over the years, it seemed those traits had only got worse.

'You had the perfect life once,' I couldn't help but remind her. 'And you threw it away so you could screw your personal trainer.'

She started sobbing again. 'I know. I'm so sorry, Gabriel. If I could take that back, I would. It's the biggest regret of my life.'

'Even more than sleeping with your sister's husband?' I asked and I saw the colour flush across her cheeks.

'Yes,' she sniffed. 'I wish I could go back and change it.'

'Well, to be honest, Jennifer, I don't,' I said.

She turned and stared at me. 'What?'

'I wouldn't change it. I forgave you for the affair a long time ago. I know that I played my part. I wasn't around as much as I should have been. But I think we both know we would have never worked out in the long term.'

'We would. We loved each other. Didn't we?'

I turned to her. 'Of course we did. But ...'

'But what?'

'I loved you Jennifer, but we weren't exactly compatible. We had nothing in common.'

'Well, sometimes, opposites attract,' she offered. 'So you and Samantha are compatible, are you?'

'Yes, actually. And besides that, she brings out the best in me.'

'Oh, God, no,' she rolled her eyes so hard I thought they might get stuck in the back of her head.

'What?' I snapped.

'Next you'll be telling me she makes you want to be a better man,' she sniped as she stuck her fingers down her throat and made an exaggerated vomiting noise.

'Well, she fucking does. But I can't imagine being with you makes anyone want to be better, Jennifer, because compared to you, most people are pretty fucking decent.'

She turned and glared at me. 'You think you're better than me? You think she's better than me?' she hissed.

'Yes! You're sitting here pregnant by your sister's husband. You claim you loved me but when we were married, you had an affair for six months behind my back. You've been to my girl-friend's place of work and sprayed disgusting lies about her all over her building.'

'Whatever,' she sniffed as she turned away from me and stared out of the window. 'Where are we going anyway?'

'To somewhere where you'll no longer be my responsibility,' I said.

She turned to me then, her eyes wide and her face pale, her mood doing another complete one-eighty turn. 'You're not going to kill me, are you?' she asked.

'For fuck's sake. Of course I'm not. Fucking hell, Jennifer,' I shook my head.

'Okay. Remember, I know who you are, Gabriel,' she said.

'Clearly not, if you think I'd kill you. Jesus Christ!'

We drove on until we turned into a tree lined street. 'I can't go back here,' she said anxiously as she realised where we were.

'Oh yes, you fucking can,' I replied as I pulled up outside her sister's house. 'Out of the fucking car.'

She unclipped her seatbelt and I got out and opened the door for her.

I walked up the path and rang the doorbell while Jennifer loitered behind me. A moment later, her sister's husband, Steve answered.

I smiled at him. 'I'm glad it's you. I've got something that belongs to you,' I said as I took hold of Jennifer's hand and pulled her towards me.

Steve started stuttering and stammering. 'She can't be here ...' he started.

'Really?' I snarled. 'She's fucking seven months pregnant with your baby, you spineless piece of shit. If she can't be here, then you'd better dig into those deep pockets of yours and find her somewhere else to be.'

Steve leaned forward. 'I can't. Emily will kill me,' he whispered. 'We're trying to work on our marriage.'

I leaned in closer to him. 'If you don't start acting like a man and take some responsibility for this mess you've helped to make, then *I* will fucking kill you,' I hissed. 'And I don't make idle threats, Steve. So step up, or I will fucking step on you. You should have thought about your marriage before you fucked your wife's sister!' I snarled.

At this point, I saw Emily's face appear at the doorway behind him. She looked drawn and tired. I felt for her, she was as much a victim in this as anyone, but she wasn't my responsibility.

'What the hell is going on?' Emily asked.

'Your sister needs support. From the father of her baby. Whether you sit back and watch the pair of them fuck you over again, is entirely up to you,' I said.

Then I turned to Jennifer. 'Your stuff is being delivered here in a couple of hours. I hope that baby of yours is healthy and you both have a great life, Jennifer, I mean that. But I will never forgive you for what you did and for the pain you've caused Samantha. I never want to see your face again.'

Then I walked down the path and closed the gate behind me as I listened to the three of them start squabbling between themselves.

CHAPTER 39

SAMANTHA

Gabriel had been edgy throughout the drive home from my office. I wondered if it was to do with what had happened earlier that morning. I had a hunch he'd been and spoken to Jennifer himself. But I didn't dare ask him about it.

I would do at some point, but I was too tired for another argument with him right then. I wanted us to get back to the way we used to be. I sat at the kitchen table and watched him as he took off his jacket and tie before he sat at the table opposite me.

'I want to talk to you about something, but I want you to know that I'm not trying to cause an argument, Sam.'

'Okay,' I eyed him suspiciously. 'I don't want an argument either, despite how hot you look when you're angry,' I said, trying to lighten then mood.

He half-smiled at me. 'Can we be serious for a minute?'

'Okay. I'm listening,' I said as I sat forward in my seat. 'What is it?'

He looked at me with those incredible green eyes. 'Why do you run?' he asked softly.

I frowned at him. I hated running. I much preferred yoga or

a good spin class. It took a second before the proverbial penny dropped. That obviously wasn't what he meant.

He stared at me intently, waiting for my answer. He was so insightful and he knew me so well. He knew why I ran when things got hard. 'Why do you think I run?' I challenged him.

'Because you're scared,' he replied. 'But I don't understand what you're scared of. I know you're not scared of me, because you wouldn't let me do the things I do to you if you were. So, what are you afraid of?'

'I'm scared of my feelings for you. Of how much power you have over me, Gabe.'

'But why? I would never use that against you. You must know that?'

I nodded as a tear slipped down my cheek. 'I know. But you don't get it.'

He stood up and knelt before me, clasping my hands in his. 'Then help me to, Sam Please?'

I reached out and touched his face. He was right. If we were ever going to have a shot at making this work, he should know what makes me tick.

'After my mum died, I promised myself that I would never be dependent on anyone again. And then I went to live with my dad, and he was so amazing. But I always tried to keep him at a distance because I couldn't have dealt with losing him too. That's why I gave him such a hard time and that just seemed to make him more protective of me. Even though I knew he loved me and was only trying to look out for me, I felt suffocated by him. I turned his life upside down and he never once complained. He gave up so much of his life for me, and I can never repay that. I felt like a burden to him and I hated it.' I stopped talking and wiped a tear from my cheek.

'You were never a burden and he never gave up anything for

you. He's your dad, Sam. That's kind of his job. He adores you and he would do anything for you.'

I nodded. 'I know that, logically. But when I was a teenager, I couldn't see the truth of it all. So I ran off to uni, didn't I? Determined to prove that I was tough and could look after myself. And then I met Jackson, and well, look how well that turned out. I ended up with a man who controlled every aspect of my life for twelve years – because I was weak. He chose me because I was pathetic. I finally found the courage to leave him and I started to feel independent and strong again. But then you happened, and my feelings for you make me feel vulnerable and that makes me feel ... weak.'

He frowned. 'Being vulnerable doesn't make you weak, Sam.'

'I know that. But that's how I feel.'

Gabriel got up from his knees and pulled the kitchen chair over so he could sit directly in front of me. 'I wish that you could see yourself the way everyone else does,' he said as he ran a hand through his hair. 'The way that I do.'

'Oh? And how's that?'

'You think that everything you've been through makes you weak, but don't you see that's exactly what makes you strong? You have been through hell, Sam, and look at you? You're successful, and kind, and compassionate, and funny. Most people would be broken by what you've endured but you've come through it with a core made of fire. You think Jackson chose you because you were weak, but he chose you because he saw the strength and the spirit in you. Where is the fun for someone like him in choosing someone who was already his? That's what he got off on, breaking you down piece by piece. He needed someone who could endure being married to him.'

'But you don't *know* that?' I insisted. 'That's your opinion ...'

'No, it's not. He told me.'

I blinked at him. 'What? When?'

'That time he phoned me and you overheard us. He took great pleasure in telling me how you would always belong to him. And that wasn't because you were weak, it was because you were anything but. He told me how long it had taken him to break you – but he was proud of himself for doing it, and that was why you would always be his property. He likened it to breaking in a wild horse,' he stopped talking then and put his head in his hands.

'God, he was such an arrogant prick! He compared me to a horse!' I spat.

Gabriel looked up and rolled his eyes. 'Is that all you took from that?'

'No,' I said softly.

'So, do you see that you're not weak at all? You're the strongest person in this room. You're the strongest person in any room. You hold all the power here, Sam. You always have.'

I swallowed. He was looking at me with such intensity that I was starting to believe him.

'Can you just promise me that you won't run, Sam? I love you with everything I have and I will always come running after you, but it's becoming fucking exhausting.'

I nodded. 'Okay. I won't run.'

Gabriel sat back in his chair again and took a deep breath. I stared at him, noting the change in his demeanour. He was edgy again. I could feel it coming from him in waves.

Dear God, what now?

'So there's something else,' he stammered.

No shit, Sherlock! I'd never seen him looking so nervous. 'What?'

'This morning, when that snarky copper referred to Jennifer as my wife and looked at you like you were my bit on the side, it fucking killed me.'

'Well, I wasn't too happy about it either, but what she thought doesn't really matter, does it?' I replied.

'It matters to me,' Gabriel said, his voice thick with emotion. 'It matters that people know who you are to me – and how much I love you.'

I stared at him. 'Okay?'

'I want to ask you something. And remember you promised not to run?'

'Okay?' I said again. *What did he want to know now?*

He knelt on the floor in front of me again, but this time on one knee as he pulled a small box out of his trouser pocket. 'Will you marry me, Sam?'

I swallowed hard and stared at him, and then at the beautiful ring in his hand and then back at him. My heart felt like it was about to lurch out of my throat. My stomach swirled and I wasn't sure if the baby had started spinning around, or whether I was going to throw up.

Marriage? That was huge. Terrifying. That was me being his wife - Mrs Sullivan and no longer Samantha Donovan. That was me belonging to him - for real.

It was also me, him and our baby sharing the same name. It was us being a family unit. It was waking up every morning with him by my side.

I told my head to shut up looking for excuses and answered with my heart. 'Yes,' I breathed.

He looked as shocked as I felt for a few seconds before he pulled me from the chair and into his arms until we were both kneeling on the floor. 'Really?' he asked.

I nodded and smiled at him. 'Yes. Really.'

He placed the ring on my finger and then he kissed me so hard that my head started to spin too.

I lay with my head on Gabriel's chest and admired my engagement ring. It was beautiful. A pink diamond set in a platinum, diamond studded band. It must have cost him a fortune, but I wouldn't have cared if it hadn't. Material things weren't that important to me.

'Do you like it?' he asked as he hugged me to him.

'I love it. When did you get it?'

'This afternoon.'

'You're a fast mover, aren't you?' I gave him a playful nudge. 'We've been together a little over a year and I'm already pregnant with a ring on my finger.'

'I'm just a man who knows exactly what I want,' he laughed.

'Hmm, you certainly are,' I said as I lifted my head to look at him. 'Can we just have a small ceremony. Just us, and my dad. And Nick, of course. And your Aunt Maggie and Uncle Hugh. What do you think?'

He placed a hand on my cheek and kissed me softly on the lips. 'Whatever you want. I honestly don't care as long as you're my wife at the end of it.'

'Do you think we can do it before the baby's born?'

Gabriel looked at me in surprise. 'I can make it happen next week if that's what you really want?'

I nodded. 'It is. When I go to the hospital to have our baby, I want to be able to say that you're my husband,' I said as I noticed he was frowning at me. 'Why are you looking at me like that?'

He shook his head and started to laugh. 'I honestly thought I was taking my life in my hands even asking you, Sam. I thought I'd have to wear you down and beg for years to get you up the aisle.'

'So, why did you ask me then?'

'Because I couldn't not. And I'm definitely glad I did.' He pulled me to him and silenced me with one of his incredible kisses. Then he rolled over until he was lying on top of me, holding himself up on his forearms to protect my rapidly growing bump. 'I can't wait to call you my wife. The sooner the better as far as I'm concerned.'

Then he was kissing my neck. Working his way down my body with his hot mouth. I groaned in pleasure as he moved his head between my legs.

He licked the length of my cleft. 'You taste so fucking good when you're full of my cum,' he growled and I whimpered.

God, I loved that filthy mouth.

He licked and sucked at my tender flesh until I was panting his name. Then he moved over me again. 'Are you okay?' he asked as he nudged at my opening.

He'd already fucked me three times that day – but I couldn't get enough of him. The more I had, the more I wanted. 'Yes,' I breathed.

He held himself up on his forearms again and eased slowly inside me. 'I'm going to fuck you like this for the rest of our days, Sam,' he whispered in my ear.

'You better had, Gabe,' I replied with a groan.

CHAPTER 40
SAMANTHA

Gabriel and Nick sat in my office while I went through the papers Nick had drawn up which would allow me to relinquish any claim I had to the Carver family fortune, and leave Milton Carver as the sole heir.

I couldn't wait to get it over and done with. I hated every single member of that family. They had brought me nothing but pain and misery and I would rather be destitute than have a penny of their rotten money.

I read through the lengthy document, pointing out the odd amendment along the way, which only drew an eye roll from Nick. He was a brilliant solicitor and I knew the paperwork would be spot on, but I felt like I had to make my mark on it somehow.

When I'd read through it twice and made my suggestions in pencil, I handed it back to Nick. 'It's great. Thanks, Nick.'

He took the papers from me. 'I'll get Sadie to make the amendments and then you can sign them.'

'I'll deliver them to Carver's solicitor myself,' Gabriel added.

I nodded. 'And then it will be done with. I never have to see a Carver for the rest of my life.'

'Here's hoping. I'll get these to Sadie,' Nick said before walking out of the office.

Gabriel sat in silence, his green eyes fixed on me and a frown on his handsome face.

'You don't think so, do you?' I asked him.

He shook his head. 'No. I hope so, but men like Milton Carver never keep their word.'

'But all he wants from me is money. As soon as he has that, he'll have no reason to bother me again. I expect he wants me out of his life almost as much as I want him out of mine.'

He stood up and crossed the room until he was standing close beside me. 'I hope you're right, Sam.'

We were interrupted by a knock on my office door. I looked up to see Simon standing there.

'Sorry to bother you, Samantha,' he mumbled. 'But do you have the file on the McKenzie case? I can't find it.'

'Oh, I left it with Sadie. I'll just go and grab it for you.'

'I can get it,' he said as his cheeks started to turn a light shade of pink.

'It's okay. I need to speak to her anyway,' I said as I stood up and walked to Sadie's office, leaving Simon standing awkwardly under the heat of Gabriel's gaze.

CHAPTER 41
GABRIEL

I watched Simon as he strolled into Samantha's office and took a seat on the spare chair by her desk. There was something about him that I couldn't put my finger on.

He acted differently around Samantha – always blushing and mumbling. When I'd first witnessed it, I'd assumed it was because he fancied her, and I couldn't exactly blame him for that. She was fucking incredible.

But the more I saw it, the more I wondered whether it was all a bit of an act. And if that was true, what was his game plan? Samantha was one of the warmest and most caring women I knew. So, was it just Simon's way of eliciting some care and sympathy from her?

'That's a nasty cut on your lip, there,' he said.

I ran my tongue over the cut. It had healed quickly and was barely visible, especially beneath my stubble. 'I've had much worse. I'm surprised you can even see it?' I said.

He pushed his glasses up his nose. 'Perfect vision,' he smiled.

'So, you and Samantha have been working together quite a lot recently?'

'Yeah, we've had a few difficult cases, and it's been good to work with her. I'm learning a lot.'

I glared at him. 'I bet you are,' I replied and he smiled in response.

There was something definitely not right about this prick. From now on, I would be making sure he never gave Samantha a lift anywhere.

I didn't trust him. My instincts were rarely wrong, and they were telling me that Simon Hardaker was hiding something. Perhaps, he would be my little side project while I looked into Milton Carver? It wouldn't take much to do a little digging on him at the same time.

Just then, Samantha walked back into the room carrying a folder. 'Here you go,' she said to Simon as she handed it to him.

His demeanour changed again as soon as she entered the room. He stood awkwardly and took the file from her.

'Thanks, Samantha,' he said quietly before slithering out of the door – like a snake. He closed it behind him and I was grateful to have her to myself again.

I reached out for her hand as she walked past me. 'Come here,' I said and pulled her to sit on my lap. She wrapped her arms around my neck and I pulled her closer to me. 'Are you okay?'

'Yes,' she said as she curled a strand of my hair around her finger. 'I feel better now that those papers are almost ready. I'll sign them as soon as Sadie makes those changes.'

'I'll hang around until they're done then, and I can drop them off myself.'

'You don't have to –' she started to say and I glared at her.

'I thought you agreed to let me deal with this?' I interrupted her.

'I did,' she said with a smile. 'I just don't want to take too much time out of your busy day, that's all. Don't think I haven't noticed how little time you spend at work since I came home.'

'Are you complaining?' I said as I pulled her hair back and kissed her neck.

'Not at all. I just don't want you getting into trouble for neglecting your duties, that's all.'

'I'm the boss, I don't get in trouble,' I whispered in her ear. 'And the only duties I'm interested in are the kind that involve seeing to you.'

She slipped her warm hand inside my suit jacket and round to my back. 'Sadie said she'll be at least half an hour with those papers. She's just finishing something else,' she purred as I continued kissing a trail along her neck.

I felt my dick standing to attention. 'You'd better go and lock that door then, baby,' I said. 'Because there is only one way I want to spend the next thirty minutes, and that's inside you.'

I saw the her skin flush pink all the way from her neck to her cheeks and couldn't help but laugh. 'I love that talking dirty to you makes you blush, Sam. But, that is why you told me she was going to take so long, isn't it?' I grinned. 'Now are you going to lock that door or are you happy to risk one of your colleagues walking in when I'm fucking you?'

She sucked in a breath but I saw the desire blazing in her eyes.

'I'll lock the door,' she said as she stood up.

'Good girl,' I said as I watched her beautiful backside walking across the room.

CHAPTER 42
GABRIEL

I pushed open the glass doors of the offices of Langley, Reardon and Barnes and stepped into the cool, air-conditioned reception of Milton Carver's solicitor's office. I walked to the large reception desk and spoke to the receptionist.

'Gabriel Sullivan. I have an appointment with Nathan Langley.'

She pressed a few keys on her computer before looking up and smiling at me. 'Fourth floor, Mr Sullivan. His secretary will meet you at the lift entrance.'

'Thank you,' I said and made my way towards the lift.

Five minutes later, I was shown into Nathan's office by his secretary. 'Can I get you anything, Mr Sullivan,' she asked politely.

'No thanks,' I said. I didn't plan on hanging around longer than I needed to.

She left the office, closing the door behind her and leaving me and her boss alone.

Nathan Langley sat at his desk. Dressed in a dark grey suit and silver tie, that matched his silver hair.

'Please, have a seat,' he indicated the chair opposite him.

I sat down and placed the brown envelope I was carrying on his desk, sliding it over to him. 'These are the papers. Samantha has signed them. She has relinquished any entitlement to Jackson Carver's estate, leaving Milton as the only living relative with a claim.'

Nathan took the envelope and removed the papers. He flicked through them and gave a cursory nod as he did. 'Everything seems to be in order. My client will be pleased.'

'It is in order,' I growled. 'So, you tell your client from me, that if he comes near me or my family ever again, all bets are off.'

Nathan smirked at me. 'It's not very wise of you to threaten my client, Mr Sullivan.'

I shrugged. 'Well, it's not very wise of your client to kidnap me and then let me live to tell the tale, is it?' I snapped.

Then I stood quickly, pushing my chair back. I smiled to myself as Nathan visibly flinched.

I fastened the buttons of my suit jacket and then I walked out of the office.

I sent a text to my driver as I was making my way to the ground floor in the lift. When I walked out of the building, the car was waiting for me, with one of my employees, Alex sitting in the back.

I climbed into the passenger seat and nodded a greeting to the two men. 'Right, let's go and see what Leroy Cain has to say for himself.'

I recognised Leroy Cain immediately. He'd been the driver of the car the day I was kidnapped. I'd spent almost an hour studying the side of his face and the back of his head and would recognise him anywhere. He had a long scar running along the left side of his face and was built like the proverbial brick shit-house. He stood up when Alex and I entered the pub. We crossed the floor and stood in front of him.

Alex introduced us and Leroy extended a hand to shake. I looked down at it, and then up at him.

'No hard feelings?' he said.

'Well, that all depends,' I replied.

'Fair enough,' he lowered his hand and indicated the stool next to him at the bar.

'I'll wait over there,' Alex said as he nodded towards a table at the back of the pub. 'Give me a shout if you need me, Boss.'

I watched as Alex walked to the empty table. He'd set up this meeting today, and also suggested that I bring him as back up, as there was no doubt Leroy Cain would have brought some. There was a part of me that still wondered where Alex's loyalty would lie if he was pushed to choose between me and his ex-squad mate, but I had brought some back up of my own tucked into the waistband of my trousers.

I sat on the bar stool and Leroy sat next to me before ordering two pints of lager from the barmaid.

'So, how long have you worked for Carver?' I asked

'Nine months.'

'Do you know he tried to have my girlfriend killed months before he kidnapped me?' I asked, remembering Anthony Garvey's attack on Samantha and feeling a wave of anger wash over me.

'I don't concern myself with the intricacies of Mr Carver's business dealings. He pays me to do a job and I do it. Men who require the services of someone like me, aren't usually very nice people. If I thought about what they did, and why they needed my protection, then I wouldn't sleep at night.'

'I got the impression none of you particularly enjoy working for him?'

He frowned at me. 'What gave you that idea?'

'He basically told you to give me a good hiding before you dropped me back home and yet none of you laid a finger on me?'

Leroy shrugged. 'We're all men who keep our ears to the ground, Mr Sullivan. We know who you are. We did the job we were paid to do. There was no reason for any of us to make a further enemy of you.'

I nodded. 'Wise move.'

'But, you're right. I can't stand him,' he said with a smirk. 'Neither can my cousin, Kelvin. Carver is an arrogant, pretentious prick. But he pays well.'

'I hear that you're a shrewd businessman, Leroy.'

He nodded. 'I plan on retiring in a few years, so I like to make the most of any opportunity that comes my way.'

'So, if I was to offer you an opportunity to make double what Carver is paying you, you'd be interested?'

'I'm all ears, Mr Sullivan,' he said with a smile.

Twenty minutes later, I downed the last of my pint and slipped off the barstool. 'It was good to meet you, Leroy,' I said.

'You too, Gabriel,' he replied as he held out his hand again.

This time I shook it. 'I'll be in touch,' I said and then I indicated to Alex that we were ready to leave.

CHAPTER 43

SAMANTHA

I picked up the TV remote and climbed into bed, snuggling against Gabriel's chest. I sighed contentedly. It was Sunday evening and we had spent the whole day together, talking, eating, watching our favourite films, but mostly having lots of very hot sex.

I traced my fingertips over the tattoos on his stomach. He had sixteen tattoos in total, mostly across his chest, back and shoulders, and I loved them all.

'I think you should get a tattoo of my name,' I laughed as I traced my fingertip along his abdomen and towards his groin. 'Right here.'

'Really? Just your name?'

'Hmm? Maybe it could say, property of Samantha Don –' I started to say but then I realised that my name wasn't going to be Samantha Donovan for much longer.

'Samantha what?' he asked with a smile.

'Samantha Sullivan, I suppose?' I said and took a deep breath.

That was the first time I'd said that name aloud. It was kind of scary, but it was mostly exciting. I had no idea how much I would like the sound of my new name.

'I like the sound of that,' he growled.

'Good. So, when are you getting it then?'

'As soon as you book us both into the studio. I assume you'll be getting a matching one?'

'Saying property of Samantha Sullivan? That seems a bit pointless,' I started to laugh.

He ran his hand across my naked behind and growled in my ear. 'Behave yourself, Samantha. Just because you know I'm not going to spank you, doesn't give you a free pass. I might just be saving all of these little misdemeanours up in my head to be dealt with at a later date.'

I shivered in anticipation. 'Well, in that case. I'll make sure to definitely not behave. I do miss that lovely soft belt of yours.'

He groaned loudly. 'Fuck, Sam! I can't wait to tie you up and turn that gorgeous arse of yours bright red.'

'Neither can I,' I said with a sigh. 'In fact, I fantasise about it often.'

He tilted my chin up so he could look in my eyes and smiled. 'What else do you fantasise about?'

'I've told you one of mine. It's your turn next.'

'You are my every fantasy rolled into one, baby,' he said smoothly.

I rolled my eyes. 'Have you ever had a threesome?'

'Yes.'

'Really?'

'Yes.'

'With two women, or another man and a woman?'

'Two women,' he replied.

'Hmm, I wonder if I need to try one then? With two men, obviously? I feel like I've missed out,' I teased him.

'There is not a fucking chance in hell that is ever happening,' he growled as he squeezed my behind and pulled me closer to him.

'Have you ever kissed a man?' I went on.

'No. Have you ever kissed a woman?'

'Yes. Two actually.'

He flashed his eyebrows at me.

'I was in college. It didn't count. It was nice though. Women have the softest lips.'

'I know,' he grinned.

'What about anal?' I asked him.

'Yes.'

'Really? Do you enjoy it?' I asked in surprise.

'Yes. Why does that shock you?' he laughed.

'Because you've never tried that with me,' I shrugged.

'Well, have you ever done it before?' he bent his head low and planted a kiss on my throat.

'No... I mean, yes, I suppose ...'

He looked up at me. 'No or yes?'

'I have. But not willingly,' I replied.

I saw his eyes darken and I suddenly regretted the turn this conversation had taken.

'Jesus, Sam!' he breathed as he ran a hand through his hair.

'Gabe, please don't. I hate it when you feel sorry for me –'

'I don't feel sorry for you,' he interrupted me. 'But you can't just drop stuff like that into the conversation and expect me not to react, Sam.'

'I know. It's just ...I hate that we can't just have a normal conversation about something without my past ruining it,' I said.

My marriage to my ex-husband seemed to crop up at the most inopportune moments.

He squeezed me tighter to him. 'It's not ruined.'

I looked up at him. 'Well, we're not talking about our sexual fantasies any more, are we? Instead, you're thinking about how you should have saved me from Jackson somehow. Or you're wondering if there is any way to torture a man who is already dead.'

He brushed my hair behind my ear. 'It's changed the conversation, not ruined it. I want to know everything about you, Sam. I am never feeling sorry for you, but yes I would like to dig that fucker up and destroy his corpse.'

'Well, there'd be no point. He wouldn't feel it,' I said with a smile.

He shrugged. 'He doesn't deserve to rest in peace though, does he?'

'I don't want to talk about him,' I said as I pulled Gabriel's face towards mine.

He pressed his lips against mine, lightly at first, before gently opening my mouth with his tongue and deepening it until I was thinking of nothing but him. I felt the familiar stirring and pulling in my abdomen and I wrapped my leg around him, pressing myself against him. I smiled as I felt his cock stiffening against me.

He broke our kiss. 'What are you grinning at?'

'You're always ready to go, aren't you?' I said as I looked down at his beautiful cock.

'And you're not?' he smiled at me.

'Hmm,' I nodded as I bit on my lower lip. 'I blame my raging pregnancy hormones though. I can't be held accountable for my actions.'

'You're really trying to blame your raging horn on our unborn child?' he said with a dramatic shake of his head.

'Not on our child, no. But on the pregnancy. That's different.'

'So, what was your excuse before you were pregnant then?' he growled. 'I can't recall ever keeping you satisfied for very long.'

'Oh, but you keep me very satisfied,' I grinned at him. 'Maybe that's why I can't get enough of you.'

'I already told you earlier, I'm not going to fuck you again tonight,' he growled in my ear.

'But why not?' I purred.

'Because I've spent almost the whole day inside you. You have a check-up tomorrow. I want you to be able to walk into the doctor's office.'

'They're not going to give me an internal and tell you off for us having too much sex, you know?' I said with a grin.

He gave me a light slap on the behind. 'Don't be bloody cheeky.'

I laughed. 'You slapping my ass is really not doing anything to help the situation, Gabe.'

'Behave then,' he ordered.

'Okay, if we're not going to have more sex, let's go back to our fantasies talk. Where were we? Anal?'

He shook his head and closed his eyes.

'How many women have you done it with?'

'I don't know,' he replied.

'Too many to count?'

'No. But I don't keep a track of these things.'

'Did you with Jennifer?'

'Sam!'

'It's a fair question. Did you and she ...?'

'Yes,' he said with a sigh.

'So, why not me then?'

He brushed the back of his knuckles over my cheek. 'I didn't know you wanted to. I wasn't sure that was something you were into.'

'Well, you never asked me. Is it because you think I'm too fragile?'

'Don't be ridiculous, Sam. It's because I can barely keep up with you as it is.'

'Well, I want to try it.'

He cocked an eyebrow at me. 'Right now?'

'Yes. Right now,' I said as I ran my hand down his chest towards his groin.

He took hold of my wrist to stop me in my tracks and narrowed his eyes at me.

'Why?'

I couldn't help feeling mildly offended. 'Why not? I don't understand if you've done it with all of the other women you've been with –'

'Not all of them,' he interrupted me.

'Most?'

'No. Some.'

'So, why not me?'

'I told you. I wasn't sure it was your thing.'

'Well, did you know if was Jennifer's thing? Or did you ask her?'

'Sam!' he snapped. 'Enough!'

I frowned at him. 'Enough? Why? I want to know why you won't do something with me that you'd do with everyone else - with her?'

'Are you seriously questioning whether I'd like to fuck your arse? Of course I would, but not now. Not when the only reason you're asking me is because you think you have to prove something. How can I do that, especially after what you just told me?'

I shook my head. 'You're wrong, Gabe. You think you have me all figured out, but you're wrong.'

'So, why then? Why now?'

I blinked at him and swallowed. 'Because I don't want him to be the only one.'

I saw the fire in his eyes as he pulled me to him, sealing my mouth with a ferocious kiss.

'He won't be,' he growled. 'I promise you. But not yet. For one thing, we have no lube.'

I looked down between us, at our bodies pressed together and grinned. 'If you went down on me right now, I'd worry you'd drown. I'm sure you can make use of some of that, can't you?'

'Hmm. But, maybe we should wait ...'

'For what?'

He nodded at my bump.

'He'll be fine!'

'Are you sure about this?' he asked.

'Yes. I want you to own every part of me,' I breathed as I placed my hand on his cheek.

'I already do,' he growled. 'Now get on your hands and knees.'

I did as he told me and he pulled a pillow beneath me, placing it in front of my arms. 'Rest your head on that baby and put that peach up in the air.'

I leaned forward, slipping my hands and forearms beneath the pillow and resting my cheek against the cool cotton. He moved behind me, running his hands ran over my backside as he sucked in a long breath.

'This sweet little ass is so sexy, Sam,' he growled. 'I'm going to enjoy fucking it.'

He slipped his fingers between my thighs, through my folds, coating them in my juices and his own cum. Then he slipped two fingers inside me and I groaned.

I was tender from our marathon sex sessions during the day, but I still craved him inside me.

As quickly as he'd slipped them in, he pulled his fingers out again and slid them up the seam of my ass. He pressed against my hole and I sucked in a breath, my hips flexing forward instinctively.

'Relax, baby,' he soothed.

I nodded and steadied my breathing. I could do this. I wanted to do this.

He pressed against my opening again and this time I pushed back against him, until the tip of his finger breached my entrance. I bit my lip as he slid it all the way inside. The feeling was strange but not unpleasant.

'That okay?' he asked.

'Yes,' I groaned.

Then he started to move his finger slowly in and out and I felt the throbbing in my core starting to grow ever stronger. A few seconds later, I gasped out loud as Gabriel slipped his cock inside my pussy.

'You're right, baby. Who needs lube when you have cream as good as this?'

He withdrew his cock, and his finger from my ass at the same time and I moaned at the loss of the feeling of fullness. But it didn't last long as he grabbed me by the hips, pressing the tip of his cock at my hole.

He pushed himself inside slowly, so just the tip was inside me. I felt the burning of his large cock stretching me open, but he stayed still for a moment, letting me accommodate to his size.

His fingers dug into my hips and I could hear his breathing growing faster.

I smiled to myself. I loved that he was on the edge. He was so used to being in complete control and I took immense pleasure in the fact that I could take him to the brink of losing it.

I pushed myself back slightly, taking in more of him and he groaned loudly.

'Fuck, Sam! Your ass is so fucking hot and tight.'

I moaned as he slid in further, the burning sensation gave

way to an intense feeling of fullness. Then his hand slipped between my thighs and he started to rub my clit.

'Gabe!' I shouted as the pressure in my core continued building, threatening to burst out of me at any moment.

He took that as his cue to pick up his pace and he started to thrust in and out of me. His balls slapping against my opening only adding to the raft of sensations that I was experiencing. I wasn't going to be able to hold on much longer.

'I'm going to come in your beautiful ass, baby,' he growled and his filthy words were my undoing.

I screamed out loud as the orgasm rolled through me, and as Gabriel rubbed out his own relief, the waves of pleasure kept on radiating from my core – like ripples in a pond.

He pulled out of me and I collapsed onto my side, breathing heavily and with my eyes closed as my head spun. I felt him lay down beside me, his ragged breathing matching my own.

'Fuck, that was intense,' he said as he slipped his arm around my waist and pulled me close.

I opened my eyes and stared at him. His beautiful green eyes were smouldering – almost black. 'I know,' I panted.

'Are you okay?' he said as his eyebrows knitted into a frown.

I nodded.

He tilted my head to look at him. 'Don't ever question how much I want you. I have never needed any woman as much as I need you, Sam. I could fuck you in every single way, in every single place, every hour of every day and it would never be enough for me.'

I breathed in. God, I loved him so damn much it hurt.

CHAPTER 44

SAMANTHA

I sat in the new luxurious leather chair in my office and spun around like a little kid. I'd ordered it weeks ago and almost forgot about it until it had arrived that morning. I'd been getting slight backache as my pregnancy progressed and this was supposed to be ergonomically designed to help improve posture, as well as being incredibly comfortable.

As I spun around, I wondered why I'd never got myself a chair like this before. They were so much fun.

Suddenly, I started to feel sick. I grabbed hold of the edge of the desk to stop myself. But even when I'd stopped spinning, the room continued whirling around me and I felt like I was going to throw up.

I looked up as my office door opened and Gabriel walked into the room.

'Hey, you,' I said with a huge smile, forgetting my urge to be sick.

He crossed the room. 'Hey, baby. You ready to go?'

'Not yet,' I giggled. 'I'm playing on my new chair.'

He frowned at me as drew closer. When he reached me, he

took hold of my chin, tilting my head up so he could look into my eyes. 'Have you been drinking?'

'No!' I snapped. 'I'm pregnant,' then I giggled again. Something about him was so funny today.

His eyes narrowed as he brought his face closer to mine. 'Jesus Christ, you're stoned!'

'No I'm not,' I shrieked. 'I would never ...'

I couldn't finish my sentence as the urge to be sick washed over me again.

He rubbed a hand over his face. 'You're fucking stoned off your face, Sam. What have you eaten today?'

'What?' I looked up at him. 'What the hell does that have to do with anything?'

'Well, I assume you haven't smoked anything. So, have you eaten anything unusual?'

'No. Just my lunch that you made me. Oh, and I had a brownie this afternoon.'

'A brownie?' he eyed me suspiciously.

'Yes,' I frowned.

'Where from?' he was scowling at me now.

'Simon brought it in for me.'

He stormed out of my office and a moment later, he was marching my poor junior partner back through my office door.

'Where the fuck did you get the brownie from you gave her this afternoon?' Gabriel barked at him while I looked up at the two of them wide-eyed. What the hell was going on?

Simon shuffled awkwardly and pulled at the collar of his shirt. His face started to flush bright red under the heat of Gabriel's intense gaze.

'My flatmate made me it,' he stammered.

'And is your flatmate prone to making fucking pot brownies?' Gabriel growled.

Simon looked at me then, his eyes wide with horror as he

put his hands over his face. 'Oh, shit! She said she'd never do it to me again after the last time. She knew I was bringing it into work. I honestly didn't think ... I would never have given it to Samantha if I'd known. I'd never have even touched it. Samantha, I'm so sorry,' he pleaded.

Gabriel jabbed a finger in Simon's chest. 'You fucking idiot! You should think about getting yourself a new flatmate if their idea of fun is to spike you with weed. You're lucky you work here and not for me, because I would sack you on the fucking spot. I should rip your fucking head off.'

Then he walked over to me.

I placed my hand on his arm as my head started to spin. 'Can you save that until later? I need to go home.'

He put his cool hand on my flushed cheek. 'Of course, baby. Come on,' he said as he pulled me up from the chair.

I leaned against him. 'I feel sick,' I groaned.

'Jesus! I thought my days of looking after you when you were stoned were long over,' he said with a smile.

As we walked past Simon, Gabriel grabbed him by his collar with one hand. 'If anything happens to her, or our baby, you'd better fucking emigrate to the other side of the world,' he said as he shoved him roughly backwards. 'I'll deal with you tomorrow,' he snarled before he guided me out of the office.

'The baby,' I started to cry when we got into the fresh air. 'What about the baby, Gabe? What if something happens to him? I can't kill this baby too?' I wailed.

The anxiety was starting to take over as I thought about my beautiful Alice. The only other time I'd been pregnant, I'd lost my baby girl at almost five months in a car accident.

Now, I was spiralling. I knew it was in part due to the weed, but what if I really had hurt mine and Gabriel's baby? How could I have been so stupid?

He pressed me up against the wall as I started to sob hysterically. 'Sam,' he said softly. 'What happened to Alice was an accident. It wasn't your fault. Our baby is going to be just fine and so are you. You've done more pot in one night before than most people do in their entire lives. I was just trying to scare him in there. I'm sorry. But you need to calm down. I'm going to take us home. I'll have someone come and check you and the baby over and then you're going to sleep this off and you'll both be fine. Okay?'

I nodded as I wiped the tears from my face. 'Okay,' I sniffed.

'Good,' he said as he planted a kiss on my forehead. 'Now, let's get you home.'

CHAPTER 45
GABRIEL

I chewed on my lower lip as I watched the midwife checking Samantha over. Rose was an old friend of my aunt Maggie's. She worked for a private health provider now and had agreed to see us at short notice as a favour. She'd brought her portable sonograph machine and had confirmed the baby's heart rate was stable and that he was, much like his mother, going to be fine after a good sleep.

I watched as she chatted to Samantha and then she called me over.

'They're both absolutely fine. But please keep an eye on her for the next twenty-four hours. And don't forget any reduced movements or any concerns, and you get straight to the hospital,' she said to Samantha.

'I will. Thank you, Rose,' Samantha said with a faint smile.

'And no more pot brownies,' Rose said as she punched me on the arm.

'Definitely not,' I agreed as I let out a long breath.

I showed Rose out and thanked her again before heading back upstairs to Samantha. She was sitting on the edge of the bed.

'You should be resting,' I said as I walked over to her.

'I know, but I feel like I'm going to be sick,' she groaned.

I stood in front of her. 'Do you want me to get you a bucket?'

'No. I'm okay. It's passing,' she said, right before she threw up all over my trousers and shoes.

She looked up at me as she wiped her mouth with the back of her hand. 'I'm so sorry,' she said as the tears sprang to her eyes.

'It's fine. I've been vomited on plenty of times before today,' I smiled at her before I looked down at myself. 'But never by anyone as beautiful as you before.'

'Oh, I feel awful, Gabe,' she groaned as she lay down on the bed. 'Did I really used to take this stuff willingly?'

I lifted her feet onto the bed and rolled her onto her side. 'Every weekend for about three years, as I recall.'

She closed her eyes. 'I must have been such an idiot.'

'An idiot? No. You were fucking adorable,' I laughed. 'I'm going to clean up and get you a drink of water. Will you be okay for five minutes?'

'Yeah,' she said sleepily. 'Have I ruined your favourite shoes?'

'No, of course not,' I said even though I was going to throw them straight into the bin.

I turned and looked at her as I reached the bathroom. It looked like she'd already fallen asleep, although she had a dopey grin on her face. I felt my heart almost burst out of my chest as I realised how much I loved her, and our baby.

She had made my life complete.

CHAPTER 46

SAMANTHA

I woke up with a throbbing head and a dry mouth. The light from the TV flickered on the wall opposite and I looked up to see Gabriel sitting up in bed.

'Hey you,' I said as I sat up, stifling a groan.

'Hey sleeping beauty. How are you feeling?' he asked as he wrapped an arm around me.

'As rough as a badger's butt-crack. How long have I been asleep?'

He checked his watch. 'About six hours.'

'Have you been sitting here with me this whole time?'

He nodded. 'I was worried you might be sick again,' he said as he brushed my hair back from my face.

'Oh, God. I was sick all over you, wasn't I?' I groaned as the memory came flooding back. 'I'm so sorry.'

'You don't have to be. If you can't vomit on me, then who can you?' he laughed.

I shook my head as my cheeks flushed with embarrassment. 'I can't believe I ate a pot brownie.'

'Well, it was hardly your fault.'

I nodded. 'It was delicious too. What the hell was Simon thinking?'

'Seems he wasn't. I mean, to not only bring a pot brownie into your workplace, but then to give it your boss, and your pregnant boss at that, is a whole new level of stupid.'

'He's not stupid. Maybe just a little naïve?'

'Or he's neither of those things,' Gabriel said seriously as he looked at me. 'Maybe he did it on purpose?'

'What? Simon? Why?' I shook my head and laughed.

'It's not impossible, Sam. So, I'm not ruling it out, and nor should you.'

'I think your job makes you paranoid,' I said to him.

He leaned down and gave me a lingering kiss on the lips before he replied. 'I'm surprised that your job doesn't make you.'

I shrugged. 'I like to see the best in people.'

'I spoke to Nick anyway, and he thinks some sort of warning is in order,' he said casually.

'What? You spoke to Nick about this?'

He frowned. 'Well, he's Simon's boss too.'

'Yes, but you did that without me, and you had no right to,' I said. How would Gabriel like it if I started deciding how his employees should be dealt with?

'Well, to be fair, you were fucking wasted, Sam. And then you slept for six hours straight. Nick phoned me and asked me what went on. What was I supposed to do, wait until you woke up to tell him?'

I shook my head and sighed. 'I didn't realise he'd phoned you. You made it sound like you and Nick had this all figured out without me.'

He placed his hand on my cheek. 'When does Nick ever make a decision without you? He can't even decide on what to eat for his lunch without your input.'

'That's not true,' I said with a roll of my eyes. 'He just values my opinion, that's all.'

Gabriel laughed and I knew he was teasing me. Nick was my oldest and closest friend and we spent a lot of time together. I loved that Gabriel never questioned our friendship, or our intentions. Not that he had reason to, but I wasn't used to a relationship where I could be so open about my friendship with another man.

I leaned back against the pillow and stared at the ceiling. I felt a sudden sadness settling over me.

'Are you thinking about Alice?' Gabriel asked softly.

I opened my eyes and nodded, blinking back the tears. I could remember the acute feeling of terror and anxiety I'd felt earlier when I thought I might have harmed the baby. It brought all of the memories of my first pregnancy flooding back to me.

I had lost my beautiful baby girl in a car accident when I was almost five months pregnant. For a long time, I blamed myself for her death – which wasn't helped by the fact my psychopathic ex-husband also blamed me every chance he got.

As the years had passed, I had come to accept that it was an accident and it wasn't my fault. But earlier today, the feelings of guilt and loss and pain had come rushing back, exacerbated by the weed, which I hadn't taken since I was nineteen and could clearly no longer handle.

Gabriel took hold of my hand and squeezed it tightly. 'Do you want to talk about it?'

'No. I'm just thinking about what could have been, that's all. I'm okay. It was the pot making me crazy earlier.'

He nodded. 'Good. You know it wasn't your fault?'

'Yeah. And actually, I was thinking about something earlier today – before the brownie incident.'

'What's that?'

'I was wondering how I could solve the problem of you

feeling like you have to find me a driver every time you can't pick me up or drop me at work.'

'That's not a problem though,' he interrupted me.

I rolled my eyes. 'Hear me out. I was also thinking about when the baby gets here. I'll be having some time off, and I can't be hanging around for you to take me places. I know I'll do plenty of walking with the pram, but it would be handy to have transport too.'

'So, what are you saying?' he asked with a frown.

I took a deep breath. 'I think I'd like to get back behind the wheel.'

His face broke into a grin. 'Really? You want to drive again?'

I nodded. 'I think it's time. I think I've let fear and guilt hold me back for too long already. What do you think?'

'I think it's a great idea, baby. And I'm going to get you the safest car money can buy.'

I smiled back at him. 'Thank you. But I can buy my own car.'

He shook his head and placed a warm hand on my stomach. 'You have given me the best gift I could have ever asked for, the least you can let me do is buy you a car.'

'Hmm. We'll see,' I said.

He rolled on top of me. 'No, we won't see. I'm buying you and our baby a fucking car.'

Before I could protest, he sealed his mouth over mine and kissed me so hard I didn't care if he wanted to buy me a fleet of cars.

CHAPTER 47

GABRIEL

I saw the old silver Range Rover parked up across the road from Archangel Securities and jogged over before climbing into the waiting car.

I knew the driver well.

He turned to me and smiled. 'Afternoon, Gabriel.'

'Phil,' I said with a nod. 'So, what have you got for me?'

'Shall we drive?' Phil asked. 'I could murder a coffee.'

I smiled. Phil was a sucker for a service station coffee. 'Let's go then. You can fill me in while you drive.'

Phil nodded and pulled his car away from the kerb.

Phil Campbell was a retired police Inspector. He'd always been open to making a few quid on the side when he'd worked for the Met, and I had used his talents on many occasions when he was still a serving officer. But, now that Phil had taken early retirement and was working as a Private Investigator, he was still as useful as ever.

'So, who shall I start with? Simon or Carver?'

'Simon,' I replied. There was definitely something not right about that little weasel and the incident with Samantha and the brownie the week before had me more convinced than ever that he wasn't all he seemed.

'There's some paperwork in the glove box for you. But, for a start, he lied on his job application form.'

'Oh?' I said as I sat forward in my seat and opened the small compartment. I took out the large brown envelope and opened it, sliding out the papers and glancing over them.

Phil had printed out the application form Simon had submitted when he'd applied for the job at Donovan Cook, as well as Simon's birth certificate and a copy of his GCSE exam results. I didn't ask how he'd got the documents. Phil was good at his job and that was why I paid him well for his services.

Samantha would be furious if she found out I was digging into Simon's past without telling her about it, but I didn't regret it for a second. I did what I had to do to keep her safe.

'He said that he went to high school in Leicester, but he grew up in Surrey,' Phil said.

'Surrey? That's nowhere near Leicester?' I snapped.

'Exactly. And that's a hell of a commute for a teenager, isn't it?'

'So he lied about where he went to school? Why?'

'Well, I wondered that myself, so I did a little more digging and found out that he was born and raised in Surrey. Never lived in Leicester and certainly never went to school there.'

I frowned at him. 'Why does he want to hide where he grew up?'

'I don't know that, but I did find some more interesting information that might be of interest to you?'

I leaned back in my seat as Phil drove us towards the motorway. 'Go on.'

'His mum died four years ago and she left him the family home. A farmhouse in Surrey, worth just shy of one million.'

'So?'

'So, his mum, Karina Hardaker, was the daughter of a postman and a seamstress. They lived in a council house and Karina left school at fifteen with no qualifications. As far as I can find out, she never worked a day in her life – at least not officially anyway. So, where the fuck did she get a house like that from?'

I turned and looked at Phil. He was a good PI and this was all part of his routine – he didn't just give the information straight out as he preferred to make a story of it.

'I'm sure you're going to tell me?' I said.

'Well, I can tell you what I pieced together at least. Simon's father was some posh twat. He was engaged to marry the daughter of someone high up - some Earl or Lord. But he had an affair with sixteen year old Karina Hardaker and knocked her up. Both families of the engaged couple were furious and paid Karina off to cover the whole thing up. As far as I can tell, she never told a soul and she bought a house with the money they gave her.'

'That can't have been the end of it though? Someone must have subsidised her all these years, or how did she get by and raise a kid?'

'Maybe? I couldn't get to the bottom of that. But, there are all kinds of rumours about the elusive Karina. Some say she made money telling fortunes, some that she was on the game, others that she lived off the various men who were in and out of her life.'

I shook my head. I wasn't sure what any of this meant yet, except that it proved Simon Hardaker was a liar. 'So, he lied about where he grew up and he's sitting on a million pound house while he lives in a tiny two bed flat-share in Dagenham?'

Phil nodded. 'Seems so.'

'Maybe he's got debts and he needs the house to pay them off?' I suggested.

'If he has, they're not to any bank or legal establishments. And the house isn't up for sale. It's sitting empty.'

'Hmm,' I chewed my lip as I digested the information. I was missing something and while I didn't know what it was yet, I would find out.

I glanced through the papers as Phil carried on driving.

'You want to know what I dug up on Carver?' he asked me.

'Tell me over a coffee when we get to Costa,' I told him.

My mind was still racing with thoughts about Simon and what the little prick was up to. There was always the possibility that he had legitimate reasons for lying about his upbringing and keeping his mother's house a secret, and because of that I wouldn't go to Samantha with my concerns yet.

But I'd be watching him like a fucking hawk from now on and there was no way he'd be giving her any more lifts to or from work.

Half an hour later, I sat across a small table with Phil at the service station. I watched as he poured his fourth packet of brown sugar into his coffee and smiled. He almost had as many sugars in his coffee as Samantha did.

'So, tell me what you found out about Milton Carver,' I said when he was done stirring his drink.

'I didn't find out a lot more than you already knew, to be honest, Gabriel. As you suspected, he's almost penniless. He blew his fortune in the States and basically partied his way through his thirties. While his father was still alive, it seemed he still got a generous monthly allowance, but after he died, Jackson Carver cut him off completely.'

'So, what's he been living on for the past four years then?' I asked with a frown.

Phil sucked in a breath. 'Rich, older women with more

money than sense. He'd seduce them, fleece them for every penny he could, and then moved onto his next victim.'

'So, he's a gigolo?' I said with a flash of my eyebrows.

'Oh, he's much more than that. My sources indicate he wasn't just financially abusive. One of his victims lost the sight in her right eye and another of his lady friends disappeared and hasn't been heard from since.'

I felt my pulse start racing. This prick was as bad as his sadistic brother. 'Didn't any of these women go to the police?'

'You know the score. It's easier said than done. Maybe they were ashamed to be swindled by a con artist? Afraid of him? There are so many reasons. And by the time these women came to their senses, he was long gone, they were probably just happy to have him out of their lives.'

I nodded. Phil was right. I knew all too well why even the strongest of women felt powerless against men like Milton Carver.

'So, in a nutshell, he's desperate for money and he's a sadistic fucker?' I said as I ran a hand over my jaw.

'Yep,' Phil replied as he took a mouthful of his coffee. 'He's dangerous, mate. I'd tell you to be careful, but I'm sure you've dealt with worse.'

CHAPTER 48
GABRIEL

I'd had one of my drivers, Scott, pick me up from the Service Station after my meeting with Phil. I had a meeting to get to in the middle of the city and it was always a nightmare to find somewhere to park.

I asked him to make a quick detour to Samantha's office. I was still planning on buying her a car but we were having trouble agreeing on the safest one. I'd seen the car I'd suggested on the front of a car magazine while I'd been waiting for Scott to pick me up and had bought it for her – along with a packet of M&M's to sweeten the deal.

Scott pulled over outside the offices of Donovan Cook.

'I'll only be a minute,' I said to him as I picked up the bag from the seat beside me. Then I opened the passenger door and climbed out before jogging up the steps of Donovan Cook. I came face to face with Samantha's business partner, Nick as I walked into the reception.

'Forgotten something?' he said with a smile.

'What?'

'Samantha only left for her appointment ten minutes ago. Did she forget something?'

I frowned at him. 'I was just dropping something off for her. She said she was in court this afternoon.'

Nick's face turned a few shades paler than it already was. 'What?' he stammered.

'Where did she tell you she was going?' I snapped.

He shook his head. 'I don't want to get in between anything–'

'Where is she, Nick?' I interrupted him.

He blinked at me. 'She said she had a doctor's appointment. I assumed you were taking her. Maybe she just decided to go on her own?' he said with a shrug.

'But she doesn't have a doctor's appointment. At least none that I know of. I spoke to her earlier to see if she wanted to me to pick her up from work and she specifically told me she'd be in court all afternoon. In fact, she told me you were giving her a lift home,' I snarled at him. What the fuck was going on and why had she lied to me?

Nick shook his head. 'I don't know what to say.'

'How did she seem when she left? Was she okay?' I barked.

'Yes, she was fine,' he said. 'I feel like shit for dropping her in it. Look, Gabriel, I don't know what's going on with the two of you, but I'd rather stay out of it. She's my best friend, and I've come to see you as a friend too. Please don't put me in the middle of the two of you.'

I scowled at him. Where the hell had she gone? My heart started to hammer in my chest.

What if something had happened to her?

I turned around without another word to Nick and walked back to the car. I took out my mobile phone as soon as I was sitting in the passenger seat of Scott's car.

My overriding fear was that she was in some danger. I opened the *find my Iphone* app on my screen and entered her details. It felt invasive to be tracking her movements, but she knew I had the app and I had her ID. If the technology was available, then I would be a fool not to use it.

'Drive,' I said to Scott as I waited for her location to show up on my phone. After a few seconds, it did. She was in a coffee shop in Chelsea, on the other side of the city. Nowhere near the court she claimed to be working in. What the hell was she doing there?

I dialled her number, my fear and anger growing each with each ring.

'Hi, Gabe,' she said when she finally picked up.

She sounded fine. I could hear the noise of the coffee shop in the background. I took a deep breath and tried to remain calm. Surely, there was a perfectly legitimate explanation for her lying to me? 'Hi, baby. Just calling to see how you are.' I said, my jaw clenched in anger.

'I'm great,' she said. 'But I'm kind of in the middle of something. Can I call you back later?'

'Of course. Where are you?' I asked as casually as I could. This was her opportunity to come clean.

'In court,' she said without missing a beat.

'Oh? Sounds a bit noisy?'

'I'm in the coffee shop on the ground floor. We're just waiting to go in.'

'Oh, of course,' I replied as my blood started to thunder around my body. *Liar!* 'I'll see you at home later?'

'Yes. I'll pick us up some steak for tea,' she said breezily, as though she hadn't just told me a blatant lie.

'Bye, Sam,' I said and ended the call.

I put my phone back in my pocket and slammed the side of my fist against the door panel.

'Something wrong, Boss?' Scott asked.

'Yes, something is very wrong,' I snarled but I didn't elaborate any further and Scott had the good sense not to ask. I had a good mind to have him drive me to the coffee shop she was sitting in but I couldn't miss my meeting. Besides that, I was too fucking angry to confront her right now. I still hoped there was a good explanation for what had just happened, but that didn't make me any less furious at that moment.

I hated liars.

CHAPTER 49

SAMANTHA

I slid my phone back into my handbag and swallowed. Why had I just lied like that? Why hadn't I just told him the truth? At least half of it? I didn't know, but I did know that the look on the face of the woman sitting opposite me was making me incredibly nervous. It was the half smile she'd given me as she'd sat down that had done it.

Smug bitch!

Jennifer Sloane had looked at me like she knew something I didn't and it made me falter momentarily. It made me doubt him – if only for a second.

'Hello, Samantha,' she'd said sweetly when she'd walked into the coffee shop we'd agreed to meet at. Just as I'd been about to respond, my phone started ringing on the table. I'd looked down to see Gabriel's handsome face flashing on the screen. I glanced around me before I answered. Did he know I was here?

Then he'd asked me where I was and I'd lied outright and that wasn't like me. I didn't lie to him. I'd only done it once before and that was when I'd told him I didn't love him and I didn't want to be with him. But that had been different – that had been to protect both of us from my sadistic ex-husband.

I had contemplated not answering at all. I'd already told him I was in court and so it wouldn't be unusual for me not to answer my phone. But it could have been something important – and if it was, he would get a message to me somehow. He'd phone Nick at my office, or the court. I'd had to pick up just in case.

When I did answer, I should have told him the truth. He would have been angry with me, but he couldn't have done anything to stop me now.

I hadn't wanted Jennifer to hear us arguing though. It would have felt like she had some insight into our lives that I didn't want her to have. I didn't want her to know anything about us. I wanted her out of my life forever. But, to do that, I needed closure.

I put my handbag on the floor and lifted my gaze to meet hers. She looked me directly in the eye.

'Hello again, Jennifer,' I said.

She gave me that cocky half smile again and I resisted the urge to slap it off her face. Gabriel had always made out that she was this meek, mild woman who was clingy and lacking confidence. But she was far from it.

I looked down at her pregnancy bump. She was close to the end now and it was obvious. I already knew that Gabriel was telling me the truth, and this was just added confirmation. But she would never know that I had doubted him again because of her.

'Just how exactly did you expect to cover up your lie for much longer than you did?' I asked her as I leaned forward. 'You're clearly a lot further on than I am. You could hide it at first, but now ...' I didn't need to finish my sentence.

She shrugged. 'To be honest, I didn't realise Gabriel would

know the exact date your baby was conceived because I didn't realise you two were separated when he and I got together.'

Her words felt like a slap in the face. 'So, you thought he was in a relationship with me, and you went after him anyway?'

She laughed. 'Went after him? He didn't need much encouragement, I can assure you.'

'You're lying,' I snapped. 'He was drunk and you just happened to be there.'

She shrugged as she took a sip of her coffee.

'And that was no coincidence, was it? That you just happened to be in his club that night? You planned to seduce him all along so you could try and convince him you were having his baby?'

'Like I said, he didn't need much encouragement. I suppose I've still got whatever it is he wants,' she said with that bloody smug grin on her face. 'Whatever he doesn't get from you.'

It was my turn to laugh now. 'You can't seriously believe that?'

She frowned at me.

'He was hurting because we'd split up. He hardly ever drinks but that was why he was so drunk that night.'

'He wasn't *that* drunk.'

'But you said yourself he was so wasted he might not have put the condom on right. That was your excuse for why he'd got you pregnant.'

She blinked at me. She had no comeback for that.

'So, I'll ask you again, how long did you honestly think you could get away with your little charade for?'

She rolled her eyes. 'I had no idea he'd be so interested in the baby's gestation and what was supposed to be happen at how many weeks. He never used to be so bloody dull. That kind of put a dent in my plan.'

'So, you just tried to destroy our lives and our relationship on a wing and a prayer? Hoping that he wouldn't even bother putting the dates together in his mind?'

'It wasn't quite as ill thought out as you think. I'm no fool, Samantha! I was going to tell him the baby was born a few weeks early. I was planning on going into the hospital alone and pretending I couldn't get hold of him. I had it all worked out. Kind of,' she said with another shrug.

'Kind of!' I spat. 'You're fucking unbelievable. Just how stupid do you think we are?'

'We,' she snorted. 'You've barely been together five minutes and you're calling yourselves a we! I was married to him, darling. I know exactly what makes him tick. I know exactly what he needs – and it's not you,' she hissed.

'Really? I don't think you know him at all, Jennifer. I think you know a small part of him. A very specific part of him that he wanted you to see.'

'You're not his type at all. He likes submissive women who will bend to his will,' she snarled. 'Has he tied you up yet? Spanked you with his belt?' she said as she sat back with a look of triumph on her face.

I sat back too feeling temporarily winded. I had to admit that stung. Knowing that he'd done those things with her too, hurt me. But of course he had. They'd been married for three years.

I looked at the woman in front of me and made my peace with the fact that Gabriel had once loved her. But I knew with one hundred percent certainty that he didn't any longer. Whatever had been between them was long over.

It was me he loved now. That knowledge suddenly made me feel like I was invincible.

I placed my left hand on the table and saw her eyes darting to my engagement ring. 'Oh, yes, I forgot to tell you we're engaged. So, he'll be my husband soon,' I said with a smile. 'I might not be his usual type, Jennifer, but I am the woman he's in love with. I am the woman who gets to spend the rest of her life with him.'

I picked up my handbag and stood up. 'I don't know what I expected to gain from meeting with you today, but I can guess why you agreed to it. You wanted to create some tension or distance between Gabriel and me. You wanted me to doubt him. To doubt us. But you've done the exact opposite. You have shown me how much I trust him.'

She looked up at me in shock, her mouth hanging open.

'Bye, Jennifer,' I said and then I turned on my heel and walked out of the coffee shop.

CHAPTER 50

SAMANTHA

I went straight home after my meeting with Jennifer and decided to make a start on dinner. My chat with her had been cathartic. I now saw her for the manipulative, desperate woman that she was.

If I was honest, I had always felt threatened by her. If not by her, than by her memory. She was the first woman Gabriel her ever loved. But, now I saw the situation for what it truly was. She was his past, and she had no place in his future. That was my domain.

Gabriel walked into the kitchen as I was just about to take the steak I'd bought for dinner from the fridge.

'Evening, handsome,' I said with a smile.

He didn't smile back. He placed his car keys on the worktop and glared at me. I could feel the anger radiating from him as he stalked across the room. In two long strides he was standing before me. I closed the fridge and looked up at him. His eyes burned into mine.

Shit!

He must have found out where I'd been today. I swallowed

and stood fixed to the spot as he held me captive with the ferocity of his gaze.

'When we first got together, you presented me with a list of your demands. Do you remember?' he growled.

I licked my bottom lip as my legs trembled. Not from fear, but from anticipation. I wondered if a part of me enjoyed pushing his buttons so much because he was smoking hot when he was angry.

'I do,' I said softly, recalling our conversation where I had reeled off all of the things I'd said I would never allow him to do. Then I had told him how I would never be his property, that he would never get to tell me what to do, and how I would never belong to him. It had been a remnant from my awful marriage and stemmed from my desire to be fiercely independent.

But over the time we'd been together, Gabriel had broken down each of those barriers one by one. He had broken me down piece by piece and rebuilt me into the woman I was now. The woman who was squaring up to this six foot two wall of muscle and anger and fire, and not for one millisecond feeling an ounce of fear or uncertainty.

I was sure of him.

Of myself.

Of us.

'Do you remember I had rules too?' he said.

'Yes,' I whispered.

'And what were they?' he said in that low growl that resonated through every cell of my body.

'That I should let you fuck me senseless at least twice a day–'

'Epic fail,' he interrupted me.

I raised one eyebrow at him. 'How so?'

'Have I fucked you every single day since you made me that promise?'

'Well, no. But that was because we were broken up. And

whilst the first time was all on me, the last time was because you fucked your ex-wife instead.'

He moved a few centimetres closer to me and my breath caught in my throat. I felt the heat from him deep in my core. The closeness of our bodies had every nerve in mine on edge and desperate for his touch. Not to mention, he looked and smelled good enough to eat.

'And what was my *only* other rule, Sam?' he asked, ignoring my attempt to get a rise from him.

I swallowed again. God, he was so bloody intense. 'Never to lie to you,' I whispered.

'So, where the fuck where you this afternoon?' he snarled.

'I went to see Jennifer,' I replied.

'Why?' he said with a scowl.

'Because I needed to speak to her. I needed to hear her side of things.'

'You didn't believe my side then?' he asked.

'Yes, I did,' I said honestly. 'But I still needed to hear it from her. I needed to know why she did what she did, Gabe.'

'So, why didn't you just tell me that?'

'You'd have talked me out of it, wouldn't you?' I challenged him.

'Yes. But that doesn't excuse you lying to me, Sam. I asked you where you were and you lied to me as though it was as easy as breathing.'

'I was with her when you called. I didn't know what else to say,' I said and suddenly I felt awful about what I'd done. I'd known it was a big deal earlier – but I hadn't realised just how angry it would make him. It was a huge red flag for him. He hated liars. So did I.

'What else do you lie to me about?' he growled.

'Nothing, Gabe,' I said as I stared into his dark eyes. 'I swear.

I'm sorry I lied to you today. And I promise it will never happen again.'

'Tell me why I should believe you?' he snapped, his eyes narrowed as he glared at me.

'Because you know me, Gabe. You know I'm not a liar, despite what happened today.'

He lowered his head and leaned close to me so his lips grazed my ear as he spoke. 'I think I've made a big mistake in being too lenient with you, Sam.'

'What do you mean,' I breathed as I felt goose-bumps prickle along my forearm.

'I told you once that I need to be in control. I told you that I wanted you to do as you're told, when you're told. I know that's not always easy for you, so I made adjustments. But, I think maybe in doing that, I've become too soft.'

He pressed his body close to mine and my insides trembled. 'I don't think anything about you could ever be considered soft,' I said as I looked down between us. His rock hard erection was currently straining at the zip of his trousers.

He moved his head so he could look into my eyes again and I swore he could see into my soul. 'Maybe? But my punishments have been,' he said and took a deep breath.

He stood there for a moment, licking his lower lip as he studied my face. I realised he was deciding what to do next. 'I need to make a call. It won't take me long. By the time I'm done, I want you naked and upstairs waiting for me.'

'Then what?' I asked as my pulse quickened.

'Upstairs. Naked,' he said as he stepped back and took his mobile phone from his pocket.

I stood on the spot staring at him.

'Now, Sam!' he barked.

I stared at him. It felt like something was shifting between us. But whatever it was, it felt right somehow.

'Okay,' I said and then I slipped past him and walked up the stairs.

I took off my dress and sat on the edge of the bed. My fingers trembled as I unhooked my bra and tossed it into the laundry basket. I wondered whether to leave my white cotton briefs on, but the look in Gabriel's eyes suggested he wouldn't take kindly to any disobedience. Naked, he'd said – twice.

I slipped my underwear down my legs and placed them on the bed beside me. My heart raced in my chest and I took deep breaths to calm my breathing. I had no idea what to expect.

I'd noticed Gabriel was wearing that beautiful soft leather belt of his, and I had enjoyed being spanked with it many times before. But, I knew from experience he wouldn't spank me while I was pregnant.

So, what did he have planned?

I was almost breathless thinking about it – but it was with anticipation and excitement rather than fear. I smiled as I realised how much I had changed in the last twelve months. I trusted Gabriel Sullivan completely.

I lay down on the bed while I waited for him. He'd said his call wouldn't take long and a few moments later, he strolled into the bedroom, still wearing that incredible suit that he filled so bloody perfectly.

His eyes roamed over my body as he removed his jacket. I watched him intently, looking for a clue as to what he had planned. What would my punishment be for lying to him today? He reached for his tie and slowly undid the knot, pulling it away from his neck with one hand.

'Are you going to tie me up?' I asked, my voice trembling as much as my legs.

'No. Because you're going to do as you're fucking told,' he snapped.

'And if I don't?' I challenged him.

He scowled at me. 'Really? You want to play games with me right now, Samantha?'

I shook my head. 'No,' I whispered.

He moved his hands to his belt next and unbuckled it slowly. I watched and shivered as his expert fingers fed the leather through the fabric.

He looked up at me. 'You know that's not happening,' he said, reading my filthy thoughts. 'Besides, that would be far too easy.'

Too easy? Jesus, what was he planning on doing to me?

I watched as Gabriel stripped off the rest of his clothes and was standing in all his naked glory. My eyes roamed over his incredible body and I took a deep breath. He walked towards the bed and crawled over me.

'Open,' he commanded as he looked down at my thighs and nudged them roughly apart with his knee.

I did as he instructed and gasped as his fingers immediately slid through my dripping wet folds. 'Why does pissing me off make you so fucking wet, Sam?' he growled.

'I don't know,' I groaned as I pressed my head back against the pillow.

He pushed one finger inside me and I moaned loudly. Then he sucked one of my nipples into his hot mouth and began to suckle gently while he finger fucked me.

I writhed beneath him. This wasn't punishment at all. It was pure pleasure. He brought me to the edge quickly with his expert touch and just as he was about to tip me over the precipice, he stopped.

He moved his head and looked into my eyes. 'Why did you lie to me?' he asked.

I blinked at him. 'I told you. I didn't want you to know I was with Jennifer.'

'But why?' he demanded.

'Because I knew you wouldn't be happy about it. I don't know what else you want me to say, Gabe,' I said.

'I want the truth.'

'I've given you it,' I insisted.

He frowned at me and then he moved down my body. He blew over my wet slit making me gasp out loud before his mouth settled over my clit. He sucked the swollen nub of flesh into his mouth as he gently nudged it with his tongue.

It was only seconds before I felt my orgasm building again. I was tempted to run my fingers through his thick, dark hair but I sensed that he wouldn't approve so I grabbed onto the pillow either side of my head as I bucked my hips against his mouth. I felt the tightening in my core as my climax kept building to a crescendo.

Then he stopped.

I groaned out loud.

He moved up the bed towards me again. His face glistening with my arousal. 'Why did you lie to me, Sam?' he asked again.

'I already told you,' I snapped.

He took a deep breath and closed his eyes for a second. When he opened them again they were full of fire. He took hold of my wrists and pinned them above my head. 'What will it take to get the truth from you?'

'You already have the truth,' I hissed.

My body was aching for him and his denial of what I needed from him was driving me crazy. He was right, this was much worse than his belt.

He pressed his cock against my opening. 'Is this what you want?' he growled.

'Yes,' I panted.

'Then why did you lie?"

'Gabe, please. You're torturing me,' I wailed. 'I've told you the truth.'

He pushed deep inside me, making me groan with pleasure as he slowly thrust in and out of me.

I was so close. I bit the inside of my cheek so he wouldn't know how near to the edge I was. Maybe I could come before he'd even realised? But he knew me and my body far too well. Just as I was on the edge of collapse, he gave a final thrust and found his own release instead.

Then without a word, he pulled out of me, leaving me feeling empty and bereft.

I cried out in frustration as the tears started to roll down my cheeks.

'You're a bastard,' I hissed.

'You've only just realised that? Now, why did you lie to me?'

I shook my head and one hand slipped down towards my clit and he started to rub slowly.

'Why?' he snapped as he continued taunting me.

I pressed my head back against the pillow and closed my eyes. This was torture.

'You want to come? Tell me the truth,' he growled.

My body felt like it was on fire. Every part of me was aching for some release and he kept denying me. I tried to move but he still had my wrists pinned above my head with his other hand, and the weight of his body held the rest of me in place. I was completely at his mercy and he wasn't going to stop until he got what he wanted.

'Because I didn't know what I would do if she'd told me you were lying,' I shouted and then I started to sob. That was the truth but I hadn't even known it myself. I felt the salty tears streaming down my face and then Gabriel was beside me again, brushing them from my cheeks with the pad of his thumb.

'So, you didn't believe me then?' he asked quietly.

'I did. I do,' I sniffed. 'I didn't tell you I was going to see her because I knew you wouldn't want me to. And then when you phoned me, I panicked. We'd just sat down for a coffee and the way she was looking at me made me feel nervous. I thought she might tell me that you were lying to me, and that you were in love with her and planning to run away together or something.'

Gabriel frowned at me. 'What the fuck?'

'I know how stupid it sounds now, Gabe. But, I freaked out. That's why I lied when you phoned me. I didn't want to argue with you in front of her. I was going to tell you tonight.'

'What if she had told you I was lying. Would you have believed her over me?'

'No. Of course not. I believe you. I always have. I panicked. That's all. I swear.'

He brushed my hair from my face before kissing me. 'Don't ever lie to me again, Sam,' he growled.

'I won't.'

He kissed me again as his hand ran down my body and found that place where I was desperate to feel him. He slipped two fingers inside me as his thumb brushed over my clit and I groaned into his mouth.

Then he broke our kiss and looked into my eyes as I started to fall apart for him. 'Who does this hot, sweet pussy belong to?' he asked.

'You,' I panted.

'Who do you belong to, Sam?'

'You,' I whispered, lost on the brink of an orgasm.

'That's right, baby. I own you,' he growled in my ear and I came apart around him, shouting his name as I found my release at last.

The room spun around me and I had barely recovered when he was crawling over me to push his huge cock inside me again.

He lifted my legs and wrapped them tightly around his waist while he fucked and kissed me to another slow, rolling climax.

As we both lay breathless, he pulled me to lie on his chest and ran his fingers through my hair. 'I love you,' he whispered. 'I was terrified something had happened to you when nobody knew where you were earlier. Don't ever do that to me again.'

'I know. I'm sorry, Gabe,' I whispered. 'You're not going to implant me with a LoJack or something now, are you?'

He laughed and I smiled at the sound. 'Find my Iphone will do just fine for now, baby.'

'Some people would call that stalking,' I said.

'Some people would. I call it protecting what I love most in the world.'

I lifted my head to look at him. 'You're such a smooth talker, aren't you?'

He grinned at me and then he placed his hand under my chin and his face turned serious again. 'Do you know why I need to own every part of you, Sam?' he growled.

'Why?' I whispered.

'Because you own every single part of me. You always have and you always will.'

I felt a rush of love for him that almost completely over-whelmed me and I rested my head back on his chest so he wouldn't see the tears in my eyes again.

CHAPTER 51
GABRIEL

I wrapped my arms tighter around Samantha and planted a kiss on the top of her head. I felt my heart rate slowing as I lay there with her. I'd been so fucking angry earlier, I'd thought I might explode.

I still hated that she'd lied to me, but I kind of understood why. I would have definitely talked her out of meeting with my lying, slut of an ex-wife if I'd known that's what she was planning on doing. I didn't need her filling Samantha's head with her bullshit. She'd done enough damage already. But whatever had been said between them, I didn't get the sense that it had caused any tension between Samantha and me.

I had been furious earlier in the kitchen. I had stood over her, my anger pulsing through my body as I'd interrogated her.

She had stood, rooted to the spot, her jaw tilted in defiance as she'd looked up at me with those huge brown eyes. I'd looked at her and saw the emotion there. Love. Guilt. Anger. Excitement? But I didn't see even a trace of fear and that realisation made me so fucking happy – and proud. After everything she had been through, she was still willing to give me everything, and like the selfish bastard that I was, I would take it all.

She had done what I'd told her to, submitting to me completely and without question while I had taken what I needed from her. I looked down at her body nestled against mine and smiled. I loved this woman more than I could ever have imagined possible and there was nothing I wouldn't do for her.

'What did Jennifer say to you, anyway?' I asked her.

She looked up at me, her eyes pink as though she'd been crying again. 'Are you okay?' I said as I cupped her chin and tilted her head so I could get a better look at her face.

'Yes,' she said with the most beautiful smile I'd ever seen in my life.

I leaned down and kissed her soft lips. I felt her pushing for more and as much as I wanted to give her what she needed, I also needed to know what had happened today. I pulled back. 'So, what did she say?'

'Nothing that you probably don't already know. She told me she'd hoped you wouldn't figure out the date issue and I honestly think she thought she could have kept her charade up forever.'

'Is that all?' I asked.

'She also said I wasn't your type, and that I could never be what you really need,' she said with a soft sigh.

I felt my heart constrict in my chest. 'What?' I frowned.

How fucking dare she! Jennifer Sloane had no idea what my type was or what I needed.

Samantha smiled at me. 'Don't worry, I told her that if she thought that, she didn't know you at all. Not like I do.'

That response took the breath from my lungs. 'You said that to her?'

'Yes.'

'I fucking love you,' I breathed.

'Good,' she grinned at me. 'Does that mean I'm forgiven?'

I grabbed her hair at the nape of her neck and tilted her head to the perfect angle before I brushed my lips over hers. 'Have you learned your lesson?' I whispered against her skin.

I heard the breath catch in her throat and I moved my other hand to her backside, squeezing hard enough to make her gasp.

'Yes, Sir,' she purred like a kitten and I felt it vibrating through my cock.

'It's dangerous to call me, Sir, Samantha,' I growled.

'Why?' she said as she ran a fingernail down my chest.

'Because it makes me want to tie you up and do really fucking filthy things to you,' I growled.

'That doesn't sound dangerous. In fact, it sounds incredible,' she smiled and I felt my cock stiffen. I sealed my mouth over hers, forcing my tongue inside as I pulled her head back to hold her in place.

I would never get enough of this amazing woman if I lived ten thousand lifetimes.

CHAPTER 52

SAMANTHA

I opened the door to Gabriel's house and stepped outside, seeing the familiar black car waiting across the road as I walked down the path. Then *he* stepped in front of me and my heart almost leapt out of my throat. He looked so much like his brother, it was like seeing a ghost. My heart hammered in my chest and my blood raced through my body. I placed a hand protectively over my bump and he looked down at it and sneered.

I raised my head in defiance. He wouldn't see an ounce of weakness from me.

'What are you doing here, Milton?' I asked.

'We're going to go for a little drive,' he said with a wide, false smile.

'The hell we are,' I spat.

Just then two henchmen got out of the car I had wrongly assumed belonged to one of Gabriel or my father's employees, and stood beside it.

'You can walk to the car, or they will drag you into it,' he indicated his head towards them.

I looked around me. The street was quiet. Someone might see me, but by then it would be too late. 'I'll scream,' I said.

'And I'll knock your teeth down your throat before anyone has a chance to hear you,' he said smoothly as he stepped closer towards me and took hold of my arm by the elbow. 'Now, get into the fucking car,' he hissed.

He marched me across the road while I was still trying to think of a way out of the situation. Then he manhandled me into the back seat until I was sandwiched between him and one of his goons. The car sped away as I sat in silence and tried to steady my ragged breathing. Stress wasn't good for the baby. Milton was just trying to scare me – make sure I didn't change my mind about the money. That was all. I kept telling myself that over and over again.

Then I thought about Gabriel and my father, and how they always seemed to be keeping tabs on me. Hopefully, they still were and they would notice I was missing as soon as possible.

'Phone!' Milton snapped as he held out his hand, interrupting my thoughts.

I took my mobile phone from my handbag and passed it to him. He pressed the button to lower the electric window and tossed the phone out of the moving vehicle.

'You didn't have to do that. I would have turned it off,' I protested.

'I wouldn't put it past that possessive boyfriend of yours to have some sort of tracking device planted in it,' he hissed at me.

I leaned back against the seat. I wouldn't put it past him either, but if he had, now it was useless. 'Where are we going anyway?' I asked as the London scenery whizzed by us.

'You'll see when we get there,' Milton replied. 'Now, no more questions. I'm fed up of listening to you already,' he laughed at his own joke and turned towards the window.

He was even more arrogant than his brother, if that were possible.

CHAPTER 53
GABRIEL

Sebastian and I walked out of Baker Securities offices and crossed the road to where my car was parked.

'That went well,' he said to me with a grin.

I nodded in agreement. We had just negotiated the takeover of a smaller security firm and had managed to retain their staff as well as keeping on their Managing Director as one of managers. It had all gone smoothly and the deal was bringing us one step closer to our plan of becoming the biggest security firm in the south of England.

I was getting into the car when my phone rang and I saw Scott Thomas' number flashing on the screen. I frowned as I noticed the time. He should be driving Samantha to work, not calling me.

I answered the call. 'What's up?'

I heard the panic in his voice as soon as he spoke. 'Boss, is Samantha with you?'

I felt the adrenaline start to course around my body and my heart started pounding in my chest. 'No!' I barked. 'She's supposed to be with you.'

I heard him swallow. 'I was running ten minutes late.

There was an accident and the road was backed up. I got to your house and she wasn't there. There was no answer on her mobile. I called her office and she's not there either.'

'What?' I leaned against the car as I felt all of the breath leaving my body. She wouldn't have gone somewhere without telling me, not after what happened yesterday. 'So where the fuck is she?'

At this point, Sebastian was staring at me with a worried look on his face.

'I don't know, Boss,' Scott replied.

'Haven't I told you never to be late picking her up?' I snarled. The anger was kicking in, drowning out the fear for now as the adrenaline started to take over. 'Be an hour fucking early if you need to be, but *never* fucking late.'

'I know, Boss. I'm sorry. But the accident was in the street right behind yours. There was no avoiding it.'

'Get your team together and wait for further instructions,' I snapped. 'If anything happens to her ...' I swallowed. I couldn't even bear to finish the sentence.

'I know, Boss,' Scott said quietly.

I put my phone back into my pocket and stared at Sebastian. 'Sam is missing,' I told him.

'What? What?' he shouted.

I watched the range of emotions flickering across his face as I dialled Samantha's phone number. The call went straight to her voicemail and I fought the urge to throw up onto the pavement. 'No answer,' I told him.

'How the fuck did this happen, Gabriel? How the fuck?' he banged his fist on the top of my car and closed his eyes in anguish.

'Look, this is obviously Milton, isn't it? So, let's do what we do best and find this prick, Seb.'

He opened his eyes and nodded. 'Where do we fucking start?'

'Let's see if she's spoken to anyone this morning,' I replied as I opened the car door and climbed inside.

As soon as we were moving, I dialled Nick Cook's number from my car. He answered on the second ring. 'Gabriel, is everything okay? Where is Samantha?'

'I don't know Nick. I think someone has taken her.'

'What?' he gasped. 'Oh fuck!'

'Have you spoken to her at all this morning?'

'Yes, earlier on, about nine o'clock. She told me she was doing some work from home and would be in at lunchtime.'

'Did she say anything unusual or something that didn't sound quite right?'

'I don't think so,' Nick replied.

'Think, Nick. Are you sure?' I snapped.

'No, she didn't. She just told me she was catching up on some admin, and then I told her that Simon had phoned in sick.'

'What?'

'Simon phoned in sick,' he repeated.

The hairs on the back of my neck stood on end. I knew there was something fucking dodgy about that prick. 'What did he say was wrong with him?'

'Said he had a stomach bug. Why? Is that important?'

'Has he ever been off sick before?' I asked.

'No. Never, although he hasn't worked for us for that long.'

'Thanks, Nick. I have to go.'

'Please tell me as soon as you hear from her,' Nick added. 'And if there's anything at all you need me to do, let me know.'

'Will do,' I said as I ended the call.

I turned to Sebastian. 'I think I know where she is,' I said and I watched the relief wash over his face.

'Where?'

'I think we were right to keep an eye on Simon Hardaker. And I think he's connected to Milton somehow. Call Scott and tell him and the team to meet us at the Holbrook services. Tell him to bring the guns from the safe. One for each of us. And tell him to bring my toolkit as well.'

Sebastian nodded as he took his phone out of his pocket. I listened to him giving Scott his orders and willed my heart to stop racing as I sped along the streets of London.

The thought that Milton Carver had his hands on her, that he had her and my baby hostage, was too awful to think about. I couldn't let the thoughts occupy my head for too long or I'd fall to pieces. I had to concentrate on my anger and my rage. I had to do what I did best, and that was finding people and fucking them up when they had crossed me.

One thing that I could guarantee, was that whoever had taken her, would feel a pain like they had never even imagined possible.

CHAPTER 54

It felt like we'd been driving for hours. We'd left London and from the road signs, it seemed we were heading towards Surrey. I wanted to ask more questions. My mind was racing with them. Why the hell had he taken me and where the hell were we going? But I knew he wouldn't answer. I wondered too if Gabriel or my father had discovered I was missing yet, and whether they had started moving heaven and earth to find me. I certainly hoped so.

'I need the bathroom,' I said as the urge to pee came over me.

Milton turned and sneered at me. 'Hold it. We'll be there soon.'

'I have a baby pressing on my bladder and I need to pee.'

He shrugged. 'Hold it, or don't. I don't care,' he said as he turned back to the window.

I frowned at the back of his head. Arrogant prick!

A short time later, we pulled up outside a large detached house in the countryside. Milton climbed out and pulled me with him. I stumbled on the gravel path but Milton walked on, undeterred. Fortunately, one of his goons held out his hand to steady me and I took it gratefully. Another goon opened the front door and the four of us walked inside.

'Can I use the bathroom now?' I asked as soon as were inside the house.

'There,' Milton said, indicating a door to the left of us.

I rushed to it and pushed it open, relieved that it was in fact a bathroom and not a broom cupboard. The minute I saw the toilet, my bladder wanted to release its load and I scrambled with my clothes, just about making it.

I sat on the toilet and looked around the small room. It was very country. Cream tiles and flowery wallpaper. A small mirror in a wooden frame hung above the basin and a pink towel was hanging over a small rail. There was a pink soap dispenser on the basin too and I got the impression that this house had something of a woman's touch. For some reason, that made me feel slightly more at ease.

A loud banging on the door made me jump. 'Hurry up. Don't make me come in there and get you,' Milton snapped.

'I'll just be a minute,' I replied as I stood up and fixed my clothes. I walked to the small basin and started to wash my hands. I glanced around at the small window to the side of me. I looked down at my bump – there was no way the two of us were squeezing out of there.

I opened the door and stepped back into the hallway where Milton and two of his men stood waiting for me.

'This way,' Milton said as he started to walk along the hallway. I followed him and his two henchmen followed behind me. We walked into the large stone kitchen where two other goons were already waiting for us.

Milton indicated a wooden chair beside a large table. 'Sit,' he ordered.

I did so, thankful to be off my feet. Now that I was no longer focused on my desperate need to pee, I started to wonder what the hell I was doing here, and I could barely stop my legs from trembling.

'Where are we? And what do you want from me?' I asked, my voice shaking as much as my legs. 'I signed the money over to you. I told you I don't want any of it.'

Milton pulled up a chair and sat directly in front of me. 'I know you did. But you see, the thing is, it's not enough,' he said as he sucked air in through his teeth.

'What?' I scowled at him.

'It's not enough that you relinquished your claim on the money. As long as you're alive, you have a claim on it.'

I shook my head. He had no clue how the law worked. 'No, I don't. And I don't want it. Not a single fucking penny.'

Milton smiled at me. If you could call it a smile. It reminded me of a shark's. It never reached his eyes. 'You say that now, but who knows how you might feel in a few months, or a few years. What if you and that little bastard need money one day?' he looked down at my stomach and I felt the urge to slap his smarmy, arrogant face.

'I'd rather beg on the streets than take a penny from you or your family,' I hissed.

He stood up and towered over me, lifting up his hand, he brought the back of it across my cheek, snapping my head back. It hurt like hell, and I tasted blood, but he would never see me cry.

'You brought my family's name into the gutter, you fucking whore!' he spat. 'I told my brother you were bad news. You came from nothing, and you will always be nothing, Samantha!'

I glared at him and he held my gaze until something caught his eye behind me. He looked up and grinned. 'Son! I'm so glad you could join us?'

Son?

Milton looked down at me again. 'I believe you've already met my son, Simon,' he said.

I turned my head to see Simon Hardaker, the junior partner from my firm, striding into the room. He walked purposefully towards me, with his head held high and his hands in his trouser pockets. He stared at me. His blue eyes ice cold and then he grinned. 'Fooled ya,' he said and then he and his father started to laugh.

There was not a trace of the nervous, caring, Simon that I had come to know. Instead, he was arrogant – and cold. Just like his father and uncle. The psychopath gene must really run in the family.

I blinked at him. He'd had me completely fooled. He had played me perfectly, knowing that his nervousness and clumsiness would endear him to me. 'Simon?' was all I could say.

'God, it's so good to finally show you who I really am,' he ran a hand through his blonde hair. 'Having to listen to you prattle on about your favourite films and watching you pine over that great big ape you called a boyfriend. It was fucking torturous.'

'You were Edward Lewis?' I scowled at him.

He smiled widely and nodded, looking incredibly proud of himself. 'Yes. I thought you'd figure it out. You're supposed to be smart, aren't you? We'd literally just been talking about that God-awful film and you still didn't have a clue.'

'But why did you do that? What the hell did it achieve?'

'That was just a bit of fun. You walk around that office like you're God's gift to fucking men, but I knew all along who you really were and what you tried to do to my family. Slut!' he snarled at me with such venom in his voice that I shrunk back from him.

'So, what do you plan to do with me then?' I asked with a shaky breath. I feared the answer but I needed to know.

'You haven't figured it out?' Simon said with a laugh.

I shook my head.

'My dear, Samantha. We're going to kill you and then we're going to bury your body on this land. No-one will find you for decades,' Milton said with a vicious grin.

I stared at him open-mouthed and then I began to shake my head. I couldn't die. Not here. Not at the hands of these psychopaths. I couldn't let them kill my child.

I looked at the four armed men who were standing in the kitchen. Surely one of them had an ounce of compassion and couldn't stand back while this pair of psychopaths murdered a pregnant woman in cold blood?

They all avoided my gaze except for the one who had offered me his hand when I'd stumbled earlier. I was sure he gave me a subtle nod. But, maybe I just imagined it? Maybe I was so desperate for him to be an ally that I read into a meaningless head movement?

'No, please? My baby.' I started to beg.

'No, please? My baby,' Simon mimicked me as he and his father started to laugh.

Suddenly, I felt a fury like I had never felt in my life. I jumped up and lunged at Milton, scratching my nails down his face and drawing blood.

'You fucking bitch,' he screamed, pushing me back down on the chair and pinning me down against it, his hands pressing on my shoulders. 'I'm going to make you regret ever hearing the name Carver.'

'I regretted that five minutes after I married your sadistic fuck of a brother,' I hissed.

He raised his hand again, but we were both distracted by a fast whooshing sound followed by a thwack. We both turned as one of his armed men clutched at his neck before dropping to the floor. Then, immediately the same sound reverberated around the kitchen and another man dropped. The two remaining henchmen withdrew their guns and pointed them at the kitchen doorway.

I turned in my seat and my heart almost leapt out of my chest with relief when I saw Gabriel and my dad walking through the door with at least half a dozen men, all of them carried guns and their weapons were trained on the men who were holding me captive. I looked back at Milton and his men. They were outnumbered, but they could take at least a few of us out before they were shot themselves. We weren't out of danger yet.

I looked back at the doorway and my eyes met Gabriel's. 'It's okay, baby. But don't move,' he said to me, holding my gaze intently, and for a moment it felt like there was only the two of us in the room.

'What the fuck?' I heard Milton bark behind me. 'You told me no-one knew about this place?'

'They don't,' I heard Simon reply.

That's when Gabriel broke eye contact with me. 'Did you really think we weren't onto you?' he snarled. 'I've been keeping tabs on you for weeks, Simon.'

'You fucking idiot,' Milton shouted and I turned in my seat just in time to see him slapping Simon around the back of the head.

Simon shrunk back from him and I couldn't help but smile.

'Train your guns on her,' Milton said to his henchmen and then he turned back to Gabriel and my father. 'She'll be dead before any of you even get a single round off.'

Gabriel looked up at the two henchmen and nodded and I watched in stunned silence as they sheathed their weapons.

'What the fuck are you doing!' Milton shouted at them.

'You can't buy loyalty, Carver. It has to be earned. The problem with hired guns, you arrogant fuck, is that they work for the highest bidder. And in this case, that would be me,' Gabriel snarled.

'You couldn't afford them,' Milton scoffed.

'Actually, I can. But the real beauty of it is I don't have to. They've already been paid from your family's estate,' Gabriel replied with a smile.

'What?' Milton sputtered.

'Samantha signed the papers to relinquish her claim, like you asked, but any outstanding debts from the Carver family will be paid for by the estate. And my shit-hot lawyer has given these fine men iron-clad, backdated contracts to ensure they get exactly what they're owed.'

'But I haven't signed any such contracts,' Milton spat. 'So, good luck proving that.'

'No, you haven't,' Gabriel said with a shake of his head. 'Because they were security employed by the Carver family estate, and they were backdated, weren't they? I just told you that, fuckwit. Those contracts were signed eighteen months ago, by Mrs Jackson Carver.'

I couldn't help but smile. Nick must have drawn up those contracts and I would happily sign them. I didn't want a penny of the Carver family money, but the fact that it was now paying for Milton's own demise was the perfect karma.

'You fucking snakes,' Milton shouted as he waved his arms around maniacally. I wondered if he would start foaming at the mouth soon enough.

Gabriel took a few steps towards me. 'Samantha. Come here,' he said and I obeyed, standing up and running over to him.

He pulled me into his arms and I melted into him, burying my head in his chest and inhaling the smell of him. 'Are you okay,' he whispered as he ran his hands over my back.

'I am now,' I said, trying not to cry.

'You two can go,' I heard my father say and then the two remaining henchmen walked out of the kitchen. I looked at them as they passed me. The one who had helped me earlier and whom I had hoped might be an ally, gave me a nod of acknowledgement before he walked out of the door.

Gabriel turned to his own employees. 'Secure them,' he barked and the kitchen was suddenly filled with men dressed in black as they restrained Milton and Simon. The two of them begged and protested – loudly.

'Fucking shut them up, will you?' Gabriel snapped. He kept my back to the room and I heard shuffling and banging, followed by a few loud groans, but then Simon and Milton's pleading stopped.

Then my father was standing beside us. He put an arm around my shoulder and kissed the top of my head. 'You're okay, now, love,' he said and I saw he had tears in his eyes.

'Can you give us a minute, mate?' Gabriel said to my dad who nodded at him and walked into the centre of the room to join their employees.

Gabriel cupped my chin and tilted my face up towards his. He ran the pad of his thumb over the cut on my lip and scowled. 'Who did that to you?'

'Milton,' I whispered.

He nodded and then he crushed me to him again. When he released me, he ran his hand down over my stomach. 'Is he okay too?' he asked.

I nodded. 'He's been playing football with my bladder for the past four hours. He's fine.'

'Good. Now, I need you to go home with your dad.'

I blinked at him. 'No. I want to go home with you.'

He tucked my hair behind my ear. 'I need to sort this out. Your dad will take you home. I'll be home as soon as I can, baby.'

'Come with me. Please. Let your men sort this out for you.'

He shook his head. 'I can't. I need to deal with this myself. And I don't want you anywhere near me when I do.'

'But, I need you with me,' I sniffed.

'Your dad will look after you until I get home, and then I will never let you or our child out of my sight again. Okay?'

I nodded. 'Okay. But please come home soon.'

'I'll be home as soon as I can, baby,' then with a final kiss on the lips, he beckoned my dad over to him. 'I'll see you both later.'

My dad put an arm around me and we walked out of the kitchen and out of the house to his car.

CHAPTER 55
GABRIEL

I watched as Samantha and Sebastian walked out of the door and then I turned back to the room. Four of my best bouncers were holding onto Milton and Simon. But, I wouldn't need them for much longer. Given what I had in mind, I preferred to work alone.

Sebastian and I had argued over who would deal with the two bastards who had kidnapped Samantha for the whole drive here. Understandably, he'd wanted to deal with the fuckers himself. They had taken the most precious person in the world to him too, not to mention his unborn grandchild. But there was no way I was going to let anyone else do what needed to be done. I had to handle this myself.

I'd known that Samantha would be terrified and anxious after her ordeal today, and although I'd hoped that Leroy and Kelvin wouldn't have let any serious harm come to her, I knew there was also a possibility she'd be hurt too. There was no way I could have sent her out of here with anyone other than me or her father. Not to mention, I was still terrified that something might happen to her, and the only man who would look after her as well as I would, was Sebastian.

I walked towards the centre of the room and started taking off my jacket. 'Strip them and tie them to a chair,' I ordered.

'Yes, Boss,' my bouncers murmured as they got to work.

Milton and Simon struggled and protested as much as they could with their mouths stuffed with rags. A few moments later, they were naked with their ankles bound to the chair legs and hands secured behind their backs with zip ties. I picked up the holdall that we'd brought along and started taking out the instruments I'd be needing.

I placed each of them on the table as Milton and Simon looked on, their eyes widening in terror each time I placed another weapon on the table – the lump hammer, the blow torch, the drill and my personal favourite – the long-nosed pliers. They could do the most damage if you knew how to use them. I made sure they got a good look at each one as I placed them down. The psychological torture could be as powerful as the physical pain.

'You can wait in the other room,' I said to my men. 'Make yourselves comfortable. I might be a while.'

They nodded and filed out of the room until I was left alone with Milton and Simon. I stood in front of them. 'Which one of you should I start with first then?' I asked.

They both nodded their heads towards the other, not realising the terror of having to watch someone else going through something that you knew you were about to endure yourself.

I stood directly in front of Simon. 'I knew there was something dodgy about you. And after that comment you made about the cut on my lip, which you could hardly even see, I've been keeping my eye on you. I looked into your past. You lied about where you went to school, didn't you? And I didn't know why until I dug a little deeper and realised that you were trying to cover up where you grew up. Trying to cover up who your mother was – and who your father was. To be honest, I hadn't worked out yet that your father was this piece of shit,' I kicked Milton in the shin as I said it and he groaned. 'But I did find out that your mother had left you this place. And thank fuck I did, eh? Would either of you like to tell me what you were planning to do to my future wife and my child?' I snarled.

Simon shook his head furiously but Milton glared at me.

I shrugged. 'Don't worry. It's probably best that I don't know. But I can promise you this,' I snarled as I leaned my head closer to their faces. 'It is *nothing* compared to what I'm about to do to the two of you.'

I picked up the lump hammer from the table and swung it down across Simon's left shin. I heard the sickening crunch of bone as his shin was smashed to pieces. He cried out through the rag in his mouth and tears started running down his face. His body had barely had time to process the pain it when I did the same to his right shin.

Milton started thrashing about beside us, screaming through his gag. 'Don't worry. You'll get your turn,' I said to him with a smile. 'Don't be so impatient.'

I placed the hammer back on the table and picked up the cordless drill. 'This bit might get a bit messy,' I warned. 'You might want to close your eyes.'

I pressed the switch on the handle and the machine whirred to life. I heard the two of them start retching into their gags. I knew that they wouldn't last very long. Their hearts would likely give out before I had caused them the amount of pain they both deserved. They were weak and they had never learned to endure real pain.

Almost two hours later, I walked out of the kitchen covered in the blood of Milton Carver and Simon Hardaker. My employees were waiting for me. Together we would set to work removing every trace of us from the house. Then when we were done, we would all change into fresh clothes and clean ourselves with a solution of hydrochloride and water before pouring two gallons of petrol around the farmhouse and razing it to the ground with Simon and Milton's corpses inside.

CHAPTER 56

SAMANTHA

My dad and I drove in silence for a while. As soon as we'd walked outside the farmhouse earlier, he had pulled me into the tightest hug he could and had just held me there for a few minutes while I'd cried against his chest, comforted by his powerful arms and his Chanel cologne. When I was done, I'd looked up to see the tears in his eyes too.

'I'm sorry I let them take you, Sam,' he said as he wiped the tears from my cheeks.

'Don't be silly, Dad. This wasn't your fault,' I reassured him. He was always blaming himself for not protecting me.

Now we sat quietly, me looking out of the window, and my father's eyes fixed on the road ahead.

'How did you know where to find me?' I asked eventually. 'You and Gabriel haven't implanted me with a LoJack, have you?'

My dad turned to me and rolled his eyes. 'No. Gabriel found out that Simon grew up in Surrey and not in Leicester like he'd told you. You know he's like a dog with a fucking bone when he gets into something, so he did some digging and he found out that he owned that house and that it's worth a fortune. Seemed a bit odd then that he lived in a poky flat in Dagenham with a flatmate.'

'So, why didn't either of you tell me about him? I worked with him every day and I had no idea.'

My dad shook his head. 'To be honest, love, we didn't know if there was anything worth telling you. He could have had legitimate reasons for not selling his family home and lying about where he grew up. We didn't realise Milton was his father until today. Gabriel has always suspected there was something dodgy about him, but he had no proof. And until he found it, he didn't want to put you in any danger by sharing his concerns.'

I nodded. I supposed I understood that. And every time Gabriel had raised the issue of Simon, I had always defended him. He'd had me completely fooled. 'I still don't get how you knew it was him though.'

'Well, Gabriel has also been digging up information on the Carver family. When Nick told us that Simon called in sick today, then it all kind of fell into place. Simon's mother was Karina Hardaker. He never knew his father, but from what Gabriel found out, he was engaged to be married to someone else at the time and the pregnancy was a huge scandal. She was paid off by his family, and royally so, to take the kid and never mention who his father was. Did you ever know why Milton was cut off from the Carver family?'

I shook my head. 'Not the details, just that he'd disgraced them.'

My dad nodded. 'It seems he had a habit of dragging his family's name into the gutter. But it all started when he was twenty and he disgraced them by agreeing to marry some Earl's daughter and then having an affair and a baby with a sixteen year old from the local council estate.'

'Karina?' I said as the pieces started to fall into place.

My dad nodded. 'The Carver's paid to keep her quiet, and it

seemed she kept her end of the bargain. Both families would have been destroyed if the scandal had got out. But, like I said, it was only the first of his many indiscretions. Eventually even that corrupt shower of fucks couldn't cover up for him any more and they disowned him. They kept him quiet with a generous monthly allowance. It wasn't until today that Gabriel realised the connection and realised that Karina must have been Milton's young mistress.'

'Wow!' I shook my head in disbelief. 'Gabriel has been busy.'

My father nodded, with an unmistakeable look of pride on his face. 'I told you – like a dog with a bone.'

'Thank you, Dad,' I said as a wave of emotion washed over me. 'If you and Gabriel weren't so good at your jobs, and so bloody protective of me ...' I wiped a stray tear from my cheek.

'Hey,' he said as he took my hand and squeezed. 'You *never* have to thank me for looking after you. It is, quite literally, my job. And now it's Gabriel's too.'

I smiled.

'I only wish I could have stayed back there and helped take care of those fuckers myself, Sam. But, I wanted to be the one to bring you home. You are the best thing that's ever happened to me, kid. Do you know that?'

I laughed. 'I do, Dad. I love you.'

'Love you too, sweetheart.'

CHAPTER 57

SAMANTHA

My dad and I were sitting on the sofa when Gabriel finally came home later that evening. He walked through the door and my heart almost burst of my chest with relief and happiness. My father and I both stood up and I walked to him, wrapping my arms around his neck.

He pulled me close to him and kissed the top of my head. I breathed in the scent of fresh air on his clothes, but he smelled of something else too – chemicals and bleach. It burned my nostrils and I took a step back from him.

'Is it done?' my father asked him.

'Yes,' Gabriel replied.

'Good,' my dad said with a nod. 'You can tell me about it tomorrow. I'm going to leave you both to get some rest.'

He gave me an extra long hug before he left and then there was only Gabriel and me standing alone in the room. I looked up at him, placing my hand on his cheek. His skin was cool under my fingertips.

'Are you okay?' I asked.

'I'm fine,' he said with a frown. 'Are you though?'

'Yes. They didn't hurt me,' I replied.

He ran his thumb down my cheek and across my lip. 'It looks like they did.'

I touched my face. 'Oh, that was nothing. I barely felt it.'

'If anything had happened to either of you,' he said, and I saw the pain on his face.

'But it didn't. You made sure of that. You were right about Milton. He was never going to leave me to get on with my life.'

Gabriel hugged me tighter to him. 'He will never hurt you again, I promise.'

'I know.'

He cupped my face in his hands. 'I really need a shower,' he said. 'Why don't you find us one of those awful romantic comedies to watch while I grab one, and I'll join you as soon as I can?'

'Okay,' I nodded.

It had been twenty minutes since Gabriel had gone upstairs for his shower. I had flicked though the movie options but couldn't decide on anything in particular. All I wanted was to curl up in his arms and be close to him.

Switching off the television, I walked upstairs and into our bedroom. I heard the shower still running and opened the door to the en-suite. He was standing under the water, his palms pressed flat against the wall and his head hanging down between his shoulders as the hot water rained down on his muscular back.

He didn't move and I stood there and watched him for a moment. I knew all too well that feeling of needing nothing but the hot water to wash over you. Despite the day we'd both had, looking at him like that gave me butterflies in my stomach. He was the most beautiful man I had ever seen in my life. Every part of his body looked like it was carved from the finest marble.

He was a work of art. But it wasn't just his body that I loved. He was kind and passionate and considerate and he always put me first. He wasn't perfect – but he was perfect for me. I was suddenly overcome with a rush of love for him.

I was still wearing my yoga pants and vest top, but I stepped into the walk-in shower and ran my hands over the large angel tattoo on his back. His head snapped up and he turned to me.

'Are you okay?' he asked as he wiped the water from his face.

'I was just missing you,' I said as I stepped closer to him.

'You're getting wet,' he said as pulled at the strap of my vest.

'I'm always wet around you,' I said with a grin.

He half smiled back at me, but it didn't quite reach his eyes. He was drifting. I didn't know the detail of what had happened after I'd left that old farmhouse today, and I would never ask, but I could well imagine. And I knew that as much as Gabriel was capable of extreme violence, to go to the place he'd had to today, always cost him something. Now he was drifting, and I had to anchor him back to me somehow.

I peeled my vest over my head and tossed it onto the floor behind me. Then, I rolled down my yoga pants and my underwear and kicked them off too. He looked down at my body, his eyes scanning my breasts and then over my bump.

I stepped towards him, until my stomach was pressed against his. He was always taking care of me and now it was time to return the favour. 'What do you need from me, Gabe?'

He slipped his hands over my waist and down to my backside. 'All I need is you,' he growled and then he sealed his mouth over mine, pushing his tongue inside and devouring me as though we had been starved of each other for weeks.

I felt the warmth pooling between my thighs as I ran my hands over his chest and down towards his cock. He was hard and I squeezed the thick shaft, making him groan in my mouth.

He lifted his head and spun me around so I was facing the tiled wall. Sliding his hands onto my hips he pulled me to him until I could feel his erection pressing into my back.

'Put your hands on the wall,' he growled in my ear.

My pregnancy bump made shower sex a little more difficult than it used to be. Previously, he would have pinned me to the tiled wall with the full weight of his body and fucked me until we were both completely spent.

He took the bottle of shower gel from the shelf beside us, and squeezed some into his palm. I moaned in pleasure as his hands moved over my body, gliding easily over my skin with the soapy lather. First over my swollen breasts, kneading them and pulling at my tender nipples, rolling them around between his finger and thumb.

I squeezed my thighs together to quell the throbbing between them, but it didn't help at all. He nibbled at my neck, his teeth grazing my skin as my legs began to tremble. My pussy thrummed with heat and the need for him to be inside me. The tension and the drama of the day was starting to get to me and I needed some of the relief that only Gabriel could give me.

We both needed it.

'Gabe,' I whimpered.

Continuing his lazy exploration of my body, he slid one hand down to my clit and started to rub slowly, circling the swollen nub of flesh.

'Is this what *you* need?' he asked.

'Yes,' I panted.

'Spread your legs wide, baby,' he instructed and I obeyed. I felt him bend his knees slightly before he slipped the tip of his length inside me. It wasn't enough. I tried to move my hips towards him but he held me in place, teasing me with his cock while he slowly rubbed my throbbing clit.

'Please, Gabe,' I cried out.

'Soon, baby,' he growled as he planted his left hand beside mine on the tiled wall. 'I'm still full of rage and I don't want to hurt you.'

'You won't,' I gasped. 'You couldn't.'

He nipped at my neck. 'Hmm. If you weren't pregnant, I would pin you to this wall and fuck you so hard you wouldn't be able to walk tomorrow,' he slipped his right hand from between my thighs and onto my stomach and I groaned in frustration. I was so close.

'I need all of you, Gabe. You won't hurt me, or the baby,' I breathed.

'Keep your hands on the wall then,' he said as he planted his right palm on the wall beside mine too, so I was caged in by his strong arms. 'And push back against me.'

I pushed back against him, locking out my arms. I gasped as he drove into me, hitting that spot inside me that had been desperate for him.

He drove into me, over and over again and I felt the orgasm building deep inside my core. He sucked on the same spot on my neck as he maintained his relentless pace, and just as he was about to come, he sank his teeth into my tender flesh.

Pain and pleasure shot through me and I finally found my own release. My orgasm tearing through my body like black powder.

He wrapped his arms around me, pulling me back towards him as my body sagged against his. My head was spinning, my legs trembling as the last of my climax ebbed away.

He turned off the shower and then he scooped me up into his arms and carried me into the bedroom before laying me down on the bed. He brushed my wet hair from my face as he straddled me.

'Are you okay to carry on, Sam?' he asked softly.

I nodded. 'Are we not done yet then?'

'Done? Baby, we haven't even started,' he grinned and I could see that my Gabe had already come back to me. Then I watched his head disappear below my huge bump and felt his hot breath on the skin of my inner thighs. He started to plant delicious soft kisses up my legs until he reached my dripping cleft before running his hot tongue through my folds.

'Have I ever told you how good you taste when you're full of my cum, Sam,' he growled.

I pressed my head back against the pillow as his tongue set to work. Hardly a few minutes had passed before he had me screaming his name.

CHAPTER 58

SAMANTHA

I placed my glass down on the table and looked around at the five faces sitting with me. They were the most important people in the world to me. Gabriel and I had been married in a small ceremony at the Registry office earlier that afternoon, with only my father, Nick, and Gabriel's Aunt Maggie and Uncle Hugh in attendance.

Afterwards, the six of us had come to my favourite restaurant, Vincenzo's and were sitting in a private booth near the back.

I couldn't help but smile. There had been a time when I'd thought that I would never marry again. In fact, the thought of being someone else's wife had been abhorrent to me. But that was before Gabriel Sullivan.

I looked at the platinum wedding band on his hand as he shared a joke with Nick and his aunt and felt a rush of love and contentment. I looked down at my own matching wedding ring, as my hand rested on my huge bump. At over eight months pregnant now, I was fit to burst. The last trimester tiredness had well and truly kicked in too, and despite it only being 8 p.m., I stifled a yawn.

Gabriel looked up and caught my eye and then he downed the last of his glass of champagne and cleared his throat. 'As lovely as it is to spend time with you lot, I think I need to take my wife home,' he said.

I smiled in silent thanks to him and we exchanged hugs and kisses with everyone before we walked out of the restaurant, with his arm around my waist. As we got outside, the most beautiful white stretch limousine was waiting for us.

'What's this?' I asked as I looked at him in surprise.

'Only the best for my wife,' he said with a grin as he opened the passenger door for me. I climbed inside and saw that Scott was the driver.

'Hi, Scott,' I said as I slid along the plush leather seat.

'Evening, Mrs Sullivan,' he said with a smile and I felt my heart swell in my chest. I could definitely get used to that.

Gabriel slid onto the seat beside me and Scott took that as his cue to raise the privacy screen so that we were alone.

'This is a lovely surprise,' I said to him, noticing the bottle of alcohol free champagne and the two flutes sitting nearby.

'This isn't the only surprise, baby,' he said as he reached down and lifted my legs, swinging them over his lap and wrapping an arm around me.

'Oh? What's the other one? Are we going to have limo sex?' I giggled.

'Not tonight,' he growled in my ear.

I ran my hand down his chest towards his groin. 'Why not?' I purred. 'We've never had limo sex before.'

He rubbed a hand over my stomach. 'Well, we will rectify that as soon as we're able to, but logistically, limo sex isn't going to be easy, is it?' he nodded towards my large bump and then started to nuzzle my neck.

'I'm sure we could figure it out. I don't mind being a little uncomfortable.'

He nipped my shoulder blade lightly and then he looked up at me. 'The first time I fuck my wife is going to be on a soft, king-sized bed. She is going to be completely naked and spread out for me, and I am going to take my sweet time.'

I smiled as my pussy thrummed with heat and anticipation. 'So, what's the other surprise then?'

'The other surprise is we're not going home tonight, baby. Or tomorrow. Scott is driving us to a beautiful lodge in the country-side, and it's all ours for two whole nights.'

I blinked at him. 'You certainly kept that quiet, you sneak. What about clothes?' I flashed an eyebrow at him. 'I know we're on our honeymoon, but I will need some.'

He laughed and his green eyes twinkled mischievously. 'I like your thinking, baby, but don't worry, I packed for us both. Scott has our bags in the front.'

'How far away is this place?' I said, stifling another yawn.

'About two hour's drive. Why don't you close your eyes and relax and I'll let you know when we get there?'

I closed my eyes and leaned against him. 'What about the champagne?' I murmured.

'The champagne will keep,' he said before softly kissing my forehead.

I nestled against him and breathed in the smell of him. He was intoxicating. I couldn't wait to get to the lodge and have him all to myself.

CHAPTER 59
GABRIEL

I looked down at Samantha sleeping in my arms and couldn't stop myself from smiling. Everything I had ever wanted in life was right here in my hands and I had never been happier. I felt like my heart might explode out of my chest. It was hard to believe that only four months earlier she had walked out on me and I'd wondered if she would ever be mine again.

When I'd asked her to marry me, I'd readied myself for the possibility that she'd turn me down. I'd been prepared for the fact that she might never want to marry me, but I'd had to at least try. I'd been completely floored when she'd said yes, and even more surprised when she'd wanted to marry quickly.

It had taken us seven weeks to arrange the wedding and every day, a part of me had worried that she'd change her mind before the event. But she hadn't, and earlier today she had made me the happiest man in the universe when she'd said 'I do.'

Now that I had that platinum band on her finger, she was mine forever.

A little over two hours later, the wheels of the limousine stopped outside the lodge that was going to be ours for the next forty-eight hours.

I gave Samantha a gentle nudge. 'We're here, baby.'

Her eyes fluttered open and she smiled at me sleepily. 'Already?'

I nodded. 'You slept the whole way.'

She blushed. 'Sorry. I must have been exhausted.'

'No need to apologise. You're working hard keeping our little boy safe,' I said, planting another kiss on her head as I gently eased her legs back down onto the floor.

I had noticed how tired she'd been these past two weeks. But I'd read that it was entirely normal in the last trimester. I felt a twinge of guilt when I thought about how I wasn't going to let her go back to sleep for at least a few hours, but it passed when she flashed me one of her winning smiles. 'I'm feeling rested now though.'

'Well, let's get in there then,' I said as I took her hand. Opening the car door, I stepped out and helped her out too. Scott took our bags from the front seat and placed them on the doorstep.

'Thanks, mate,' I said to him.

He nodded. 'No problem, Boss. I hope you two have a wonderful break. One of boys will drop your car off here in the next few hours. They know you're not to be disturbed though,' he said with a knowing smile.

'Thank you, Scott,' Samantha smiled at him, making him blush.

Scott had a bit of a soft spot for her. He'd been her driver for a while and I trusted him with her life, which said a lot about the kind of man he was.

Scott walked back to the car and I bent and scooped Samantha up into my arms.

She laughed out loud. 'What are you doing?'

'Carrying you over the threshold,' I smiled.

'But this isn't our house.'

'It is for the next two days. And don't worry, I'll carry you over the doorstep of our own house too when we get home.'

She giggled and then placed her hands on my face before giving me a soft kiss.

'God, I fucking love you, Mrs Sullivan,' I growled.

'I love you too, Mr Sullivan,' she purred and my dick immediately stood to attention. If I didn't get some part of my body inside her soon, I'd go crazy.

CHAPTER 60

Gabriel put our bags on the large king-sized bed as I looked around the lodge. I loved that it was all open plan and we could wander freely from the kitchen to the bedroom and to the sitting room with the huge log fire.

I was looking out of the large window that led out onto the decking when Gabriel came up behind me and slipped his arms around my waist. I turned in his arms and he pulled me as close as he could, given my large bump.

'As soon as the baby is old enough to stay with your dad for a few nights, I'm going to take you on a proper honeymoon. Somewhere very hot, and very secluded,' he said as he started to trail soft kisses along my collarbone.

'Oh, really?' I breathed.

'Hmm,' he mumbled against my skin. 'Somewhere, where your entire wardrobe for the trip would fit in your handbag.' I shivered as he grazed his teeth along the delicate skin of my neck. 'But for now, two nights in this beautiful lodge, with a log fire and a fully stocked fridge, will do.'

'It will do?' I breathed. 'It sounds like heaven to me.'

He moved his head and looked into my eyes. 'Oh, it will be,

baby,' he smiled as he unzipped my dress before pushing the soft material over my shoulders. It landed in a pool of cream fabric at my feet. He took hold of my hand and helped me step out of it and then he looked down at me and sucked in a breath. 'You are so fucking beautiful, Sam.'

I rubbed a hand over my bump. 'I'm enormous,' I laughed.

'You have never been sexier, Mrs Sullivan,' he growled as his eyes flashed full of fire.

Then he bent his head and kissed me, softly at first, gently exploring my mouth with his tongue as his hands glided over my back and down to my backside, where he slipped them inside the band of my cream lace underwear. I ran my hands over his solid chest and to the buttons of his shirt. My fingers trembled as I started to unbutton each one. We had done this a thousand times, but this felt different and I was almost breathless with anticipation.

Usually, he preferred to undress himself, and more often than not, while I was already naked and in a post orgasmic haze, but he didn't stop me, or even try to help. He kept on kissing me softly until my heart was pounding in my ears.

When his shirt was open, he obliged by taking off his platinum cufflinks and I pushed the crisp white cotton over his shoulders until it fell onto a heap on the floor.

My hands ran over his muscular chest and I broke our kiss to take a small step back and look at him. I had never seen anything so beautiful in my life.

He was exquisite.

Just looking at him made my knees feel weak. I thought back to the first time I'd met him, eighteen years earlier. He'd been standing shirtless and bleeding in my father's kitchen and I'd barely been able to take my eyes off him then either.

I could hardly believe that he was finally mine. I loved him so much, it made my heart feel like it would burst. And not only that, I knew that he loved me too. I knew that he would do anything for me. He made me feel safe, and protected, and that was something I'd never thought I would feel again.

I reached for the fastener on his trousers and unclipped it, before unzipping his fly. Slipping my hand inside the soft fabric of his boxers, I took hold of his stiff, hot cock and squeezed.

He groaned softly as he placed a hand on my chin and tilted my face up to look at him. 'Do you have any idea how much I love you?'

'Yes. Almost as much as I love you,' I replied.

He smiled at me and I thought that I had never seen him so happy. 'You ready to be fucked, Mrs Sullivan?' he growled.

I nodded. 'Always.'

EPILOGUE
SEBASTIAN

I grabbed a bottle of Budweiser from the refrigerator and walked into the garden of Gabriel and Samantha's new house, with my sleeping grandson, Max, cradled against my shoulder.

They'd moved out of the city four weeks ago to this sprawling six bedroomed house set in two acres of land. Samantha said she wanted to fill the place with children and now that Max was almost five months old, I wondered how long it would be before she was pregnant again.

She had taken to motherhood like a natural, and Gabriel adored being a father. I sensed him slipping further and further away from the life that he and I had built for ourselves and although I missed him, I was glad that he was stepping back.

I wanted better for my daughter and my grandchildren, and I knew that he was the man who could give them it. When I saw how happy he made Samantha, it made me love and respect him even more than I already did. He'd been my best mate for twenty years, and had always been like a brother to me. But now he was my son-in-law too, and he fit that role better than any he'd had before.

I placed Max down in his Moses basket and sat on the chair beside him.

I couldn't help but smile as I watched Samantha and Gabriel. She had come so far in the last year. No longer jumpy and defensive, she had opened her heart up again completely, and she was quite literally glowing with happiness. Gabriel rarely took his eyes, or his hands, off her, and I knew that he was happier than he'd ever been in his life too.

As for me, I adored spending time with my grandson, Max, and couldn't wait for them to add to their brood.

Perhaps I would be a better granddad than I'd been a father? I often wondered whether I should have had more children. At forty-nine, I was probably getting too old now, but grandchildren would do me just fine. Besides, I had never met a woman that I'd been happy enough with to want to have more kids.

I fell in love hard and fast, and out of love just as quickly. Maybe it was never really love at all? Maybe they made it too easy for me? I'd never had any problems meeting women and getting them into bed. But I'd never met a woman who challenged me, or made me work for her affections. Not since Samantha's mother, Alice, and that had been a very long time ago.

I sipped my beer and watched the guests milling about, chatting to each other and laughing. There were only half a dozen people invited to the barbecue to celebrate the house move. Gabriel's aunt and uncle, Maggie and Hugh, as well as Samantha's friends from work, Nick, Sadie, Beth and the new partner the firm had just taken on – Lauren. At least I thought that was what her name was, I hadn't met her yet.

I knew she was only a year older than Samantha and an old friend of hers and Nick's from university. She was American but had come to England to do her law degree and then had gone back there afterwards for a few years.

Samantha was planning to reduce her caseload and her working days when she finished her maternity leave, and as they'd also needed a replacement for Simon, her and Nick had decided to take on a new managing partner.

Samantha had told me that Lauren was the perfect fit – she didn't do relationships and didn't want kids. She worked hard and she played harder. Donovan Cook was now Donovan, Cook and Hayes.

I couldn't see her in the crowd though and wondered if she'd decided not to come.

I closed my eyes and took in a deep lungful of clean country air. There was something nice about being in the countryside and out of the city. I could get used to this myself.

I heard footsteps beside me and opened my eyes to see an absolute fucking angel standing in front of me. I blinked as the sun shone behind her, framing her face like a halo. Long dark curls and even longer tanned legs stretching out of the sexiest little skirt I had ever seen in my life. She had curves like a country road and I couldn't stop my mind from wondering what it would be like to run my hands over them.

'You must be Sebastian,' she said with a voice as smooth as honey. She smiled as she extended her hand. 'I'm Lauren. I don't think we've met.'

'No, I don't think I've had the pleasure,' I said as I sat up straighter and reached out my hand to hers. Her skin was warm and soft and my hand engulfed hers.

'Samantha never told me her dad was such a silver fox,' she said with a grin as she sat on the chair beside mine.

I laughed out loud. I liked her already.

'So, why are you sitting here all on your own?' she asked as she took a sip of the glass of wine she was holding.

'I'm not on my own. I've got my wingman,' I nodded towards Max in his basket.

She peered over to look at him. 'Aw, and an adorable little wingman, he is,' she said with a wink and I noticed that her eyes were the most incredible shade of blue.

I nodded in agreement.

'It's great that you can give him back to his parents when he starts crying too, right?' she said with a wicked grin and I laughed again.

'You certainly know how to make a first impression, Lauren,' I said to her as I tried to stop my eyes from lingering on the exposed flesh of her thighs as she crossed her legs.

'Oh? And is that a good or a bad first impression?' she asked with a flash of one eyebrow.

'Oh, bad. Most definitely bad,' I winked at her and she tossed her head back and laughed out loud. Suddenly, this day was taking a very interesting turn.

LAUREN

I closed my eyes and tilted my face towards the sun. I couldn't help but smile as I crossed my legs and could almost feel Sebastian's eyes roaming over my thighs.

Who would have thought Samantha's father would turn out to be so freaking hot? I knew all about him and the kind of man he was though.

A player.

A gangster.

My business partner's dad.

I hadn't expected him to look like he did at all. Dark hair peppered with silver. Huge brown eyes that crinkled at the corners when he laughed. A strong jaw framed by a perfectly trimmed beard.

And those forearms!

Damn!

He looked like he could hoist me up over his shoulder with one hand and not even break a sweat.

I opened my eyes and glanced sideways at him. He sipped his bottle of beer and I looked at his large hands as they gripped the drink firmly. I felt a flush of heat as I had a sudden image of him peeling off my panties with them.

I could feel the energy radiating from him. He was seriously hot. I knew that he loved women – and he was a serial cheat. But that was fine by me. I wasn't looking for anything serious. I didn't do relationships. I didn't do falling in love. Not since I'd had my fingers well and truly burned.

Maybe Sebastian Donovan would be just perfect for a bit of fun?

BONUS EXTENDED EPILOGUE
SEVEN MONTHS LATER

I placed my hands on the railing as I looked out over the beautiful Italian countryside. It was an incredible view. Tilting my face up to the sun, I closed my eyes and enjoyed the feeling of it warming my skin.

Even in my wildest dreams, I had never imagined I could ever be this happy. True to his word, Gabriel has booked us a honeymoon to Sorrento as soon as Max was old enough to to spend a few nights with my dad. And at almost twelve months old, he was becoming a character. Handsome like his daddy and full of mischief like him too.

I adored our son. Sometimes, I looked at him and felt like my heart would burst. I still enjoyed my work, and I loved my dad and my best friends, but Max and Gabriel were what I truly lived for. Despite that, I had happily packed him off to his grandpa for three nights so Gabriel could whisk me away to this incredible villa.

We had landed two hours ago, and I was missing Max already, but a quick call to my dad confirmed that our son was having the time of his life with his doting grandpa. So, I had changed into my bikini, leaving Gabriel to make a few calls, and headed out to the amazing garden.

I heard soft footsteps behind me and smiled as I felt Gabriel's warm, rough hands sliding over my hips and onto my stomach.

He pressed his lips against my ear, his stubble grazing the delicate skin on my neck. 'Your arse looks fucking incredible in that bikini,' he growled and my insides melted like warm butter.

I pushed myself back against him, rubbing my behind over his semi hard cock and enjoying the feeling of his hard muscular chest against my bare skin. I had chosen the skimpiest bikini I could find. It was barely a couple of pieces of string and a few scraps of material, and I knew it would drive him crazy when he saw me wearing it.

'It's a good thing we have our own pool, baby, because there is no way I want anyone else seeing you in this,' he said as he slipped his hands lower, his fingers reaching beneath the flimsy material. 'It's obscene.'

'It's perfectly acceptable,' I giggled. 'And I thought I could wear it if we go to the beach later?'

I heard the growl rumble in his throat as his fingers slid further southwards until his whole hand was almost inside my bikini bottoms. 'Not a fucking chance, Sam. I'm keeping you prisoner in this villa for three whole days.'

I groaned in pleasure as his fingers glided through my folds and he started to circle my clit with just the right amount of delicious pressure.

He sucked in a breath. 'Why are you soaking wet already? Have you been thinking about me, and all of the filthy things I'm going to do to you this week?'

'Yes,' I whimpered as he continued circling the sensitive nub of flesh. I opened my legs slightly to allow him easier access and he smiled against my skin.

'I love how much you want me inside you, Sam,' he chuckled! 'So, tell me, what filthy things have you been thinking about?'

'You know exactly what I've been thinking about,' I breathed as he continued to torture me.

'Tell me, baby. Tell me what you want me to do?'

'I want you to fuck me, Gabe!' I panted.

'Well, that's a given, baby. I'm going to fuck you in every single way, in every hole and on every surface of this house.'

His words vibrated through my core and I felt a rush of heat. I ground my hips against his fingers, desperate for more of him. Desperate to feel him inside me.

'I'm going to make you come on my tongue, my cock, and my fingers,' he growled as he slipped one inside me.

I groaned out loud at the relief of having some part of him inside me and rewarded him with a rush of wet heat which made him groan against my neck.

'I've brought my belt with me too,' he said as he added a second finger and I clenched my walls around him.

God, I loved his soft leather belt. He used it to restrain me or to spank me, and both of those things drove me crazy. Not to mention, they turned him into even more of a sex demon than he already was.

'You're a sexual deviant,' I groaned.

'Me? You're the one who's creaming all over my fingers at the mention of my belt. I'm going to put you over my knee later, and spank your beautiful peach until it turns cherry red.'

'Gabe,' I hissed as he pressed his thumb against my clit and the jolts of pleasure ricocheted through my body. I pressed back against him, rubbing my backside over his stiff cock and he groaned in my ear.

'Not yet, baby,' he growled as he pulled his hips back slightly.

He slid his free hand into the back of my bikini bottoms,

gliding over my backside and between my legs. Then his other hand moved back to my clit as he pushed two fingers inside me. I cried out in pleasure as he started to work me into a frenzy with both of his skilled hands. My walls clenched around him as I squeezed his fingers, trying to take more of him. I could barely concentrate as he pressed on my sensitive pressure points.

My orgasm was building and building as he kept me teetering on the edge. I held onto the railing as my legs started to tremble violently.

'Gabe, please!' I begged.

'Come for me, Sam,' he ordered, and as always, my body obeyed him.

I felt the rush of cream onto his fingers as my climax rolled through my core, all the way down to my toes. He wrapped one of his arms around me as he continued gently rubbing my clit with the other.

I shivered against him. 'Jesus, Gabe,' I hissed.

'And we haven't even started yet, baby,' he whispered against my ear.

I had barely recovered from the earth shattering orgasm, when Gabriel scooped me up into his arms and walked us over to the pool area. He lay me down on one of the soft padded sun loungers before standing over me.

'Jesus! That bikini is even more dangerous from the front,' he said with a flash of his eyebrows. 'You are fucking beautiful, Sam' he growled as he started to peel his swim shorts down over his thick, muscular thighs. A few seconds later he was standing naked in front of me.

I licked my lips as I looked at him, drinking in his body. All taut, toned, rippling muscle, and tattoos - even looking at him my womb contract! And if that wasn't enough to have me drooling, his huge cock was standing to attention, with a delicious bead of pre-cum glistening on the end.

'You're pretty hot yourself, Gabe,' I purred. 'Now get down here and fuck me!'

He narrowed his eyes at me before shaking his head. 'So impatient.'

He dropped to knees instead and wrapped his hands around the back of my thighs, pulling me down the lounger towards him. Then he looked up at me smiled as he pulled on the ties at either side of my bikini bottoms and the tiny scrap of fabric gave way in his hands.

He tossed it over his shoulder and it landed with a faint splat in the pool behind him. 'Sit up,' he ordered and I silently obeyed, watching him as he untied my top too, his deft fingers working quickly. As soon as he'd removed it, he tossed that behind him into the pool too.

'I hope you're going to dive in and get them for me,' I flashed an eyebrow at him. 'I told you I'm wearing that bikini to the beach later!'

'The fuck you are! You're not going anywhere Mrs Sullivan,' he growled. 'I told you, I'm keeping you here as my sex slave for the next three days.'

'Deviant!'

'You know it, baby,' he laughed softly as he dipped his head lower and rubbed his nose along the length of my wet folds. 'You smell fucking delicious, Sam,' he growled. 'I will never get enough of this delicious pussy.'

I shivered in anticipation as I felt his warm breath on my skin. My husband was a magician with his tongue and I considered myself a very lucky lady. He parted my lips with his thumbs and then licked the length of me, from my hot opening right up to my clit.

'Fuck!' he hissed.

I felt a rush of cream as he rimmed my clit. I ran my hands through his hair as he sucked and nibbled me, alternating between my clit and my hot entrance.

'Gabe!' I panted. 'Please let me come?'

'Soon, baby,' he groaned. 'Let me taste you some more. I can't get enough of you.'

I started to grind myself against him, desperate for the release he withheld. My blood pounded in my ears and my heart hammered in my chest. I could feel perspiration beading on my forehead and my top lip as I panted and groaned.

'Gabe!' I cried out.

I looked down at him and saw the look of pure devotion and enjoyment on his face and it was so hot, I thought I might pass out. He was the King of cunnilingus! He loved it as much as I did.

Just as I thought I could take any more, he tightened his grip on the back of my thighs, pulling me closer to him and sucking my clit hard into his mouth. I climaxed with a violent shudder as it crashed over me in wave after delicious wave.

I lay there, panting for breath and shaking as he crawled over me, pulling me back up the sun lounger with him, until he was nestled between my thighs and his cock was nudging at my wet channel.

'You okay, baby?' he growled, his face glistening with my arousal.

'Yes,' I breathed as I wrapped my arms around his neck.

'You ready to be fucked hard now?'

I looked into his eyes, full of passion and fire and nodded. 'Always.'

He smiled at me. 'Always,' he whispered before he slammed into me, pinning me to the chair as he gave me everything he had.

'So. Fucking. Wet!' he hissed as he thrust in and out of me, pounding into me and driving at the sweet spot inside me until I felt another orgasm building and another rush of cream coated his cock.

'Fuck, Sam! You're close, baby. I can feel you squeezing me,' he grunted. 'Can you come for me again? I want it all from you. Every last drop.'

I threw my head back against the padded cushion and shouted his name as my third orgasm ripped through me like black powder. My walls clenched around him as I milked his cock with my spasms.

'Fuck!' He hissed loudly as he found his own release.

We lay on the sun lounger together - completely naked, and completely sated. Due to its size, I was practically lying on top of Gabriel and he had his huge arms wrapped around me. I traced my fingertips along his new tattoo on his chest - Samantha - etched right over his heart. I let out a long, contended sigh.

'You okay?' he asked as he ran his hand over my arm.

'Hmm, better than okay. I'm perfect!'

'You certainly are,' he said as he planted a soft kiss on the top of my head.

'Thank you,' I said softly.

'For what? Making you come three times in forty minutes?' he chuckled. 'Don't thank me just yet, baby, I'm going to fuck you in that massive pool as soon as I catch my breath.'

'You're a sex maniac,' I said with a roll of my eyes, although his words made my pussy clench in expectation.

'It's not my fault I find my wife completely fucking irre-sistible, is it? I could fuck you every second of every day and it wouldn't be enough, Sam,' he growled.

I pressed myself tighter against him, my thigh draped over his stomach and my groin pressed against his hip. 'As incredible as that sounds, I didn't mean that.'

He laughed again. 'Okay. Then what did you mean?'

'I meant thank you for everything. This holiday. Max. Our life. For being you. For putting me back together again,' I breathed, feeling overcome with a rush of emotion.

He sucked in a breath. 'You're welcome, baby. But, I think it's me who should be thanking you.'

I looked up and into his beautiful brown eyes and he tucked a strand of hair behind my ear. 'My life was completely empty before you, Sam. You make me happier than I ever imagined I could be. Besides, you made me a dad, and I fucking love that.'

'Maybe, I should make you one again?' I flashed my eyebrows at him. 'I didn't start taking my pill again after my period last week. I know we talked about it, and I meant to tell you, but with planning for the trip, and –'

'Sam!' he interrupted me. 'You know I want more kids. I was just waiting for you to be ready.'

'I'm ready,' I said with a smile.

He grinned back at me. 'Fuck, I am going to love trying to knock you up again!'

'Do you remember how horny I was when I was pregnant with Max?' I started to laugh.

'Fuck, yes, I do. You were a sex maniac. I could hardly keep up with you.'

'I wasn't a sex maniac,' I insisted.

'You fucking were. But then, you still are,' he growled as he pulled my face to his and sealed his mouth over mine, kissing me fiercely until I was panting for breath.

When he broke our kiss, he pulled back and looked into my eyes.

'I love you, Sam,' he breathed.

'I love you too, Gabe.'

I nestled my head back against his chest and watched the sun setting over the mountains in the distance. Little did I know, Gabriel had just given me another amazing gift, and our beautiful baby girl would be born just under nine months later.

ABOUT THE AUTHOR

Sadie Kincaid is a steamy romance author who loves to read and write about hot alpha males and strong, feisty females.

Sadie loves to connect with readers so why not get in touch via social media?

Join Sadie's reader group for the latest news, book recommendations and plenty of fun. Sadie's ladies and Sizzling Alphas

Sign up to Sadie's mailing list for exclusive news about future releases, giveaways and content here

ACKNOWLEDGMENTS

I'd love to thank all of the wonderful women who have supported me to write this book - my beta readers, ARC reviewers and the wonderful writing community. With a particular mention to TL Swan and the Cygnets who are an amazing and inspiring group of women.

I also need to give a special mention to Sue and Michelle who have championed Sam and Gabriel's journey from the outset, and who I'm eternally grateful to. And also to Edie, for her advice and her friendship.

To my incredible boys who inspire me to be better every single day. And last, but no means least, a huge thank you to my husband, who is my rock and my biggest supporter.

I couldn't do this without you!

ALSO BY SADIE KINCAID

He is the King of L.A, and she is his queen. Alejandro and Alana Montoya are hotter than hell in Sadie's L.A Ruthless series. Available on Amazon and FREE in Kindle Unlimited.

Fierce King

Fierce Queen

If you'd like to read about the hotter than hell Irish Mafia, Ryan Brothers and their computer hacker, Jessie, you can order the New York Ruthless series on Amazon now:

Ryan Rule

Ryan Redemption

Ryan Retribution

Ryan Reign

Made in United States
North Haven, CT
05 January 2024

47099994R00200